BOOKS BY WILL MURRAY

Nick Fury, Agent of S.H.I.E.L.D.: Empyre
Doc Savage: Skull Island
Tarzan: Return to Pal-ul-don
Tarzan: Conqueror of Mars
King Kong vs. Tarzan
The Spider: The Doom Legion
Spider: Fury in Steel
The Spider: Scourge of the Scorpion
The Wild Adventures of Sherlock Holmes, Vol. 1
The Wild Adventures of Sherlock Holmes, Vol. 2
The Wild Adventures of Cthulhu, Vol. 1
The Wild Adventures of Cthulhu, Vol. 2
Master of Mystery: The Rise of The Shadow
Dark Avenger: The Strange Saga of The Shadow
Wordslingers: An Epitaph for the Western
Forever After: An Inspired Story

FORTHCOMING:

The Wild Adventures of Sherlock Holmes, Vol. 3
Secret Agent X vs. Dr. Death
Knight of Darkness: The Legend of The Shadow

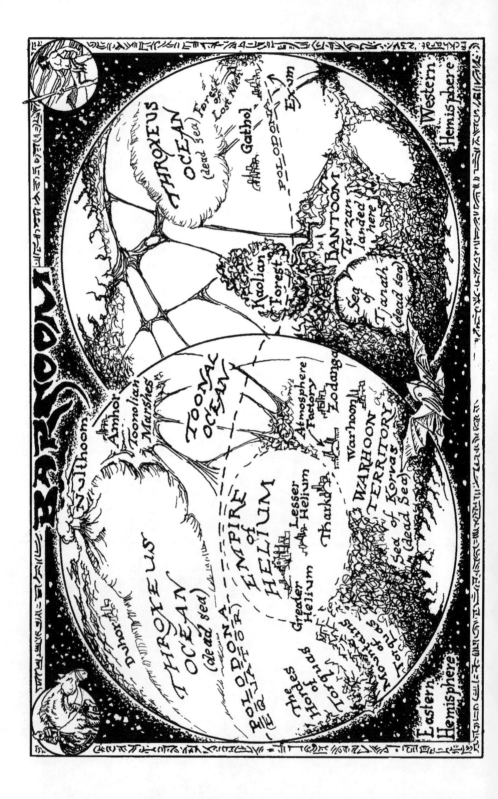

The Wild Adventures of Edgar Rice Burroughs™ Series 12

TARZAN ®
BACK TO MARS

By
WILL MURRAY

Cover illustrated by
Joe DeVito

Altus Press • 2023

THANKS TO

Gary A. Buckingham, Christopher Paul Carey, Jeff Deischer, Joe DeVito, Dave McDonnell, Don O'Malley, Stephen Payne, Ray Riethmeier, Jim Sullos, Jess Terrell, Cathy Mann Wilbanks, and Edgar Rice Burroughs, Inc.

COVER ILLUSTRATION COMMISSIONED BY
Richard Burchfield

First Edition — July 2023

DESIGNED BY
Matthew Moring

Like us on Facebook: "The Wild Adventures of Tarzan"

www.edgarriceburroughs.com
www.adventuresinbronze.com

For Jim Sullos, who believed in us…

And who took the Wild Adventures in
exciting new directions….

TARZAN: BACK TO MARS

Chapter 1

HOMEWARD BOUND

ALL THINGS come to an end, as they inevitably must. Lives, loves, even dreams ultimately reach their culmination. Nightmares as well. This is the immutable law of all creation.

And so it was in the late summer of 1945 that the Second World War ceased to trouble the world. Soldiers who had been forged in the furnaces of battle were mustered out of service and duly returned to their families, forever altered in body, mind and spirit.

Not the least of these defenders of freedom was Royal Air Force Group Captain John Clayton, otherwise Lord Greystoke. For his service to the Crown, he was presented with his decommissioned and unmarked black P-40B Tomahawk warplane and allowed to fly home to Africa, unescorted.

Yea, Tarzan of the Apes was winging his way homeward.

The flight from Cairo was a tedious one until Clayton refueled at Addis Ababa in Ethiopia, after which the mountainous terrain ceased unrolling beneath the ebony wings of his shark-mouth-painted aircraft, and a zone of desert wastes came and went. Then the magnificent greenery of the African jungle stretched out as far as the eye could behold to the south.

Pushing back the glass canopy to let in rushing air, Tarzan drank in the mingled smells of the jungle—odors he had not inhaled in a long time. The welcoming scents of familiar trees and animals, both friendly and otherwise, greeted him.

The ape-man was flying too high to detect the spoor of Numa the lion or Tantor the elephant. Because these were the scents he missed most of all, he drove downward until he was skimming the treetops and the myriad jungle smells filled the open cockpit, charging his lungs with oxygen and reinvigorating his brain with strong memories.

Clayton wore his fur-colored Sidcot flying suit and boots, but once he was on the ground, he would shuck them off and become the demi-god of the forest savage Africa had made him, Tarzan, Lord of the Jungle.

A bull elephant seemed to trumpet loudly in salute. Tarzan knew that Tantor could not recognize him from the jungle trails far below. Still, it was a welcome sound. Throwing back his head, he gave vent to the riveting hunting cry of the bull ape, and no sooner had that cry resounded, than the jungle came alive with a wild chorus of answering calls, which all but drowned the roar of his rotary engine. Some were calls of welcome, but others told of fear—fear that the bronzed Tarmangani was returning to his domain after a long absence.

Tarzan smiled at the cacophony of sounds. This was his realm. This is where he belonged. His years of military service finally had come to an end. And a deep longing to return to his family and estate soon would be sated.

There was much to smile about. Lady Jane, his wife, would be waiting for him. And his faithful Waziri warriors. Perhaps his son Jack would have returned from his own service by now. That remained to be seen.

Reaching Kenya, Tarzan turned toward Lake Victoria and the Greystoke estate.

It would not be long now. The boots encasing his feet would be discarded, the uniform stored away, perhaps never to be worn again. For Tarzan had grown weary of civilization's latest war.

For the medals in a small wooden box under his seat, John Clayton cared little. Deeds were what mattered. Of what use were medals to Tarzan of the Apes, whose magnificent chest was always bared to Usha, the wind?

As Clayton completed the turn toward the southwest, he spied a flash of sunlight against distant wings.

At first, Tarzan thought little of that fleeting flash. Since the war had broken out, aircraft were a common sight in the African skies. Ever alert, he kept his eyes on it as it flew lazy circles under the equatorial sun.

After a time that very aimlessness drew the ape-man's interest, for the aircraft was not behaving as it should. It seemed to skim about, as if unpowered by a motor. Perhaps it was a glider, but the wings were not the flat wings of a glider, he perceived. They reminded Tarzan of the gull wings of a Royal Navy Corsair Mk, but these bent wings did not appear to be painted the regulation sky gray.

Determined to reach home while he had sufficient fuel, John Clayton chose not to investigate the strange sight. But that turned out not to matter.

Evidently, the pilot spotted Clayton's aircraft for, in the middle of executing a slow turn, it abruptly shifted its course and commenced beating in his direction.

Here, Tarzan's interest was piqued. The metallic craft appeared to be flapping its wings in a rhythmic and regular fashion!

At first, Tarzan questioned the reality of what he saw. Kudu the sun, burnishing those distant wings, could play tricks on the brain and the eye, even upon those of Tarzan of the Apes. And the way the other ship seemed to drop into a flat glide, and then canted and jinked about like a great bird transitioning between gathering air under its wings and stretching them out again to skim effortlessly, it was difficult to discern clearly at the distance involved.

Inevitably, the two aerial objects closed with one another, and behind the goggles of his leather flight helmet, the gray eyes of Tarzan widened in surprise.

For this was no aircraft!

Yes, it gleamed like metal. It appeared to be formed of metal. But this weird thing was in the shape of a great long-necked bird, the size of which brought to mind the Roc of the Arabian Nights tales. Two gleaming crystal disks served as eyes, and seemed to regard him with a brittle intelligence.

SEEING THIS clearly, Tarzan drove his all-black Tomahawk toward the approaching apparition.

The bird-like creature of metal shifted to meet him. Almost immediately, they fell on an intercept course.

Tarzan advanced his throttle. Collision seemed almost inevitable. Banking his moaning aircraft to starboard, he hoicked it around again, circling the other winged thing.

There was no question but that it was a bird encased in metal, entirely unlike any other avian of Africa. More astonishingly, a man in silvery armor sat perched upon the back of the bird, between its widespread wings and behind the goose-necked head, guiding it somehow, as if astride a horse.

Tarzan could see the man was seated on some type of wood and leather saddle and his feet were encased in metal devices resembling boxy stirrups nothing at all like those normally seen on equine saddles.

In the brief seconds in which Tarzan took in the fantastic sight, the ape-man saw that the man was encased in smooth armor of some whitish metal suggesting platinum. Moreover, he was equipped with a bow of peculiar design. Reaching back over his shoulder, the armored warrior took out a fletched arrow from a quiver at his back.

In a flash of movement that was more practiced than swift, the bowman let fly. With a distinct *thunk*, an arrow sank into the fuselage of the speeding Tomahawk, just behind the fierce shark's mouth painted on her nose radiator scoop. It caused no harm, having missed the motor entirely.

Banking, Tarzan came around for another pass.

The winged mount was necessarily slower than the engine-driven warplane, so Tarzan was forced to throttle back as he swept in for another look.

As he did so, Tarzan threw the greenhouse canopy forward, locking it in place. It was well that he did so. For the next arrow smashed one of the glass panes at his shoulder without penetrating further. Slipstream forces snatched it away.

Engine howling, the Tomahawk swept around once more and Tarzan got behind his avian antagonist. Now the bowman would have to turn completely around in his saddle in order to let fly.

The Tomahawk's guns were charged with full belts, but the ape-man chose not to reach for the trips that would send 30-caliber lead screaming at the amazing aerial rider from her four winged-mounted Browning guns.

Clinging to the other's tail, Tarzan could see that the man's arm was composed of the same whitish metal that sheathed the bird. His sharp gaze studied the winged thing, and it became obvious that it was not a living bird of stupendous size but a cunning machine fashioned to *resemble* a bird of impressive size.

Here and there, it was decorated with scarlet streaks, suggesting feathers. A single red-metal plume stuck up from the back of its head, suggesting both an antenna and the feather decoration of an Apache brave. But the creature was not alive. How the rider controlled it was unclear.

Staying on the reddish tail, Tarzan was able to study the man's face. This was no native of Africa. His face was extraordinarily pale, almost as white as an albino man. It did not seem that the fellow could have long been in the Dark Continent, for his skin was neither burnt red nor bronzed by the sun.

A helmet encased the rider's head. His features were regular without being distinctive. The ape-man could not discern his nationality. There was nothing about him suggesting a country of origin.

Twisting in the saddle, the armored man nocked his arrow to his bowstring, and Tarzan sent the Tomahawk into a dive as another bright-feathered shaft whistled over his glass-shielded head.

Coming up from beneath, he could see the wings flex and beat, then fall into a posture that permitted it to glide extended distances. Somehow the mechanical bird was capable of staying aloft through a series of simple repetitive actions.

Extending from its smooth belly were two sets of talons. They appeared to be fixed in place, like aircraft landing gear. The talons were splayed outward, as if to enable the bird to land and hold itself upright.

Tarzan was considering what to do about the situation. He did not care to shoot down the intruder. Nor was he of a mind to chase it to its rookery. More than anything else he yearned only for his home estate.

But curiosity is a powerful thing. And Africa was Tarzan's home. Such a strange intruder suggested trouble coming from a new direction.

Pulling back on the stick, Tarzan sent the warbird's snarling nose upward. It shot past the gliding machine of metal. Reasoning where there was one, there must be others—and that all birds that ever lived must return to their nests, whether they were living or otherwise—the bronzed giant decided to give chase.

Reaching an altitude of six thousand feet, Tarzan leveled off and began tracking the bird from on high.

In response, the rider attempted to urge his unliving steed upward to match Tarzan's altitude. But the metallic mount appeared not to possess such a capability. It rose laboriously, fell, rose again, and settled back into what appeared to be its comfortable cruising altitude.

It was perhaps a strange phrase to employ when considering a metallic steed and armored rider armed only with a bow and arrow, but it seemed to fit the circumstances, improbable as they were.

Unable to match the altitude of the Tomahawk, the bird-rider decided to return to his business, whatever it was. He struck out toward the west, in the direction of Lake Victoria.

Where before, the bird-man seemed to be exploring, now he showed signs of having a definite destination.

Whether he might have reached it or not would never be told. For not long after, two more metal birds rose from the jungle canopy to join the first. They fell into an arrowhead formation, with the first bird making the point.

They, too, attempted to rise and challenge Tarzan's shark-mouthed warplane. But they lacked the ability. Now the ape-man had three quarries to track.

For nearly an hour, Tarzan patiently followed. The metallic birds showed no signs of fatigue, nor did they slacken in their majestic pace. What motivated or propelled them was a mystery.

Once or twice, a rider would twist in his saddle and send a shaft skyward. But it fell far, far short of the droning Tomahawk.

One gray eye on his gas gauge, the ape-man realized that his fuel supply would give him limited time to pursue these fantastic fugitives. He could not afford to run empty over the jungle where suitable landing spots were rare and taking off again was almost impossible.

Reluctantly, Clayton broke off the chase.

Turning his howling propeller southward, he resumed his original course, looking back from time to time until the three metal birds were no longer in view.

This uncanny development was something that former Group Captain John Clayton would set aside for now.

Later, at the appropriate time, Tarzan of the Apes would investigate these strange new inhabitants in his jungle....

Chapter 2

ARROW UNKNOWN

L ITTLE NKIMA the monkey was the first to know of Tarzan's return.

The monkey was bored. He had been bored for a long time now. He missed his master, but there was nothing he could do about it.

And so he went about his monkey business, climbing trees, throwing rocks at animals that were his betters, eating grubs, and hiding from any trouble he managed to manufacture due to his own predilection for mischief.

The drone of the approaching airplane caught his attention.

Spread out in the high branches of a banyan tree, Nkima sat up suddenly and his tiny brown head swiveled this way and that. Curiosity seized him.

The noise of an airplane motor here in this part of East Africa known as Kenya was unexpected. The monkey was not ignorant of airplanes in and of themselves. But such things were so rare that his attention was immediately arrested.

Scampering to the top of the tree, he poked his head above the uppermost leaves of the closely-packed crown, beady eyes searching the sky to the north.

At last he spied the plane. It was black. The monkey did not know that color was unusual in aircraft, but it was a shade that was nevertheless ominous. He began to chatter with nervous concern.

Hunkering so that only the top of his head and dark eyes poked above the canopy, Nkima tracked the approaching craft. From time to time, he shivered. He did not know why he shivered. Little Nkima did not know why he did many things. He just did them.

The black airplane was flying low. As he watched, it seemed to descend even lower. This was not something that met with the cowering monkey's approval. For it possessed a gaping fanged mouth large enough to devour a tiny creature such as Nkima!

Ducking his head even farther, he craned his small skull backward and stared straight up, dark eyes wide.

The black-winged monster flashed over his head. Nkima became very, very still.

But in the next instant, he exploded into manic activity. For as the droning monster passed by, down reverberated a familiar sound.

It was the weird hunting cry of the great apes of Africa!

Nkima knew that call. When voiced by the Bolgani, it meant danger. But this was no Bolgani. This was a cry he recognized emanating from a throat he knew well.

Tarzan of the Apes had come home!

Chattering excitedly, Nkima scrambled down to the base of the banyan tree, ran some distance, and leaped into another tree, this time swinging from limb to limb, then tree to tree, covering a short distance until at last he reached the heart of the vast farmstead of his master with its bungalows and surrounding huts and outbuildings.

Attempting a landing on an airstrip of packed dirt, the black aircraft had dropped to tree-top level.

Running to and fro were the Waziri warriors who guarded and maintained the Greystoke estate. And out from the bungalow came fair-haired Lady Jane Clayton.

With glad cries of joy, they rushed toward the makeshift landing spot.

The black warplane struck ground, bounced slightly, then settled as it rolled away airspeed. At the last moment, it seemed about to run out of runway and pile into the jungle at the other end.

Abruptly, it skewed about, coasting to a final stop. The three-bladed propeller ceased turning. And a last cough of smoke belched from the engine cowling exhausts briefly obscuring a name painted in red on the nose: *Kala.*

Immediately, the aircraft was surrounded by joyous Waziri warriors who made way for the lithe blonde white woman who was the mate of Tarzan.

Out from the cockpit stepped the Lord of the Jungle, not quite recognizable to Nkima's eyes, for Tarzan was wearing unfamiliar clothes and his hair was covered by a leather helmet. This he removed after he stepped off the wing.

Little Nkima gave a glad cry when he saw Tarzan embrace his mate and turn her around as they walked arm in arm toward the main bungalow, laughing Waziri tribesmen and women forming a joyous procession around them, giving shouts of praise and happiness.

Rushing toward them, Nkima jumped into Tarzan's arms, chattering happily.

"Hello, Nkima," greeted Tarzan in the language that the monkey understood. "How have you been keeping?"

Lady Jane Clayton laughed. "Keeping? He has been a constant bundle of trouble. But look how glad he is to see you again. I'm glad. We all are."

"It is wonderful to be home," returned Tarzan. "All is well?"

"The jungle has been peaceful. The war has not come close. We have been very lucky."

"And Jack?"

"I received a telegram from him five days ago. He was given his discharge papers. It's just a question of when he will arrive."

"It will be good to see him after so long."

Arriving at the bungalow, Tarzan mounted the veranda and addressed his faithful warriors.

"Muviro, prepare a feast. A homecoming feast."

The aged headman, Muviro, smiled broadly. "I would have had the feast ready, B'wana, had I but known the date of your return."

Tarzan smiled. "I would have sent a telegram had I thought it would arrive in time. It was quicker to fly straight home. Now go, while I change out of these confining clothes."

Jane said, "I have a fresh shirt and ducks ready for you."

Tarzan laughed without mockery. "Jane, after so many months wearing this flight suit and uniforms like it, the last things I want to wear are the raiment of civilization. There will be time enough for that later."

Jane smiled. "You have not changed a bit. The war has not suppressed your spirit."

Tarzan looked momentarily serious. "The war was a terrible thing, but a necessary one. I'm glad to put it behind me."

AN HOUR later, it was Tarzan of the Apes who stepped out of the bungalow, wearing only a loincloth of deerskin. His steely, sun-bronzed muscles rippled in the light of day. Fresh scars crisscrossed his limber figure, Jane saw. She said nothing about them. They were to be expected of a soldier returning from war.

The only accoutrements he wore were a gold locket and chain. Inside was concealed cameo portraits of his parents. His father's hunting knife he had brought back from the war, but it was not necessary to wear this during a feast.

The feast included deer steaks and roast boar, and it went well into the night. The Waziri cavorted in their dance of welcome. Nkima chattered and jumped from Tarzan's left shoulder to his right shoulder, sat upon his head, clinging to the bronze giant's black hair with tiny fingers unwilling to let go.

In the morning, Tarzan spoke as Kudu the sun was rising behind him, "I intend to take a war party north."

Jane looked taken aback. She brushed a wick of blonde hair from her brow. "A war party! But the war is over."

"The world war is over," Tarzan said seriously. "But as I flew home, I encountered a strange sight. Three warriors in armor riding the backs of giant birds made of metal. They fired arrows at me. They do not belong to Africa. I do not know where they came from. But they patrol the forests of Tarzan unchallenged. I must discover what their business is."

"Can't you put it off for another day or so?"

Tarzan considered this. "If I knew what they were doing here, I might be leisurely about investigating them. But it is better to meet trouble before it worsens than to confront it after it has gotten out of control."

Jane smiled. "You never change."

After the feast was done, Tarzan walked back to his dull black warplane. From the maw of its shark mouth, he extracted the single arrow that had struck home.

Holding it up to the moonlight, the bronze giant examined it closely. It was not African. The arrowhead was of metal. The end was fletched with feathers he did not recognize. They belonged to no African bird.

There was something about the workmanship that stirred a memory that he could not immediately place. The wood was exceedingly hard, but it was not an African hardwood. Of that, he was certain.

That night, Tarzan slept and dreamed a procession of dreams that left him puzzled upon waking. He barely could remember them. But there was a great deal of familiarity that clung to his mind after he awoke to greet the rising sun.

Chapter 3

Waziri War Party

TARZAN SLIPPED out of bed, leaving Jane to finish her night's sleep. He went out on the veranda of the bungalow and looked out over his sprawling estate. It had been well cared for in his absence. This gave him great satisfaction. But there was other work to be done.

Going to the mahogany and bamboo house of Muviro, the wrinkle-faced headman of the Waziri, the jungle lord found the old man already awake.

"My aging eyes are again pleased at the sight of you, B'wana," said Muviro sincerely.

"It is good to be back among friends," returned Tarzan. "But now there is work to be done. Assemble a party of your finest warriors. We will ride northwest, where strange metal birds circle like shining vultures and warriors unlike any I have ever seen ride them to an unknown purpose."

"White men?"

Tarzan nodded. "They are too white for Africa. They are from someplace other than here. It is best if we investigate now, rather than await developments that might not be pleasant."

"It will be as you say, B'wana. Will you require a horse?"

"The best one available. For it will be a long ride. Pick a suitable one for yourself."

"I am not too old to march with my warriors," Muviro returned stiffly.

To that, Tarzan laughed. "I count on you to be fresh when we reach our destination, Muviro. I will not have you tire yourself out unnecessarily."

"As you say," said the old man, suppressing a smile of relief, for he did not truly wish to march on foot. But Muviro was too prideful and stubborn to do otherwise unless ordered.

Breakfast was simple: Ostrich eggs and boar bacon. Jane cooked it herself and Tarzan silently gave thanks for having wed a woman who could prepare such a delicious meal. Later, there would be leisure enough to kill fresh game during the march.

An hour after he had risen, the bronzed giant mounted a great white stallion, then rode the magnificent beast to the clearing where Muviro sat upon his own steed, surveying his assembled warriors.

They were a clean-limbed group of blacks, the cream of the Waziri tribe.

Turning in his saddle, Muviro advised, "At your command, B'wana."

"We are missing someone," said Tarzan simply.

Muviro looked puzzled, his wrinkled face gathering into a tight web.

"Who is missing? All who are of age and able of limb stand before you. Name this person you consider to be recalcitrant."

Tarzan's smile was reassuring. "For this expedition, I would be pleased to have Jad-bal-ja accompany us."

Relief washed over the old man's face, and he snapped out a command in his language to one of his men, who went and opened the low hut where the golden lion had passed the inter-mittently-rainy night.

Tarzan already had visited the black-maned creature he had raised from a lion cub. So this was not a reunion, but an expression of brotherhood.

Jad-ba-ja soon padded into view, the black warrior striding beside him unafraid.

"Jad-bal-ja!" called out Tarzan. "We hunt now. You will hunt with us."

As if understanding fully, the great golden lion took up a position next to Tarzan's white stallion. The horse was well trained. It did not quiver at the smell of the powerful feline.

Satisfied, Tarzan turned his horse around and urged it ahead at a canter. Muviro called out commands, and his warriors formed a double file behind his own mount. They struck out for the northwest.

With Jane watching proudly, the war party soon put the Clayton land holdings behind them.

Hours passed as they pushed north, then struck west toward Lake Victoria.

Studying the passing trees, Tarzan refrained from springing from his saddle and leaping into the leafy aerial aisles. There would be time enough for that later.

Behind him, the Waziri sang war songs whose cadence kept up their spirits. They were proud to follow the jungle lord, even if they did not fully understand the mission.

"What shall I tell them, B'wana?" asked Muviro at one point.

Without humor, Tarzan replied, "Tell them we are hunting birds."

"They will think that we intend to eat them, and will be disappointed."

"Then tell them that these birds are as large as any aircraft they ever saw."

"They may not believe me. No such birds inhabit Africa."

"Inform your warriors that these birds are made of metal, yet flap their wings like vultures."

"Perhaps it is better that I say nothing," decided Muviro.

"I will leave that up to you," returned Tarzan. He had no reservations about the bravery of his blacks. They would charge into any battle, with or without him. Perhaps it was better that they not know too much too soon. Especially inasmuch as Tarzan himself possessed so few answers.

ALONG ABOUT afternoon, hunger began to creep into their bellies, and Tarzan abruptly turned his mount around and declared, "Break camp here. I will find meat."

"My warriors could hunt," suggested Muviro.

Tarzan shook his head firmly. "No, let them rest. I will find game."

Guiding his stallion toward a large tree, the bronzed giant stood up in his saddle, then vaulted into the handiest branch. Pausing there briefly, he crouched like an ape and then uncoiled his mighty muscles, propelling himself up into higher branches, sprinting along the thicker ones, then leaping from tree to tree, his sensitive nostrils seeking the smells of game he had not had the luxury of hunting in many a year.

Far and wide ranged the ape-man. He scented the riotous spoor of the jungle, drinking them in the way that civilized men imbibe fine wine or inhale choice tobaccos. These were intoxicants Tarzan of the Apes had all but put behind him. He had little desire for them, nor did he often indulge. He sought only the freedom of the jungle and the bounty that teemed all about him.

Soon enough, the jungle lord smelled antelope. The wind was bringing it from the west. So Tarzan plunged west.

Finding the crown of the tallest tree in the area, he stood atop it and his gray eyes scanned his surroundings. His sense of smell was so keen that it guided his vision, and not the other way around.

A flash of antelope fur showed in a nearby swale.

Sighting it, Tarzan dropped down and then began swinging from limb to limb the way the great Mangani apes had taught him in childhood. He moved with a swift surety that would have astonished a civilized man. His fingers never failed to grasp a handy branch, yet he gripped each perch only briefly as he used it to launch his limber body into the next tree.

Finally, the ape-man reached the point above a jungle trail and watched as the antelope made its unwary way toward him.

It stopped and sniffed the air. The antelope smelled him. A nervousness caused his fur to ripple. But Wappi did not see man as his great enemy. They feared the lion more. And Wappi did not look into the trees for danger. Not from men.

So it was that Tarzan of the Apes flashed downward out of the tree and landed upon the animal's muscular back. One sinewy bronzed arm wrapped around its thrashing neck while the other pulled the knife out of its scabbard and sent it plunging into the antelope's fast-beating heart.

One strike was all that was necessary. The Wappi shuddered its entire length as Tarzan rolled it into the dirt and then, using the edge of his blade, slit its throat.

For a moment, the ape-man reverted to his savage youth, and placing one foot on the still-warm animal, lifted his head and vented the terrifying victory cry of the great apes.

The jungle seemed to freeze at that sound.

Then Tarzan sank to one knee and drank of the antelope's flowing life's blood.

Once he was satisfied, he began carving out juicy steaks to carry back to the Waziri camp.

Muviro already had ordered that a fire be built, and soon gouts of meat were being roasted over sticks.

Seated in the circle, Tarzan ate his meat raw. He threw a piece to Jad-bal-ja the golden lion, who chewed hungrily before swallowing the juicy bit.

"There is not enough for you," said Tarzan. "You should hunt your own meat."

Understanding the strange language that Tarzan used among animals, the great lion stood up and slipped off into the leafy expanse.

When he returned an hour later, Jad-bal-ja smelled of wild
boar and found a spot in the dirt where he could lick gore off
his paws. The lion appeared content. His master had returned.
All was well, so far as he was concerned.

After that meal, they assembled anew and pushed farther
north.

They marched until long after sundown, then bedded down
for the night under the protective watch of the golden lion.

At daybreak, they were again marching, eating such wild
fruit as they could pluck while they made their way through
the leaf-shaded trails.

Before the sun could fully rise in the east, the smell of fresh
water reached their nostrils. The wind was coming from the
west, carrying with it the distinctive freshwater smells of Lake
Victoria.

"We are nearing the spot where I encountered the metal
birds," the ape-man advised Muviro.

"We are ready," the old man responded.

Daylight was turning the forest a smoldering red when
Tarzan smelled something unfamiliar. He brought his horse
up short, and turned it around.

"I smell men."

"Black men, or white?"

"These are not blacks. But they do not smell like any white
men I have ever encountered."

Despite his puzzlement, Muviro nodded.

"Hold your warriors here. I will scout," said Tarzan, taking
up his bow and setting it so that the wooden part lay against his
back, held in place by the catgut string, which pressed against his
massive chest. His antelope hide quiver was packed with arrows,
including the strange one he extracted from his warplane.

Tarzan again took to the jungle lanes, moving from treetop to
treetop, lifting his black-haired head above the greenery, scan-
ning the tree line in all directions. All about him was a waving

sea of leaves. But his eyes were not on the jungle canopy. He was searching the vast cloudless sky.

The smells reaching his nostrils confused his senses. These were not the smells of African animals, but some other types. The ape-man had not expected this.

In his long life, Tarzan had ranged the length and breadth of the Dark Continent and had encountered every species it harbored. And even some species not known to modern scientists. In the lost land of Pal-ul-don, there had been saber-toothed lion-tiger hybrids and gigantic triceratops.

These were heavy, alien odors. But not the smell of dinosaurs. Of that, he was quite certain. Puzzled but curious, the Lord of the Jungle moved from tree to tree until finally he saw something circling in the sky in the direction of Lake Victoria.

The sun was by now sinking low. But the light was still good.

This winged thing caught the ochre rays of the dying sun, making them flash and burn.

Lifting his voice, Tarzan gave vent to a challenge that carried far above the treetops.

Abruptly, the wheeling metal bird took notice. Or rather, its rider did. For suddenly, they were beating in his direction.

Tarzan waited patiently. He knew the power of curiosity. And the danger thereof.

Disengaging his bow from his back, he drew an arrow from his quiver. Its tip had been whittled to a sharp point and hardened by fire. This, he fitted to his bowstring, but kept the shaft pointed at the jungle floor.

The ape-man's gaze searched the approaching form. As it resolved, he could again see the strange lines of a giant metal bird and astride its back, a pale-faced man in whitish armor.

Tarzan made no move as the fantastic form drew nearer and nearer. When he could see the bright blue of the man's eyes, he lifted his bow and pulled back on a string so taut that only one of his feral strength could draw it fully. Sighting carefully, he released the fletched end.

The missile flew up, but it rebounded against the right wing of the metallic bird, falling to earth without leaving a mark.

Tarzan drew another arrow and repeated the operation, this time aiming for another spot. Again, the arrow failed to penetrate the silvery metal.

Frowning, the ape-man shifted his quiver around until he could select an arrow by sight instead of by feel. Spying the weirdly-feathered arrow, he plucked it free and studied the arrowhead. It appeared to be forged of the same metal as the circling bird form.

Nocking it, Tarzan sent the shaft whistling skyward.

The sound when it penetrated the wing rang like steel piercing hard metal. The slow-flapping wing seized up, and the rider was suddenly fighting to stay in his saddle. The pseudo-bird dipped, spun, and commenced a downward spiral that could not be overcome.

By the time bird and rider crashed into a spreading nut tree, Tarzan had dropped to the ground and was racing for the spot it struck.

In one hand he clutched his father's hunting knife. But he had no intention of using it unless it was necessary to do so. For if the armored warrior survived his fall, he would have to deal with the Lord of the Jungle on Tarzan's terms.

Chapter 4

"Refuse and Die"

TARZAN OF THE APES found the great metal bird
smashed at the bottom of the tree into which it had
plunged. The act of crashing through the branches had dislodged
several heavy boughs and stripped one wing from the colossal
form.

Knife in hand, the ape-man approached warily.

He found the wood and leather saddle partially dislodged
from its straps, but the saddle was empty. Circling the fallen
bird-form, Tarzan discovered that the armored warrior had been
thrown clear. He lay in a heap, arrows thrown from his broken
quiver were strewn all about the grassy bush.

The warrior was in no condition to fight back. He lay on his
back, barely moving. The ape-man could see the rising and falling of his chest and knew that he still breathed.

Still wary, Tarzan padded closer. He spied the man's exceedingly pale face still encased in its helmet. As Tarzan's shadow
fell across the fellow, his limbs quivered and struggled to budge.
He seemed unable to move them very much.

"Who are you?" Tarzan asked in English.

The warrior did not respond. His wide eyes stabbed wildly
about. Tarzan smelled no blood and so did not think the other
was gravely injured. Perhaps his back was broken. It seemed so
to the ape-man.

Recognizing that the warrior lay helpless, Tarzan knelt at his
side, after first sheathing his hunting knife. He studied the man

closely, but could make nothing of his features. Above his strikingly blue eyes, where the helmet lay flat against his forehead, Tarzan descried a strange symbol painted upon it.

It was a white triangle, flat at the top, surmounted by a half-moon of red. The device meant nothing to Tarzan. It belonged to no nation he knew.

Reaching under the man's chin, the bronzed giant found the strap and unbuckled it. Off came the surprisingly-light helmet, revealing a shock of blond hair.

"Speak," commanded Tarzan.

The pallid warrior struggled to speak. Placing a hand under the man's head, the ape-man lifted it and repeated his command.

"Speak!"

Squaring his jaw, the strange warrior began to mumble words. They were initially incomprehensible. Tarzan leaned in, the better to hear them.

Slowly, comprehension dawned over the ape-man's bronzed features. He began to recognize words. They were not in English, or any of the common languages of this world. Tarzan had not heard such syllables in more than a decade. At first, he doubted his own recognition, but as the man continued speaking, struggling to form words, it became clear that he was speaking in the common language of the planet Mars, called by its inhabitants Barsoom.

Summoning up his own knowledge of that alien tongue, Tarzan asked, "You are a soldier of Barsoom?"

"I am. How is it you know this, bronze face?"

"I have been there," said Tarzan flatly. "I did not like it. Your skin is not red, but white. And your eyes blue. Do you belong to the Orovar race?"

The man nodded.

"What are you doing on the planet Earth?"

"Who speaks thus to me?" the Martian demanded indignantly.

"I am Tarzan of the Apes. Known on Barsoom as Ramdar—Red Scar."*

"I have never heard of you, Ramdar."

"I am a friend of John Carter, Warlord of Helium."

"I have never heard of John Carter. I do not know him."

"Why have you come to Earth?"

"To make a new home here."

"There are others with you?" demanded Tarzan.

"Many. All warriors. The women will follow in another ship."

"What manner of ship?"

"It is not permitted that I speak of it. Only that I warn you to stay away from our colony. We will defend it with our last breath."

"This is my jungle. I am known as Tarzan here. Tarzan, Lord of the Jungle."

"Do you claim authority over this entire continent?"

Tarzan shook his head vehemently. "No one owns Africa. But I am the guardian of this reach."

Blue eyes blazed defiantly. "You would do well to stay away from us, then, Tarzan. We have come too far to be turned away. And besides that, our ship was damaged in landing, its motor exhausted. We are unable to return to Barsoom. Nor do we wish to go back to that dry and dying world. Here, you have plenty of water. Trees. Fruits. Fish and other game. Here we will live as our ancestors once did when Barsoom was young and green and wet."

Tarzan of the Apes heard these words and understood their import fully.

Once before, he had been transported to the red planet and dwelled upon it for a time. It had been an ordeal. Mars' great oceans had long ago evaporated. Water was scarce. Jungles rare. Cities and the ruins of abandoned cities lay scattered here and there. It was a planet of war, with different races fighting for

---

* *See* Tarzan, Conqueror of Mars *by Will Murray.*

dwindling resources. He could well understand why this man of Mars had come to Earth in order to start anew.

During the time Tarzan had struggled to survive on that dying world, he had come to understand that they did not possess the knowledge to venture beyond its thin atmosphere. That Martians had developed the ability to escape to Earth was a disturbing revelation. If these invaders could establish a colony, the ape-man knew that others would follow.

"Where is your encampment?" he demanded.

"I will never tell."

Tarzan's knife came out of its scabbard, and he laid its sharp edge against the fellow's jugular vein. He lifted the man's head by its crop of pale hair and said in a dull growl, "Point in the direction of your camp. Or die."

"I cannot lift my arm," the warrior said, his eyes going to his right arm.

"Lift your other arm."

"I cannot lift either arm. The gravity of Jasoom is too strong. I have not gotten used to it. The armor I wear is treated with a special ray that counters gravity. Sufficient pieces have fallen off that I cannot move my limbs."

Tarzan considered this and realized it was true. On Mars, whose gravity was less than that of Earth, the ape-man quickly learned that he would spring high into the air at the slightest step. It took some practice in adjusting to this freakish fact until he could simply walk in a normal fashion.

For this warrior of Mars, the reverse must be true.

Dropping the man's head and regaining his feet, Tarzan gathered pieces of the armor and set them in their proper positions until the man's right arm was fully encased.

"Point to your camp," repeated Tarzan.

"I refuse."

"Refuse and die."

"You will kill me anyway," sneered the other. "I still refuse."

Tarzan did not care to kill the man until he had extracted the truth from him. On reflection, the ape-man did not feel that killing this intruder into his jungle was a necessity. He was entirely helpless and could not fight back.

"You came from the direction of the great lake called Victoria," Tarzan stated. "Therefore your camp must be near its shores."

"You did not hear that from my lips," the white warrior said grudgingly.

Having learned what was necessary, Tarzan went and gathered up the scattered arrows. Some were broken, but many were not. Now he understood why they seemed so familiar. The design was not something he had ever seen, but the wooden shafts were made of skeel, a hardwood he had come to know on Barsoom.

Once he had gathered up a clutch of arrows, the ape-man studied the fallen metal bird. He saw clearly that the shell of the thing was made of the same metal as the warrior's armor. It was exceedingly light, lighter than aluminum. And he understood how it was able to fly even though it was a product of the Martian world.

Taking hold of his spent arrow with both hands, Tarzan carefully worked it around until the shaft came free of the fallen metal bird. He studied the steel tip. It was still good.

"I do not wish to kill you," said Tarzan, returning to his fallen foe.

"I do not wish to die. But I cannot move without all of my armor."

"If I restore your armor, would you give me your word to accompany me wherever I go?"

"I refuse. I am loyal only to Nulthoom."

"Is that the name of your chief?"

"I refuse to say."

"So be it," said Tarzan. "I will leave you here for the vultures and jackals to devour."

"I do not know what those things are."

"Eaters of carrion. Is that the fate you wish for yourself?"

The warrior from Mars made an effort to shake his head in the negative, but it barely moved. It was clear to the ape-man that he had given up on his life.

While Tarzan considered what to do about his alien prisoner, Jad-bal-ja broke through the brush and approached, sniffing warily.

The Martian jerked his eyes to the left and saw the approaching beast.

"Is that a banth of Jasoom?"

"In a manner of speaking," replied Tarzan. "It obeys my commands. It is a meat eater. If I tell him to, he will consume you."

"I do not wish to be eaten by that Jasoomian banth."

"You have no say in the matter," returned Tarzan coldly. "I could run you through with a spear and let Jad-bal-ja devour such portions of you as pleases him."

The man closed his eyes. He shuddered. The thought of being consumed alive had penetrated to his dazed brain.

"Do with me what you will," he sighed stubbornly.

"You are brave, therefore I will let you live," decided Tarzan. "For now."

Stooping, he gathered up the man in his arms and, turning, walked back to meet with Muviro and his men, who were trotting up with their spears and shields at the ready.

"I am taking this man prisoner," announced Tarzan.

"He is wounded?" asked Muviro.

Tarzan nodded. "To what degree, I cannot tell. But he cannot move his limbs."

"His back is no doubt broken," decided Muviro.

"I think not," returned Tarzan. "But we will lay him across your saddle. You may ride behind me."

"I am tired of riding," scoffed the old man. "I will walk until I am tired of walking. But I am grateful for your offer, B'wana."

Tarzan laughed as he threw the Martian across Muviro's saddle and secured him there with a woven-vine rope taken from a saddlebag.

Once finished, Tarzan stated, "We will seek this man's encampment."

Muviro was looking the man's face over, frowning at what he saw.

"What nation birthed him?"

"No nation known to Africa," said Tarzan. "He comes from a very distant place."

"What is that place called?"

"Barsoom."

Muviro fingered his withered chin thoughtfully. "I have never heard of it."

"It is known by another name. One that you do know."

"What is that name, Tarzan?"

"Meriki, which some call Mars."

Muviro searched the jungle lord's sun-bronzed features for any hints of humor.

"I do not know whether to believe the big B'wana or not," he said finally.

"Believe me or not," returned Tarzan, "the truth is as I speak it."

"In that event, I believe you. But what does it mean?"

"It means," said Tarzan vaulting back into his own saddle, "that the people not born on the Earth have come to Africa to conquer it. This is not permitted. They must be returned whence they came, or slain."

"From the look in the B'wana's eyes, I believe he intends the latter course of action," murmured Muviro.

"That," stated Tarzan firmly, "is up to the men from Barsoom. Let us ride while there is still light."

Chapter 5

"I Smell Strange Beasts"

NIGHT WAS falling and the jungle was changing. The verdant and riotous colors gradually shaded to gray and the common noises of day went away, to be replaced by the more sinister sounds of night and those that hunted by night.

Working through the jungle trails, with Tarzan riding in the lead astride his stallion, the Waziri procession became more watchful.

Marching beside Tarzan, and clutching his spear, Muviro asked, "Will we make camp for the night?"

Tarzan tasted of the air and shook his head. "I smell strange beasts. They are not far off. We will ride until we make contact with them."

Muviro sniffed the air. "I do not recognize these odors."

"That is because these are not the odors of Africa, but of another world entirely."

"Do you recognize the spoor of these beasts, B'wana?"

Tarzan said, "I scent banth. It is like a lion but with ten legs."

Muviro's wrinkled mouth quirked tightly. "Why would it need so many legs?"

"Because there is so little game on Mars and such great competition for food, ten legs are necessary to race across the dead sea bottoms and catch prey."

Muviro grunted. "Why would these men from another world bring such beasts here?"

"Perhaps as food. Possibly for other reasons."

Tarzan turned around in his saddle and asked the prisoner in his own tongue, "I scent banth. Why is such a monster on Jasoom?"

"It got loose. We do not control it."

"Did your people also bring thoats?"

"I will admit this," said the other grudgingly.

"Thoats do not belong upon this world. They were not made for the jungle."

"Yet they are here," rejoined the other stubbornly.

"Tell me," said Tarzan, "how are you able to make the metal birds fly where you wish?"

"There's no harm in telling you, Ramdar. Built into their skulls is a mechanical brain. Through this, we use brain waves to direct the scout-bird in its flight. The upright metal feather atop its skull serves as a receiving antenna."

"In all my time upon Barsoom, I never saw such a steed."

"They are a new invention."

"And the ship that brought you here? It too is recent?"

"It was the first of its kind. Before very long, there will be others."

"How long have you been on Jasoom?" asked Tarzan.

"Not long enough."

"What do you mean by that?"

"Our scientists believe that if we persevere, we will eventually adjust to the heavier gravity of this planet and will not need specially treated armor in order to move about."

His eyes fixed on the way ahead, Tarzan absorbed this intelligence.

Another question occurred to him. "Why did you pick this continent to found a colony?"

"Our telescopes showed us how large it was. And there was a beautiful broad lake in the center. We wish to dwell on the shores of that lake because we understand that it would provide us with fresh water and eventually, we might expand to the eastern coast of Jor and resume building great sailing ships as our seafaring ancestors had done in the young days of Barsoom."

"What do you mean by Jor?"

"It is the name Nulthoom gave to this continent."

"The name you use is incorrect. This is Africa."

"Once Nulthoom conquers it, this place will be called Jor."

"Is Nulthoom your war chief?" pressed Tarzan.

The blond-haired warrior of Barsoom declined to answer.

Tarzan turned his attention to the smells ahead. Among them was an odor he never thought he would smell again, the musky scent of a thoat, the Martian equivalent of a horse, although it bore very little resemblance to an earthly equine, possessing a preposterously wide maw at one end and a broad flat tail at the other.

Frequently, the ape-man scanned the skies for loitering metallic birds. But the only winged thing he spied was a circling vulture.

Tarzan fixed his attention on the vulture. He knew Ska the vulture as well as he did Manu the monkey and the great apes. He knew Ska's ways and habits. This lone vulture was circling something that was dying. There could be no doubt about that.

Sniffing the air, the ape-man sought to understand what manner of creature was approaching its death. Mingled with the metallic smell of fresh blood was another he knew well. Omtag, the giraffe.

Dismounting, Tarzan told Muviro, "I must investigate this."

RUNNING DOWN the trail, the jungle lord veered into the underbrush, and he once again took to the trees. A series of leaps, followed by some artful swinging, brought him to a clearing surrounded by nut bushes where a full-grown giraffe lay on its side, panting but otherwise unmoving.

After dropping lightly to the ground, Tarzan approached the majestic creature and saw that its eyes were half closed.

Death was near. Investigating its body, he found many puncture wounds. These were not made by knives or spears.

"Swords did this," said Tarzan to himself.

Swords were uncommon among the African tribes, the ape-man knew. And no local tribe hunted giraffe for meat. Nor did any black native or hunting party of black men kill giraffes for sport. This was not the work of whites, either. Safari hunters would use rifles.

It was inescapable that men from Barsoom had committed this atrocity. For Tarzan knew that the sword was the chief weapon employed by the warring races of the red planet.

There was nothing that could be done for the giraffe, except to put it out of its misery. Whispering words of reassurance, the bronze giant extracted his knife as he knelt and ended the poor creature's suffering with a swift stroke across its mottled throat. The giraffe shuddered once, then seemed to collapse into itself.

After wiping the gore from his blade on the animal's pelt, Tarzan returned to the trail and caught up with Muviro and his warriors.

"A giraffe was slain by a war party armed with swords. Those we seek will be armed with swords, as well as with bows."

"Do we also face guns?"

"I do not know," replied Tarzan. "But it is possible. My knowledge of the white men of Mars is limited. They may possess rifles and pistols. But this one we have captured does not."

Unexpectedly, Jad-bal-ja growled.

Tarzan turned his head and saw the tufted tail of the golden lion whipping about and snapping in anger. His hackles were lifting. There was no mistaking that warning sign. Danger was approaching.

"What is it, Jad-bal-ja?" the ape-man asked in the language jungle denizens understood.

But the golden lion did not reply. Instead, he gathered himself and launched his sleek body into the brush.

There came from the near distance an incredible conglomeration of snapping, snarling, and other violent noises. The sounds were unmistakable. Two animals locked in mortal combat.

Jad-bal-ja gave out a mighty roar. And in response, there followed an answering roar, even mightier! It was a terrible reverberating sound, one never before heard across the African plains.

Tarzan knew that nightmare roar.

"Muviro! Lend me your war spear. I must go!"

The old man handed up his spear. Tarzan took it, saying, "Keep your men on the trail. Do not stray."

Without waiting for a reply, Tarzan of the Apes sprang from the saddle and vanished into the choking greenery where two titans roared and howled out their terrible fury.

Chapter 6

BEAST OF BARSOOM

CLUTCHING MUVIRO'S war spear, Tarzan broke a trail toward the terrible sounds of animal combat.

No surprise touched his bronzed features, but in his mighty chest, his heart executed a strange leap of shock when he came upon them.

Locked in mortal combat before him was his faithful golden lion and a creature he never expected to encounter in the African wilderness.

It resembled nothing so much as a lion as seen in a nightmare. For its many-fanged mouth resembled Gimla, the crocodile. It was hairless, except for a bushy mane about its throat. It was longer than an African lion, its torso so elongated it appeared to be distorted.

The banth stood on its back legs, which numbered six, three on each side, while its smooth-skinned upper torso reared up and two sets of paws raked and swiped and clutched at Jad-bal-ja, who had also stood on his hind legs, striking back and blocking the other with its own massive paws and claws.

This was a banth of Barsoom. It outweighed Jad-bal-ja by a quarter ton, but its ungainly physique was not to its advantage in Earth's heavy gravity.

The two animals snapped and snarled at one another as their claws dug and raked hide. Although outclassed in size and weight, Jad-bal-ja more than made up for that disadvantage in his greater agility.

33

Both contending animals appeared equally ferocious. They ripped and raked at one another, the banth's protruding emerald orbs fearful while the lion's deeper green eyes held a killing light.

Locked together, the two brutes jockeyed about, kicking up dirt, and giving vent to their terrible cries while straining to remain upright in the face of their opposite's onslaught. For to give ground, they knew, was to submit to death.

Tarzan could see that the golden lion was holding its own, but the banth had the advantage of its four clutching paws. Its great mouth yawned to reveal needle teeth that were far more terrible than Jad-bal-ja's fanged jaws.

Those vicious teeth lunged for the lion's throat. Tarzan could see that his faithful feline could not long withstand and evade their snapping threat.

Plunging in, Tarzan took his spear in both hands and drove it into the banth's hairless flank, seeking the heart.

So consumed by animal fury was the banth that he did not feel the spear tip tunneling through his vitals. He snapped once, but the golden lion swiped at one protuberant eye, deflecting the attack.

On Mars, Tarzan had been able to manhandle banths with relative ease. But here on Earth, he did not have that advantage in superior physical strength. Yet the banth was hampered by the greater gravity, and Tarzan could see that it struggled to keep its upper torso and head erect.

Giving the spear a twist with both powerful hands, Tarzan jerked the weapon this way and that until he found a beating heart.

Only then did the banth recognize his peril. By then it was too late.

Throwing back its weird-shaped head, the leonine monster gave forth a mournful howl, one that foretold of death.

Hearing this, Jad-bal-ja saw his opportunity. His gaping jaws lunged for the banth's throat, clamped down, and came away clutching a great bloody gout that left behind a bleeding cavity too terrible to permit survival.

The howl was choked off before it could trail away.

"Back, Jal-bad-ja," commanded Tarzan.

The obedient lion released his hold and jumped back.

Leaving the spear, Tarzan stepped away as the banth rolled over on its side, and began convulsing in its death throes. His long tail beat the African earth, while ten padded feet quivered spasmodically.

Knowing that it was doomed, Tarzan ignored it, and went to the golden lion.

"Let me see to your wounds," he said gently.

The golden lion sat still as the ape-man investigated its tawny fur, examining claw wounds, rips, and abrasions.

None were serious, but all required attending. Disappearing into the foliage, Tarzan found some leaves that he knew had medicinal properties. He rubbed these together in his hands, which brought forth the healing juice. He applied these leaves one by one to Jad-bal-ja's wounds.

Once he was done, he signaled for the lion to follow him.

When they returned to the trail, they found old Muviro and his men patiently waiting, leaning on their spears. They had heard the sounds of combat, and the tenseness in their muscular bodies suggested that they would have plunged into the fray had Muviro commanded it.

Tarzan went to the captive Martian tied to the saddle and demanded, "Why would you bring a banth to Jasoom? They cannot be tamed or ridden."

The pale-skinned Martian said, "It will do no harm to tell you this. It was brought to hunt the wild animals that would otherwise trouble our people. It was also thought, due to its lightness and sleekness, to adapt to the gravity of Jasoom. My people believed that it would serve us to see how well it fared."

"What other animals have your people brought here?" Tarzan demanded of the man.

"You will meet them soon enough," the other retorted, then fell silent.

"You forget upon whose land you dwell," warned Tarzan, a growl in his tone.

Suddenly, Muviro cried out, "B'wana! Behold!"

Tarzan turned toward the call. The native was pointing to the sky.

There, three of the white metal birds were flying in a triangular formation, gliding in their direction, wings beating in synchronized unison.

Reaching for his quiver, Tarzan removed a clutch of captured arrows, saying, "Give one arrow each to your archers, Muviro. Use no other arrows."

Muviro took the alien quills and distributed them among his archers.

Tarzan picked up his own bow and nocked one of the Martian arrows into the gut string.

"When they are near enough to be certain of success," he told the bowmen, "let fly!"

Muviro's archers separated from the rest, who were spearmen, took up positions and fitted their arrows to strings.

Then they waited. They knew that to point their bows to the sky would be to warn their foes. They wanted them to draw nearer, unaware of the danger.

Tarzan held his own bow at the ready, with the arrowhead pointing downward.

The three metallic birds sighted the double column of black warriors and began dropping lower, the better to study them. If they suspected danger, they did not behave that way.

"Aim for the wings," cautioned Tarzan. "The riders will be difficult to unseat."

As the ape-man watched, the mounted warriors in white armor took up their own bows and fitted arrows into them.

"It is war," whispered Muviro.

Tarzan nodded, his keen gaze studying the approaching winged steeds.

Then he called out, "Release!"

He brought his own arrow up, and loosed it.

Behind him, the Waziri archers unleashed a whistling storm of shafts.

Seeing the rising threats, the mounted Martians did not quail. Instead they unleashed their own arrows, which came flying down in a thin deadly rain.

Two Waziri warriors were struck, one mortally.

But the metal birds received the worst of it. Their wings became quilled with Martian arrows.

At once, the strange steeds began pinwheeling in the sky, struggling to maintain altitude, but each fell into hapless flat spins.

One after the other, they crashed splinteringly into the jungle.

"Spearmen, follow me!" said Tarzan. "Muviro, see to the wounded."

"Yes, B'wana."

TARZAN LED the company of spearmen into the jungle and found the crashed birds, one by one. The first rider had broken his neck in the fall. There was nothing that could be done for him.

The second still sat upright in his saddle, his smashed avian steed beneath him. Sighting the approaching force, he swiveled his helmeted head and attempted to nock an arrow. Only then did he realize that his bow had been broken in the fall.

Climbing out of his stirrups, he drew a short-sword from its scabbard, and stood ready to meet his assailants.

Tarzan pulled up short, and spoke in the universal language of Barsoom.

"Kaor! Surrender, for you are outnumbered."

The expression on the helmeted man's face was one of blank astonishment. Before he could respond to the fact that a man of Jasoom spoke his own tongue, a grim determination came over his too-pale features.

Apparently realizing that he was greatly outnumbered, he lunged forward, the point of his blade held low, plainly intent upon disemboweling the bronzed giant.

Tarzan's hunting knife licked out, deflecting the other's first feint, whereupon the warrior lifted his blade, turning it sideways, and executed a sudden half-turn. The sword's edge sliced in, aimed for the ape-man's neck in a stroke meant to decapitate his enemy.

Seeing this danger to their war chief, the spearmen of the Waziri spoke the language of death.

The swordsman was impaled by flying spears where he stood. The force threw him backward, and he sprawled across his saddle, quivering, his sword falling from lifeless fingers.

Tarzan stepped in, took the sword, and examined it. He recognized the workmanship. These were Orovars, the white race of Mars, whose swords were unique among all the contending races of the red planet.

"Follow me," he told his spearmen.

They soon found the third Martian. He had been thrown from his saddle and lay flat on the ground, pieces of his armor scattered everywhere.

Tarzan strode up to him, looked down and said, "I am Tarzan, lord of this jungle. Speak your name."

The man may have been too dazed to be surprised to hear his own tongue being spoken to him. So he answered naturally, but with an effort.

"Ban-Dun-Thur."

"Where is your camp?"

"Not far."

"How many strong?"

The Martian looked from Tarzan to the blacks behind him and said simply, "Too strong for you and your black panthans."

"These are my fiercest warriors," snapped Tarzan. "They are not mercenaries. Now answer truthfully."

"Fifty strong."

"What weapons do they wield?"

"Swords. Bows. Spears."

"No rifles?"

"I do not know that word."

"Guns?"

The man shook his head. Suddenly, his lips became moist and red, and he began coughing.

Tarzan reached down and felt of his chest. Many ribs were broken. Too many.

"You are dying," said Tarzan.

"If I am dying, at least I have seen the great lake of Jor and drank of her pure waters and consumed her sacred fish. When my brethren come to this world, they will take up my sword and carry forth my name."

"If that is your belief," said Tarzan coldly, "then you die in vain. I will not permit invaders from Barsoom to take up residence in my jungle."

"You cannot stop us."

"I have stopped you, and your fellow warriors. Now I go to finish off the rest of your unwelcome force."

"I curse your name then."

"Better you save your imprecations for the vultures who will soon find you."

"I do not know that word vulture."

"You will know them when you meet them. If you are still breathing."

With that, Tarzan turned his back on the dying invader and led his spearmen back to the Waziri headman and his forces.

Muviro had finished tending to the wounded and now asked, "What news?"

"Three have been vanquished. The force we face is half a hundred strong."

"Twice our number," said Muviro. "It will be a battle."

Tarzan showed the old man his sword.

"Spears against swords. Arrows against arrows. We will make camp and await the falling of night. After we have eaten, I will scout."

Chapter 7

MONSTERS FROM MARS

FOR THEIR evening meal, the warriors of Muviro scattered to hunt in pairs.

Before an hour had passed, they returned with wild boar, red deer, and turtle. The campfire was built, then the game was dressed and the meat roasted and passed around on the tips of arrows.

Tarzan took a cut of roasted deer to the bound prisoner, asking, "Are you hungry?"

The other declined to answer, but the truth was in his pitiful blue eyes.

"Tell me your name and I will see that you eat," stated Tarzan.

"Gor-Dun-Ree. I will tell you no more."

"It is enough." The ape-man signed to one of his Waziri to feed the captive, then returned to the fire.

Chewing on a knot of turtle meat, Muviro turned to Tarzan squatting next to him and remarked, "The campfire will attract attention, B'wana."

Tarzan nodded. "This is my desire."

"I will watch the skies while you eat."

"There is no need, Muviro. If the enemy is wise, they will seek us by land."

"They may not be wise."

"They may not have any more metal birds to send aloft," suggested Tarzan. "But we will soon see."

Once more, Jad-bal-ja scented danger before anyone else. The golden lion had dragged a piece of deer from the campfire in order to eat it raw. He stood off from the others, not wishing to have his eyes and nose bothered by the smoke of cooking.

The smoke also concealed from Tarzan the smell of nearing danger.

So it was that when the golden lion gave out a roar of warning, Tarzan and his warriors sprang to their feet, seizing such weapons as they had at hand.

Tarzan went to the nearest tree and climbed it monkey-style, soon reaching the upper boughs.

There was a commotion to the west. The plodding of many heavy feet entwined with a cacophony that included the creaking of great wheels and the snapping of tree branches created by the passing of beasts too broad-bodied for the narrow forest trail.

Tarzan had heard that sound before.

Diving back to earth, he sought Muviro and said, "War chariots approach. They will be drawn by great beasts resembling elephants, but alien to your eyes. Explain this to your men. Let them know what to expect lest they be frightened by the uncanny aspect of these monsters from Mars."

Joining them, Muviro addressed his warriors in their own language. He gestured expressively, making the nature of the threat as clear as he was able.

Mounting his horse, Tarzan declared, "I will run ahead to meet these intruders. Follow, but keep a safe distance."

Calling out to Jad-bal-ja, Tarzan summoned the golden lion to his side. Together, they raced along the jungle trail which twisted and turned, making it difficult to see the way ahead except where moonlight painted the path.

Soon, the ape-man smelled the musky odor of zitidar. It was another scent he had never expected to again inhale. But it confirmed what his ears had told him concerning the trouble coming his way.

The horse began to scent the odor and commenced trembling. The dumb beast did not recognize the smell assaulting his nostrils. And because he did not recognize it, a natural fear overtook him.

Tarzan reassured him with a strong stroke against the side of his neck and the horse continued on, still nervous, but reassured by his master's touch.

Over the sound of its hooves, Tarzan listened carefully, trying to piece together the number of war chariots he faced. Four appeared to be their number. From experience, he knew that Martian chariots were not one-man affairs, but carried multiple warriors.

The ground began to shake under the relentless pads of oncoming zitidars.

When he sensed that he was very close to making contact, Tarzan piloted his mount into the forest underbrush and dismounted. Urging it to move away from the trail, the ape-man leapt into the trees, found a leafy coign of vantage, and there he waited, unseen.

On the other side of the trail, where Jad-bal-ja had been directed to conceal himself, the golden lion crouched, tufted tail switching in anticipation.

The first war chariot plunged around the turn of the trail in a mad cacophony of sounds. The beast was not so large as Tarzan had expected, yet hanging branches bent and broke as they grazed its pale form. It was clad in white armor. Moreover, it was more shaggy than any zitidar he had encountered on Mars. Through gaps in its armored plates, the visible fur was white as cotton discolored by jungle dust.

Behind it rolled an exotic war chariot crammed with soldiers in elaborate white armor, holding spears at the ready. The driver also clutched a war spear, since reins were not part of the Martian war-chariot array.

Watching, Tarzan crept out along a stout branch, until he was lying on his naked belly over the trail.

The first chariot swept under him in a cloud of dust.

Giving a bloodcurdling cry, Tarzan drew his knife and dropped into the midst of the packed warriors, found chinks in their armor, and impaled exposed throats, while his powerful leg muscles kicked the startled men off the back of the rolling contrivance.

On the other side of the trail, the golden lion pounced on the unprepared zitidar. Pandemonium resulted. The elephantine beast was brought up short, and the still-rolling chariot collided with the beast's shaggy hindquarters. It lifted its twin trunks and made a trumpeting call of distress.

The collision knocked Tarzan off his feet, but he soon regained his footing. Turning, he saw the second chariot bearing down.

Although its zitidar was not moving at a pace greater than a heavy trot, it could not stop short, and so trampled the surviving Martian warriors who had the misfortune to fall into its path.

Springing for the oncoming zitidar, the ape-man landed on the top of its helmeted head. The warriors of the second chariot saw him and began shouting in anger and consternation.

As they lifted their spears to their shoulders preparatory to chucking them, the bronzed giant crouched down on the zitidar's back, turned and, using his knife, slashed the straps that held the gigantic helmet in place.

Kicking the massive contrivance away produced an instantaneous effect.

The beast's head became heavy and its jaw smashed to the earth, bringing it up short and causing the second chariot to career before colliding into its immobile bulk.

Tarzan went among the warriors and made short work of them. Their armor was not sufficiently tight to prevent the keen edge of his blade from seeking bone and muscle.

Behind them, a third chariot rocked to a halt, and the warriors let fly with their spears, which Tarzan evaded with an agility that caused the anger on their faces to collapse in shock.

Many spears landed point-downward and stuck up like haphazard fence posts. Yanking the fallen shafts from the ground, Tarzan turned and hurled them, one after the other, back at those who had dared to attack him in his own forest.

That was enough for the third charioteer. He got their vehicle turned around on the jungle trail and fled in weaponless panic. In their terror, they tore off so violently that they threw a wheel, crashing the chariot broadside against a clump of trees.

Dismounting in fear, they melted into the jungle, thus delaying any alarm that might be raised and preserving for Tarzan the element of surprise.

BY THIS time, Muviro and his spearmen had arrived, and they fell to finishing the job that the golden lion was energetically enjoying. The feline was worrying the zitidar's throat as it flailed about with its serpentine trunks but was unable to defend itself. Spears and arrows found lodging in the crevices between the plates of white metal that sheathed the terrible beast.

When it was over, they turned their attention to the surviving zitidar. But Tarzan intervened, blocking their weapons with an upraised hand, saying, "Spare this animal. It will be useful."

Lowering their weapons, the warriors gathered around the felled creature and took stock of it.

Its resemblance to an elephant was marked, but also general. The massive head lacked a mouth. Instead, a double trunk dominated the brute's face. Its eyes were a pale blue, and very round, as if expressing an unwavering surprise.

Muviro walked around it once and then addressed the ape-man.

"In the books of your library, I have seen pictures of a creature like this. One resembling an elephant, but of an entirely different species. The name given by white men was woolly mammoth."

Tarzan nodded. "Yes, this one resembles a woolly mammoth. It is different than the zitidars I saw upon Mars. This one has two trunks, and its eyes are socketed in its skull and not set at the end of flexible eye stalks. But it is a zitidar."

"Why does it have six legs?" asked Muviro.

"The beasts of Mars possess more legs than the beasts of Earth," replied Tarzan. "I do not know why. But their evolution is different than ours."

"This one cannot lift its head."

"Without its armor, it is unable to move on the Earth."

"What will you do with it, B'wana?"

Tarzan recovered the helmet and said, "On Mars, the driver controlled these beasts through the force of his thoughts. I will restore the helmet and see if it will take me to the interloper base camp."

"They will know we are coming," cautioned Muviro.

Tarzan replied, "They will know one of their war chariots is returning. They will not know Tarzan of the Apes is driving it. Bring the prisoner. I will place him in the chariot. Your warriors will follow at a distance. This way, we will have the element of surprise until we attack."

Muviro went to consult with his warriors as Tarzan took the great helmet off the dead zitidar and used it to encase the skull of the one that survived.

After a short time, the Martian monster lifted its head and gathered its sextuple legs, slowly and painfully regaining its feet.

First checking the chariot, then climbing on board by its open back, Tarzan took a position at its ornate head, then sent a mental command to the ungainly beast. What had worked on Mars might not work on Earth. But there was only one way to determine that.

The beast blinked its weirdly vacant blue eyes and plodded ahead several steps, then started to turn. Laboriously, it made a circle on the jungle trail until its elephantine head was pointed back in the direction of its coming.

Signaling to Jad-bal-ja, Tarzan climbed aboard the chariot and took a position at the front. He had collected one of the fallen warrior's helmets and placed it on his head. Immediately he felt a strange sensation as if his head was trying to lift off his shoulders.

After a few minutes, the sensation dissipated.

Jad-bal-ja climbed into the chariot obediently and sat down upon his haunches.

Lastly, Muviro came up on his horse, and several warriors seized the captive Martian and removed him to the war chariot's floor. Eyes anguished, the bound prisoner pushed himself as far away from the magnificent black-maned lion as possible without tumbling out the open back.

"Follow at a respectful distance," Tarzan told Muviro. "I do not want the enemy camp to see you before it is necessary."

"Yes, B'wana."

Tarzan focused on the back of the zitidar's shaggy head and thought a simple command: *Return to your village.*

With a rolling of its powerful shoulders and hairy haunches, the zitidar began plodding ahead. It moved unsteadily at first, but soon fell into a rolling gait that brought Tarzan's memory back to his first days on Barsoom when he had discovered a driverless chariot led by a zitidar much more fantastic in physical form than this one. That chariot had been enormous, for it belonged to the four-armed green giants of Mars. This was sized for a normal-sized man, yet it was still spacious.

For nearly an hour, the mastodonian beast patiently dragged the creaking chariot along the jungle trail, never deviating from its path nor making any sound of its own. Tarzan could see that, even with the armor that counteracted Earth's gravity, the powerful beast yet struggled to move its six legs in proper coordination. At times, it nearly stumbled. At other points, a padded foot dragged briefly.

Studying the creature, Tarzan realized it had to belong to a part of Barsoom other than that which he had experienced. Evolution had given it a shaggy coat of snow-white fur and the flexible eye stalks that had denoted the species of zitidar he had earlier encountered were wholly absent.

This implied that this beast belonged to a latitude of Barsoom where predators were few. Casting his mind back to his Martian experience of a dozen years before, he recalled that the terrible banths roamed the moss-covered dried sea floors. Those areas were warm during the day but quite cool at night. This beast seemed more fitted for a less temperate climate.

All these observations were unimportant for the task at hand. Tarzan made note of them in case they proved important later.

At last, the jungle trail devolved into a grassland. The smell of Lake Victoria was very close now. Halting at the verge of the savanna, the ape-man cast his gaze ahead where the lunar light bathed the plain, which was dotted with palm trees.

He perceived nothing that did not belong there, but smells reaching his nostrils told of human habitation. Not black men nor white men. Therefore, men of Mars. The heavy stink of the Martian eight-legged steed called the thoat was also strong in the night breeze.

Mentally commanding the zitidar to come to a halt, Tarzan waited for his Waziri to catch up to him.

Once they did, he stepped off the chariot and addressed them.

"Dawn will break soon. The camp of the enemy may sleep, or it may not. I will advance. You will wait here. Listen for my call."

"What if the call does not come?" asked Muviro sincerely.

"If the call does not come, it may mean that I am dead. But it is more likely that it will mean that I am treating with the enemy. I do not wish to lose any more warriors than necessary. If these men of Mars can be reasoned with, I will reason with them. But if they are like the prisoner, they are stubborn and willful, and will not listen to reason. Therefore, I mean to slay them to the last man, for they do not belong on the Earth, and their beasts will ruin this area. We cannot afford to let either multiply, which is their plan. Africa belongs to the Earth. It does not belong to Mars."

"Shall I send a runner back to the estate," asked Muviro, "so that reinforcements can be dispatched?"

"They will not arrive in time," returned Tarzan, "but it is a sound idea. Do it."

"Go in safety, B'wana," whispered Muviro.

Turning away, Tarzan untied the Martian prisoner and placed one of the light metal helmets on his head so that he could stand erect.

"You will stand at the head of this chariot," he instructed.

"What if I refuse?"

"My knife will find your heart."

Gor-Dun-Ree considered that for a moment, and the steely glint in Tarzan's eyes told him that the ape-man issued no idle threat. He meant it.

"You ask me to betray my people," he pointed out.

Tarzan said, "If you tell them I come in peace, to parlay with them, I am prepared to talk of peace. If they do not want peace, then I will make war. That will be up to them. Do you understand?"

"I understand that you are a man who does not throw his words around lightly. I believe you. And because I believe you, I will trust you to keep your word up to the point when peace is no longer in the offing."

Tarzan nodded. Turning away, he sent a mental command to the zitidar, which promptly lurched ahead.

The soldier of Mars looked momentarily taken aback.

"It obeys you?"

"I am Tarzan, Lord of the Jungle. This is my jungle. This beast, therefore, falls under my rule."

"You impress me, Tarzan."

Tarzan did not acknowledge this compliment from an enemy. His gray eyes were fixed on the moonlit path ahead. They did not glance back once, as if the ape-man did not fear his captive.

Noticing this, Gor-Dun-Ree took silent umbrage. On his own world, he was a lesser noble, and did not consider this bronze-skinned barbarian of Jasoom to be his equal, much less his superior. He would have his revenge, if he could.

Chapter 8

"Escape is Impossible"

DAWN WAS again breaking when the zitidar-drawn chariot rolled onto the grassy plain facing the eastern shore of Lake Victoria.

As it creaked along, a fresh cloud of odors reached Tarzan's nostrils. They were the putrid smells of death and rotting elephant meat.

Before long, they came across the rotting carcass of a bull elephant and then, beyond it, another. Botflies buzzed about these corpses.

Addressing his prisoner, Tarzan asked, "Why do you slay those elephants?"

"They were uncooperative," replied the other.

"Explain," snapped Tarzan, a growing anger rising in his naked breast.

"These animals resemble our zitidars," grunted Gor-Dun-Ree. "So we thought to tame them as beasts of burden. But they refused our mental commands. They were mere dumb brutes. And since we sometimes consume the flesh of zitidars, we butchered them as food."

"Elephants are not zitidars," retorted Tarzan, "And you had no right to slay them, for here they are not hunted as game, except in emergencies."

"I have tasted their meat. It was interesting. The flavor is nothing like zitidar."

Tarzan tamped down his rising anger. There was no place for it now. But it was an example of why he could not permit these Martians to build a settlement here. The ape-man had seen how the jungle trees on either side of the trail had been damaged by the passing of their massive war chariots, for the zitidars were too broadly built for certain portions of the path. He would not have his jungle bespoiled by outsiders. Tarzan would make that clear to them.

Farther along, they came upon the rotting remains of another giraffe.

"Your people did this?" demanded Tarzan.

"That animal was not very tasty," replied Gor-Dun-Ree nonchalantly. "It was also uncooperative. But it was not suitable as a beast of burden. So we slew those we found and left them where they lay for the banth."

Tarzan said nothing. He was not pleased. Although himself a mighty hunter, he hunted within the laws of the jungle and by its unwritten rules. One killed for food and in self-defense. But not wantonly. Animals were not slain because they were inconvenient. It was their jungle as much as it was the land of those who lorded over it.

Finally, in the full light of day, they came to the settlement.

A thorny boma had been erected within sight of the palm-shaded mudflats edging Lake Victoria. Within were a cluster of strangely shaped thatched huts built of bamboo and palm fronds reinforced by what appeared to be girders and other metallic forms salvaged from some type of machine.

In the center sat a more elaborate hut whose roof was of circular metal. On it was written in the hieroglyphics of Barsoom one word: *Jor.* Tarzan took it to be a piece of the hull of the craft that had carried these pale Martians to Earth, and Jor the name of their ship.

Smells of frying fish were everywhere. These interlopers clearly had been taking advantage of the plenty offered by Lake Victoria. Tarzan understood why. On dying Mars, few waterways survived. Fish were consequently rare. No doubt the lake's abundant carp, perch, and rock bass were considered a delicacy by Martian palates.

A thorn corral had been built for the glossy eight-legged thoats, whose monstrous heads were carried a dozen feet high on their long, massive necks. They were more pale than the slate and yellow-footed species of his acquaintance. Two other zitidars stood in another corral. They had been unhitched from their chariots.

Turning to the golden lion, who was now following the chariot quietly, the ape-man spoke words that no other human could hope to comprehend. Green eyes blinked back in silent understanding, and Jad-bal-ja slipped away, seeking concealment in the bush verging the savanna.

"Announce our coming," commanded Tarzan of Gor-Dun-Ree. "And no tricks. My blade has tasted the blood of many, both man and beast."

Cupping his hands over his mouth, the Martian called out.

"Kaor, I have come with a prisoner," he shouted.

Tarzan's blade touched the back of his neck, just under the rim of the protective helmet.

Turning, Gor-Dun-Ree asked, "What would you have me say? If I tell them that I am your prisoner, they will not welcome you."

"Tarzan is no man's prisoner."

The other shrugged as if it didn't matter.

From out of the huts came groups of helmeted Martians. Some gripped spears, some had swords belted to their sides. All wore harnesses marked with the strange device of a white triangle topped by a red half-moon.

Three men advanced bearing long-barreled rifles.

"You told me there were no rifles," growled Tarzan in a low voice.

"I lied to you."

The men with rifles fanned out and pointed their muzzles at Tarzan from three different sides.

Tarzan raised his voice in their language. "I come in peace. Lower your weapons."

The men declined to do that. They shifted about on their feet, keeping their muzzles trained upon the ape-man's bronzed figure. His sinewy musculature impressed them greatly.

"Come to a halt, Gor-Dun-Ree," one of them said.

Gor-Dun-Ree gave the mental command that compelled his shaggy armored zitidar to lurch to a halt.

"Dismount, prisoner."

Tarzan stepped off the back of the war chariot. No fear showed on his bronze features. His flinty eyes raked the others.

"Walk ahead."

Tarzan complied, but his right hand never strayed far from the hilt of his hunting knife.

Gor-Dun-Ree stepped off behind him and said, "This is the one who slew our malagor scouts."

"Do you deny it?"

"This jungle is under my guardianship," returned Tarzan coldly. "You are all interlopers, killers of innocent animals. You do not belong here. But I come to discuss how this matter might be settled."

"Ro-Dun-Bo will decide this matter," said one. And he switched his gun muzzle toward the central hut that dominated the bizarre boma, indicating that Tarzan should go there.

Tarzan walked toward the elaborate hut. He stepped in after a guard pulled aside the door covering, which was of tanned zitidar hide.

INSIDE SAT a burly man whose broad features were dominated by icy blue eyes under blond brows. He wore armor that was decorated with strange designs, and had the air of a military man. His chair was formed from scrap metal, yet it suggested a barbaric throne.

"I am *Tarzan-ko-do-raku,* here called Tarzan of the Apes."

"I am Ro-Dun-Bo, utan of this expedition. How does a man of Jasoom speak the language of Barsoom?"

"On your world, I was known as Ramdar. I ruled a tribe of great white apes."

Ro-Dun-Bo laughed roughly. "It is impossible. The great white apes are too ferocious to be ruled even by a man of your stature. Impossible!"

"Nevertheless, it is true."

"Are you a king in this land?"

Tarzan shook his head firmly. "No."

"A warlord then?"

"I am war chief of the Waziri tribe. My warriors are camped beyond the savanna. They await word of me. If they do not hear, they will descend upon you and wipe you out to the last man."

A mock-serious expression came over Ro-Dun-Bo's pale countenance.

"You say you come in peace, but you bring warriors."

"I bring the strength to enforce my will," stated Tarzan unequivocally.

"Very well, speak your piece."

Tarzan fixed him with his unwavering regard. "You have come from Barsoom. To Barsoom, you must return. This is not your land. And this is not the planet of your birth. You have already caused harm to the jungle. You must return to your own planet."

"That is your demand?"

"It is," replied Tarzan flatly. "And in this jungle, the law of Tarzan is inviolate."

"Even if I were to accede to your demand," stated Ro-Dun-Bo, "it would be impossible to do so. The vessel that brought us here is no more. We cannot return to Barsoom. And we have no intention of doing so, even if we could. It is the decision of Nulthoom to relocate to this land entirely. Your request is denied."

"This means war," warned Tarzan.

"We have come prepared for war. We have planted our flag here. We will not surrender to you or to anyone else. That is final."

Tarzan studied Ro-Dun-Bo for a long minute without speaking. At his back were two men with radium rifles. These had been at the ready, but now at a signal from their leader, they were lifted and pointed at his back, one at each shoulder blade.

Tarzan could not see this, but his ears told him what had transpired.

"They will not shoot at this close range," he said to the utan.

Ro-Dun-Bo gave a half-smile. "What compels you to say that, war chief of Jasoom?"

"Because I know they fire radium bullets, which explode upon contact. Their fury would rip through my body and injure yours. They dare not fire."

A flicker of concern showed on Ro-Dun-Bo's previously placid face. Glowering, he said, "Take him out and slay him."

"I refuse to move," said Tarzan.

"Then I will gesture, and you will be shot on the very spot where you stand."

Without warning, Tarzan sprang for the man's throat, wrenched him around, and ripped the helmet off his head. Ro-Dun-Bo toppled forward. Tarzan grabbed him up and held him before him as a human shield.

"Lower your weapons!" he commanded.

The two riflemen hesitated.

Tarzan's knife came out of its scabbard and found Ro-Dun-Bo's pulsing jugular. High on the ape-man's forehead, an old scar sprang to life, livid as flame.

"My blade will open his throat if you do not depart," growled the ape-man.

"Go—go!" stammered Ro-Dun-Bo.

The men departed, leaving Tarzan and his prisoner alone.

Ro-Dun-Bo grunted, "I do not know what you intend, Jasoomian, but surely you understand that this colony has been surrounded. Escape is impossible."

Instead of replying, the ape-man threw back his head and gave out the war cry of the bull ape.

Hearing this, Ro-Dun-Bo's knees turned to figurative water and he almost slipped from Tarzan's grasp, for the sound terrified him deep into his marrow.

In the near distance, the resounding battle cries of the Waziri tribe could be heard.

And Tarzan smiled the fierce smile of a born hunter.

Chapter 9

SKIRMISH

DRAWING HIS blade away from his captive's throat, Tarzan half turned, dragging the Martian leader with him by sheer strength.

He drove the blade point into the banth skin at the back of the hut, ripped up and then down, creating a vertical slit large enough to slip through. Through this, he pushed Ro-Dun-Bo and leaped out behind him, gathering him up as if he weighed no more than a child.

"Are all men of Jasoom as strong as you?" gasped the military ruler.

"Quiet!" admonished Tarzan, and carried the man away.

Moving to a better point of vantage, the ape-man saw his Waziri warriors stream out of the jungle edge as the Martians scattered to their mounts.

Those who had thoats available to them leaped upon their backs and began to charge in the direction of the attacking blacks. These men had radium rifles, and they began firing almost as soon as they were firmly on their sleek, slate-colored backs.

Two black spearmen fell immediately, causing Tarzan to release his captive and spring into smooth action.

Pelting out from the cluster of huts, the ape-man ran to overtake the thoat-mounted warriors. But before he could get far, Orovar swordsmen intercepted him, and the bronze giant found himself in the swirling thick of combat.

58

With his strong right arm, he blocked the sword arm of one warrior and plunged his blade into the other's breastplate. Wrenching it out brought forth a fountain of blood. The jungle lord turned and slashed the throat of another.

This man's sword fell from his fingers, but before the blade could touch the ground, Tarzan caught it by the hilt. Now properly armed for a sword fight, he holstered his hunting knife and transferred the long blade to his strong right hand.

There ensued a rapid battle of contending blades. Sparks flew as glittering blades smashed and banged against one another. Men grunted in their deadly exertions.

The swordsmen were well practiced in their art, but Tarzan's strength was greater than theirs and his blade the equal of any that sought his vitals.

He smashed one swordsman back, decapitated a second with a blinding backswing, then removed the right hand from yet another. Staggered by the savage fury of the ape-man, the overwhelmed foes fell to the ground as one.

Free of battle, Tarzan threw away the blade with a disdainful gesture and raced for the charging thoats.

Radium rifles were cracking, and a Waziri warrior fell even as others released their deadly spears and arrows, his body blown apart by the explosive round.

Immediately, Tarzan's heart sank. Fleet as he was, swift as a gazelle, he could not clear the intervening space and overwhelm the mounted riflemen. One after another, Waziri spearmen hurtled backward to spill their vital fluids on the grass.

Some survivors raised their shields before them, but no African shield could turn a radium bullet. Or any other bullet for that matter.

An expertly cast spear rose from the strong right arm of one black warrior, and when it came down again, it ran through one of the mounted Martians. He reeled in his saddle, pale features aghast, and fell over dead before he hit the ground.

Charging out of the bush, Jad-bal-ja pounced on him and began worrying the body until he was certain it was dead. Lifting his head, bloody jaws agape, he looked for a fresh kill. But a radium bullet, detonating just short of striking fatally, forced the golden lion to recoil. He roared sullen defiance as he retreated into the bush, his tail switching in anger.

The Waziri likewise were forced back into the bush, harried by arrows and explosive rounds while mustering Martians were assembling in their war chariots.

For a moment, it seemed hopeless. Even Tarzan's vaunted strength and speed could not overcome the distance or the greater numbers.

Changing course, he ran toward one of the war chariots, jumped into it, and took from the warrior his spear. This he hurled into the air.

The distance was too great, however. It fell short, quivering upright where its point struck the ground.

Looking about, Tarzan sought another spear with which to try again.

Sharp eyes fell on another war chariot, but it was charging in his direction. The driver lifted a sword with the clear intent of sweeping in and removing his enemy's black-haired head.

Steeling himself, Tarzan prepared to fight for his life. He could not do that and go to the rescue of his Waziri.

A savage snarling caught his attention. Glancing over quickly, he saw Jad-bal-ja bounding into view. The mighty lion fell upon a group of enemy who were stalking his Waziri, scattering them before his roaring fury.

On his bronzed brow, the ancient battle scar flamed red, and into his gray eyes came another kind of fire.

In the din of battle, Tarzan did not hear the drone coming from the south. His entire attention was on the oncoming chariot and the massive zitidar pulling it along.

As it closed, the enemy sword lifted high, and Tarzan saw that the Orovar's intent was to cleave him from shoulder to hip.

Hunting knife in hand, he set his steely leg muscles to leap into the chariot and strike first.

But before the bronzed giant could spring to defend himself, the swordsman jerked in place, reeled, and fell over, and the zitidar broke from its harness. The chariot shattered into pieces, one wheel detaching to go rolling away, while the frightened beast blundered on, trailing its traces.

Tarzan sprang out of the way of the bounding wheel, then circled about to see what had transpired.

He heard the howl of an airplane motor, and looked up.

ABOVE HIM, his P-40B Tomahawk was climbing, its wing-mounted Browning machine guns smoking. Banking low, the black warplane executed a strafing run against scattering mounted warriors, tearing them to pieces in a stitching lash of lead.

Stumbling and mortally wounded, the thoats slid along the bloody grass, throwing their riders.

Yelling war cries, Waziri warriors descended, making short work of them with their spears.

The fierce-fanged Tomahawk pulled out of its strafing run, circled smartly, and executed another pass.

Yet another chariot shattered into pieces, and then the Waziri overran the settlement, exacting their revenge. Although their numbers had been diminished, the Orovar company had also taken significant casualties.

Moving among the scattered foe, Tarzan's recurved blade plunged in again and again. He gave no quarter. His blade drank blood to its guard.

When it was over, he thought of the utan, Ro-Dun-Bo.

The bronzed giant found the man standing amid a bloody heap of his dead warriors, a sword clutched in his shaking hand.

Tarzan walked up to him unafraid. "Lay down your sword."

"I will never lay down my blade. It is my life."

Tarzan regarded him without expression.

"Lay down your weapon or I will take it from you."

A snarl of a smile distorted Ro-Dun-Bo's overconfident face.

"A mere knife against an Orovar sword. I will gladly accept the challenge."

"As you wish," said Tarzan. He stepped in, feinted once with his knife, stepped around and evaded the first thrust from his opponent.

"You are swift," grunted the utan.

"Swifter than Ara the lightning," returned Tarzan flatly.

Ro-Dun-Bo made a derisive sound deep in his throat. He took Tarzan's words as mere boast.

The ape-man proved him wrong in his assumption.

Lunging suddenly, Tarzan's short blade licked out and scored a long red line along the other's arm where bare skin showed between two segments of armor.

Ro-Dun-Bo retreated in surprise, then Tarzan slipped his blade into its sheath. During that brief interval of astonishment, the ape-man wrested his opponent's sword from his hand by main strength.

"How can this be?" gasped Ro-Dun-Bo, a stupefied expression on his face.

Tarzan's answer was to plunge the utan's sword point into his own vitals, and then removing the red blade by kicking the mortally-wounded man away with one bare foot.

Ro-Dun-Bo fell backward, clutching his belly, and his hands turned brilliantly red. His stunned eyes soon rolled up in his head, and so he died.

Turning his bronzed back on his fallen foe, Tarzan went to his Waziri warriors and asked, "Do any enemy survive?"

"No," replied Muviro. "Jad-bal-ja has torn out the throats of the wounded."

"Where is the captive, Gor-Dun-Ree?"

"Dead. Three enemy arrows impaled him."

Satisfied with this report, Tarzan turned his attention to the circling black Tomahawk.

As he watched, the warplane's pilot seemed to be seeking a suitable place to land. Soon, he found one, overflew it once to inspect it visually for obstructing rocks or other impediments, and then came back around and landed the aircraft roughly but safely. It bounced four times before it rolled to a halt. The propeller jerked to a halt with a final cough of engine smoke.

Tarzan raced to the idling plane, and when the pilot threw back his glass canopy, the ape-man was not entirely surprised at the familiar face poking out.

"Jack!"

"Greetings, Father," replied the son of Tarzan, who was also known as Korak the Killer.

Climbing onto the starboard wing and dropping down, Korak ran over and embraced his father, saying, "It is good to see you again."

"Obviously, you have returned from the war."

"Mother told me of your expedition. I saw a perfectly good aircraft sitting there and decided to take it up for a joy ride."

"Doing so may have saved many lives, including my own," said Tarzan sincerely.

Looking back at the shark-mouthed Tomahawk grinning fiercely under the African sun, Korak said, "I am almost out of fuel. I do not think there is enough to return home."

Tarzan laughed. "It is enough that the Tomahawk saw one last mission."

With that, father and son went to take stock of the dead and wounded.

Muviro said, "The wounded are not so bad off they cannot march home. The dead we must bury here."

"How many dead?"

"Five."

"We will give them proper burial," said Tarzan somberly.

"And what of these others?" asked the old man.

"Let the vultures have them. Any beast that they brought from their world must be slaughtered. They cannot be allowed to breed, or to escape into the jungle."

The Waziri used their spears to slay the thoats, as well as the last of the zitidars. This was accomplished with grim efficiency. Moving among the slain beasts, Jad-bal-ja sampled their flesh out of curiosity. But none seemed to appeal to the golden lion.

Tarzan roved about, looking for the ship that brought the Orovar Martians to Africa. He found pieces of it. Much of it had been salvaged in order to build the huts. Some sections had been cast into the waters of Lake Victoria. Crocodiles basked in the placid waters beyond these partially submerged fragments, which appeared to have been sunk to discourage the reptiles from coming ashore at this encampment.

Once the ape-man was satisfied that the Orovar enclave was no more, he conferred with Korak.

"There are no survivors. But we are not done. For more are coming just like these pale-skinned intruders."

"What can be done about it?" asked Korak.

"I can think of only one thing. But it is something I hesitate to do."

"I've never known you to hesitate, or to shrink from any task."

"For this task, I must overcome a deep reluctance. I cannot stop people from another world from coming to Earth while I yet stand upon it."

Korak's eyes blinked without immediate comprehension. Then the full import of his father's words dawned upon him.

"Do you intend what I imagine?" he asked.

"If I must return to the red planet to preserve Africa from invasion," said Tarzan grimly, "then I will do it. But the thought does not please me."

Chapter 10

GRIM DECISION

A WEEK passed.
Another feast was held, this one lasting three days. The celebration was for the safe return of Jack Clayton, Korak the Killer, from his war service. The family of Tarzan had been reunited at last.

The dead were duly mourned and normal life resumed on the Greystoke estate.

One morning, Tarzan gathered Lady Jane and Jack in the dining room of the long bungalow.

"I've made my decision," he announced. "As much as I dread to do so, I must return to Barsoom. I can see no other course of action. The next ship might be larger and carry a greater force of men. It will be easier to stop them before they depart than to fight them once they reach the Earth."

Jane looked at her husband with deep concern. "How do you know that you can return?"

"I do not yet know. But I was taught how to translate my spirit from Barsoom to Earth. I believe the process may work in the reverse. I can but try. But before I do so, a place must be prepared for my body to rest safely. I have directed Muviro to build a raised vault of teakwood into which I will lay my body down. It will be sealed against insects and animals."

Jack said, "We could raise an army to meet the next incursion."

"And we could no doubt defeat them," said Tarzan. "But at what cost in lives? And what about those that follow them? And the company that comes after them? If it is possible to stop them before departure, whether by force or persuasion, the matter will end there. For if the inhabitants of Mars, which is dying, have discovered a means to reach Earth, there may be no end to them."

"Can you do this alone?" asked Lady Jane.

"I will enlist, if I can, John Carter, who is my friend. He is renowned among the red race of Mars. But he is from Earth. I do not think he would agree with this invasion. But I must find out. If he will not help me, then I must do it alone."

Lady Jane sighed. "I can see that your mind is made up. And when your mind is made up there is no remaking it."

"I can see no other course of action that preserves Africa from being overrun by these outworlders," stated Tarzan firmly.

"I'm just getting used to you being home, and now you are deserting me again," said Lady Jane mock-seriously.

"I will return as soon as I am able."

"The last time, you were marooned on that frightful world for many months."

Tarzan nodded his head. "That time, I did not know there was a way to return home. So long as I live, I should be able to leave Mars, as I did before."

"And if you should perish on Mars?" pressed Jane.

"Then such will be my fate," replied Tarzan solemnly. "Perhaps my soul will be able to visit you one last time, long enough to kiss you goodbye."

Jane's pensive expression spoke more eloquently than the words she did not utter.

Korak asked, "When will you go?"

"Once the vault is finished. I will not delay. I do not know when the next Orovar ship will leave Mars. But if I can intercept it, I will."

"You should not go alone this time, Father. I will accompany you."

Tarzan shook his head somberly. "Since we cannot know when the next ship might arrive, I count on you to welcome it properly while I am away. I must return to Mars alone. That is the only way." The ape-man's gray eyes showed a hint of humor. "Aside from those reasons, Meriem will be coming from London before long, and you should be here to welcome your wife, whom you have not seen in more than a year."

Jack laughed. "I could never get the better of you in an argument. Your points are irrefutable. I will remain on Earth then."

THE BUILDING of the vault took almost a week. It was constructed to be both watertight and insect proof, but not sealed from the outside air. Screened vents were artfully constructed so that air circulated properly, They would also keep the enclosure as cool as the African climate permitted.

Inspecting it, Tarzan was satisfied. "This is an improvement over the last time, when my body was buried in the earth but did not decompose."

"Will you need any special care?" asked Jack.

Tarzan said, "Only protection from the elements. It will be as if I were in a coma. Dead, yet also alive."

"How long should we hold out hope for your return?" asked Lady Jane, her eyes brave but holding back a sad light.

Tarzan considered that question. Finally, he said, "Indefinitely. If I do not return, let this be my final resting place."

Korak the Killer said nothing to that.

Eventually, the hour came when Tarzan was ready. An iron door at one end of the vault stood open and a woven grass mat had been placed on the hardwood platform floor.

After hugging and kissing his wife goodbye, then shaking his son's hand, Tarzan waved to the watching Waziri as if in farewell.

"I shall return," he said.

Then he delivered himself inside. His family took one last look at him and then quietly closed and locked the iron door.

Turning to his mother, Korak said somberly, "I do not know how to feel about this. He is going somewhere, yet he will remain here."

Lady Jane patted him on the shoulder, saying softly, "We will hang a lantern on the veranda. It will remain lit, the flame burning for as long as we must wait."

After all had retired for the night, Jad-bal-ja the golden lion padded out of the jungle, discovered the vault, sniffed around its squared lines and, upon recognizing the familiar scent of the true Lord of the Jungle, took up a recumbent position at the end where the iron door was affixed.

Like a living sphinx, the faithful lion sat there for a long time, watchful and patient. Finally, the necessity for sleep made him drowsy, and he lowered his great black-maned head to the jungle floor and closed his emerald eyes....

Chapter 11

BACK TO BARSOOM

THE METHOD by which John Clayton conveyed himself to the red planet cannot be recounted here. Truth be told, it was so mysterious that he did not understand it himself. Having been taught how to decamp Mars for Earth, returning to that dying world was simply a matter of reversing the process.

All that may be revealed was that it involved lying down in a dark place where interruption was impossible and focusing on his distant objective. Seeing Mars fully realized in his mind's eye was merely the initial step.

There came a sharp, taut snapping, as of a steel wire that had parted, after which consciousness evaporated instantaneously.

The interval of oblivion experienced by Tarzan of the Apes could not be measured by the mind of man. It began as a darkness as abrupt as the closing of an electrical switch, followed by a rushing sound suggesting something passing through infinite space.

Upon awakening, Tarzan felt thick grass at his back. This was his first sensation. It was not his expectation. Opening his eyes, he looked upward and beheld the sun. It was smaller and less bright than the sun that shone down upon Earth, the brilliant solar orb called Kudu in the language of the great apes of the African rainforest.

Sitting up, Tarzan looked about and was relieved to discover that he sat naked in a lush valley. The tall grass around him was not green but a weird purple, bearing fern-like fronds of red

69

and yellow. This was a grass he knew covered certain patches of Barsoom, known on Earth as Mars. This hardy growth was tough in texture.

Inhaling, he found the air to be breathable. The ape-man took a deeper breath, charging his lungs with oxygen. He felt alive once more.

Tarzan knew better than to leap to his feet. The difference in gravity would catapult him some forty feet into the air. So he took stock of his surroundings.

He seemed to be in a valley. The air was filled with unusual smells, none of which he recognized. Except one. Flowing water. The air was neither cool nor warm, but something in between. A breeze blew that caused the skin of his arms to bunch and creep. Or perhaps it was the riot of alien smells entering his nostrils that produced that visceral reaction.

Very carefully, using both hands pressed against the purple sward, the ape-man gathered his strong legs beneath him and, with extreme care, climbed to his feet.

He felt lighter than his more than two hundred pounds and in a strange way, buoyant. It was as if he was suspended in some invisible fluid.

Rotating his head, Tarzan looked about in all directions. Streams were present. These he knew to be rare on Barsoom. There were no signs of life that were not vegetable in nature.

During his previous sojourn upon the red planet, Tarzan's adventures had been confined to the southern hemisphere. He could not tell from looking about where on this weird world he had come to be. But the climate appeared to be temperate. This was fortunate because Tarzan knew that, as on Earth, the Martian poles were covered in ice fields. Without proper protection, he might not last long in either environment.

Taking great care, the ape-man took a single step, stopped, then took another step. The grass beneath his bare feet was springy, but his entire body also felt springy, as if it would require no effort to propel himself skyward.

A dozen steps he took, getting used to his powerful body as it was on Barsoom. The memories of his prior experience on Mars came flooding back to him. And his muscles remembered how it was to traverse the dying planet.

After walking for a short time, Tarzan gave a light leap. The kick propelled him twenty feet into the air, whereupon he landed without losing his balance.

Adjusting to the Martian gravity would be easier this time, he realized. Withal, it would still take some time. So he confined himself to walking and listening, his gray eyes taking in his strange surroundings.

The bronzed giant knew he was fortunate to land where he did, even if he did not know where on the surface of the dying planet he had found himself. So much of Mars' surface consisted of the desiccated dead sea bottoms, barren of life and dotted with the deserted ruins of ancient cities, harboring little game and even less edible vegetation.

Studying the trees in the distance, Tarzan recognized the sompas tree, whose fruit was edible. Nut-bearing skeel and sora-pus trees were also in evidence. He was not now hungry, but the ape-man knew that he would require food eventually.

Soon enough, his careful progress took him to the verge of the trees, and he saw in the distance a stone-walled enclosure, from which a tall domed tower reared. The tower reared some sixty feet high and was a dull gray. But the dome was faced with decorative glass that reflected the sun, producing bright shards and rays of light.

This appeared to be a habitation. He searched the sky for signs of the boat-shaped Martian fliers the red men of Barsoom piloted. He saw nothing of that type. The cloudless skies were clear.

Nevertheless, a settlement meant people and the possibility of assistance, for he must find John Carter as soon as possible.

Working through the forest, Tarzan listened for any sounds suggesting danger. Not all races of Barsoom were civilized like the red men. There were the green-skinned Martians who were half savage. And there were others he had not encountered but had heard about from the red and green men, among them men so black they made the natives of Africa seem pale by comparison.

Tarzan understood, too, that the various races were often at war with one another. Not all would be friendly to his advances. Nor would they necessarily cooperate with his desire to find the city of Greater Helium from which John Carter ruled his empire.

And so the ape-man trod cautiously for many reasons, only one of which was to keep from careening through the thin air due to a misstep.

Previous experience in the remote Forest of Desh in the southern hemisphere of the red planet had taught the bronzed giant that no plant or animal, no matter how innocent-looking it might appear, was safe to approach. Insects whirred and darted about him, some of which he recognized, but all of which Tarzan avoided.

Observing one particular winged specimen, which appeared to have a stinger at its tail, he saw it drift by an unusual creeper that draped across a group of trees. As the insect approached one drooping loop, weird eyes popped open in the plant, and hands not quite as large as his own, flexed. One snapped shut, capturing the unwary insect, apparently consuming it in some fashion.

This uncanny vine did not appear to present danger to someone of Tarzan's size and might, but it discouraged the ape-man from taking to the treetops.

In avoiding the trees, the Lord of the Jungle moved too close to another plant that was approximately the size of a thorn bush. This was a stunted tree, and its gnarled and woody branches ended in voracious jaws.

One of these snapped at him, and the ape-man lashed out, striking it with his fist, causing the entire plant to shudder and recoil in shock. All of its jaws closed tightly, as if afraid to dare again disturb this powerful and aggressive passing prey.

Tarzan continued on. After a time, he heard a familiar sound—the smash and clank of heavy swords wielded by determined combatants.

HALTING, HE listened, detecting the ring of only two swords. The duel seemed to be coming from the north.

Padding barefoot as noiselessly as he could, the ape-man moved in that direction, keeping low.

As he drew near, the swordplay became more violent. He listened for the grunt and heavy breathing of warriors in battle, but curiously heard nothing of the sort. Only a series of blowing sounds smacking of air being pushed through and out open pipes.

This strangeness only increased his caution. Tarzan was a brave hunter on Earth and had not left his courage behind. But he was also an intelligent man. He understood that one faced the unknown with a healthy respect.

Two men fighting for their lives naturally would make appropriate noises. Sniffing the air, he failed to scent fresh blood as well.

Crouching even lower, Tarzan decided to avoid calling attention to himself.

Pushing through the underbrush, at last he reached a point where he could separate thick leaves and peer from concealment.

What the ape-man saw registered with a sharp shock in his brain. Two men had squared off in a circular patch of dirt that obviously had been cleared for the purpose of a duel. Nothing grew in that patch, which was some twenty feet in diameter. Surrounding it, the thick grass had been shorn close to the ground.

The two men were strapping fellows with well-developed physiques of the pantherish type. Their muscles were not knotty. They wore the kind of leather harnesses that most Martian races

in his previous experience wore. Their skins were reddish and
dusky.

As he watched, their blades lifted and clanged against one
another, blocking and ringing, then sweeping back before rushing forward again.

It appeared that neither man had yet scored. No blow had
landed on their naked skin. No blood dripped from any point
in their epidermis. The combatants seemed at an impossible
stalemate, banging and slashing fruitlessly.

It seemed nearly impossible that two men could wield such
powerful swords without one landing a blow upon the other.

When Tarzan's eyes lifted from their muscular torsos and
clean limbs gripping the pommeled hilts of their weapons, his
amazed gaze encountered a sight even more incredible than this
bizarre stalemate.

One of the swordsmen lacked his head!

The shock on the ape-man's face was momentary. But it registered. His disbelieving eyes narrowed, as if to see more clearly.

Tarzan observed the duel from a position that showed the
battling foemen facing off against one another. He could see
both clearly.

The first man he studied was entirely headless. Yet no blood
spilled from his neck. His bare chest was clean except for the
perspiration of exertion.

Shifting his gaze to the other opponent, the ape-man saw
that, incredulously, the other swordsman was also headless!

His eyes naturally went to the much-trodden dirt at their
shifting feet, seeking their fallen craniums.

It was ridiculous to think that they were still fighting without their heads. But no heads were in evidence upon the ground
where they fought so vigorously.

It was madness, of course. Tarzan had seen many bizarre
sights upon Barsoom during his previous visit. But this one
seemed to exceed credulity to the point where the ape-man
questioned the reality unfolding before him.

Casting his vision around, Tarzan looked for some explanation for this mad sight.

He soon found something that only made the vision even more impossible. Beyond the dirt circle, seated in a closely-shorn ring of the purple grass, sat two short platforms with abbreviated seats upon them, one on either side of the combatants.

In those seats sat what appeared to be the missing heads. These crania looked over the arena of combat with lidless, staring eyes.

Tarzan studied them. They were a strange grayish-blue color and not at all like human heads, being much larger in circumference, and possessing vertical slits instead of a pronounced nose. Their unblinking eyes bulged as the oblate heads shifted about, watching the two champions go at one another with a strange silent ferocity, punctuated by the rush and wheeze of their breaths escaping the tops of their open windpipes.

There was a palpable expression of concentration on each of these heads. Their mouths were puckered tightly with expectation. Whatever they might be, these bodiless monstrosities were entirely immersed in the combat they were witnessing.

Back and forth, sideways and back, ever circling, the two combatants strove to gain the advantage over the other, but to no clear avail. They fought and fought, rivulets of perspiration rolling down their limbs. They appeared to be tireless, yet neither could achieve any advantage. It was as if they had some perfect perception of their opponent's moves, even before they made them, despite the fact that, lacking heads, they could not possibly see their opponent.

Tarzan could only watch this preposterous duel to its conclusion. He could not imagine what it would be. But none of it made sense to his earthly mind.

The duel ended with a singular lack of drama.

Simultaneously, the headless swordsmen broke off, lowered their blades and stepped back. They took stances of men at attention, as if waiting for something.

As Tarzan watched, the tableau grew even more bizarre.

On either side of the arena, the grotesque bluish-gray heads rose up on six spidery legs. Like grotesque crabs, they scuttled onto the tough purple sward, carrying pairs of chelae high before them, suggesting the fore-claws of lobsters.

Simultaneously, the two headless men turned in place and walked over to meet the approaching ambulatory heads.

When each pair of creatures met, the headless humans knelt, as if in obedience, and the walking heads crawled crab-like up their sweat-streaked backs and took positions upon the blood-less stumps of their necks, which were fitted with thick collars. As they settled into the leather collars, they inserted a group of tentacles growing from the base of their skulls into the open stumps as they settled in, and Tarzan received the impression that they joined with the headless creature's nervous systems through those clumped appendages.

Now joined as one, each individual rose to his feet and walked back to the dirt arena, where they placed one free hand upon the shoulder of the other in what Tarzan knew to be the universal sign of greetings and friendship among the races of Barsoom.

Turning, they started walking side-by-side toward the nearby walled settlement, their former animosity apparently aban-doned.

Tarzan decided to follow them at a respectable distance. He did not know where they fit among the races of Mars, these unfamiliar hybrid beings. But they seemed civilized after a fash-ion.

Tarzan gave them time to progress some distance, then he crept out of the forest and, keeping low, followed their progress. Yet as he did so, the breeze carried their odor to him, and it made the skin along his arms and legs bunch and creep.

There were those on Earth who believed Tarzan of the Apes to be fearless. Perhaps he was in one sense. Yet no man is entirely fearless when facing the unknown and encountering something beyond his understanding.

The ape-man was brave enough to track these creatures, but not foolish enough to engage with them until he knew more of their nature. For he was wise in the ways of the weird world called Barsoom.

Chapter 12

"I Come in Peace"

A S THE uncanny pair moved away, they conversed and their speech reached the alert ears of Tarzan.

At first, the ape-man had difficulty understanding their words, for while they spoke in the universal language of Barsoom, their strange mouths uttered queer syllables in accents and cadences difficult to follow. But as he listened Tarzan's understanding increased.

"Perhaps the next time, one of us will defeat the other's rykor," declared one without resentment.

"You said that the last time, Vrok. But we have become too practiced in the art of telepathically controlling our rykors. They fight fearlessly because they cannot see what they are doing, and they lack the brains to comprehend their peril. So they blindly risk life and limb. Which makes them perfect warriors, for they respond to our thought commands without fear or hesitation."

The first speaker laughed in an ugly chittering manner.

"We are the first of our people to learn to control our rykors without mounting them first. As we grow more proficient, one of us will discover a way to defeat the guard of the other. It is inevitable, Jeo. Just a matter of time and practice."

"I will not entirely disagree with you, Vrok. But it remains to be seen how long it will take until one of us is victorious and the other will need a new rykor."

They seemed to be discussing their slave bodies as if they represented an entirely different species, thought Tarzan. Upon reflection, the ape-man realized that they probably were. These headless bipeds were nothing like the strange forms he had encountered on Barsoom in the past, and, although he had ranged far, by no means had he traversed the failing red planet in its entirety.

Another man might have questioned whether he had arrived at his proper planetary destination, but not Tarzan of the Apes. His jungle-honed sense of smell confirmed that this was indeed Barsoom. The air had a distinctive mixture of odors he recognized from past experience.

As Tarzan tracked the two weird figures, they drew toward one of the circular enclosures dominated by a narrow tower.

The bronzed giant could see that the walls appeared to be faced with plaster, but inset with prismatic glass. This hinted of a civilization of a high order, similar to the cities of the red men.

These weird beings with their detachable heads were not quite as red as the Barsoomians he knew. They were several shades paler, but still, their skin possessed a reddish tinge, suggesting that they might be related to the red Martians, whom Tarzan had dubbed the Gamangani.

Following at a respectful distance, the ape-man saw that they were rounding the enclosure. Before long, a heavy wooden gate came into view.

Now Tarzan faced a choice: To let them pass through the gate or to intercept them before they could enter. His chief concern was to determine where upon the face of Barsoom he had arrived. Was he near Helium, the seat of John Carter, Warlord of Mars? If so, this knowledge would provide a starting point in his quest.

The ape-man had attempted to reckon his present latitude by the sun, but to no avail. It had been many years since he had trekked this world, and without knowing the positions of the stars, he could not calculate where on the red planet he stood.

Considering his options, Tarzan decided it would be more expedient to confront the pair rather than follow them into the unknown confines of the rounded enclosure.

Coming out of his half crouch, the ape-man pelted ahead, and almost immediately the buoyancy that he knew since his arrival upon the red planet was felt keenly.

There was no point in resisting it. With a kick, he launched himself into the air, passing high over the heads of the fantastic hybrid warriors, twisting as he did so.

The parabola of his leap brought him down upon the high purple grass between the closed gate and the two men.

Once they beheld him, they stopped dead in their tracks, looked at one another, and without another word, drew their swords. With these gripped firmly in hand, they charged.

"Kaor!" greeted Tarzan. "I come without weapons and therefore in peace."

The two did not halt their charge, but raised their weapons high, clearly intending to inflict downward strokes upon the bronzed giant.

The ape-man did not wait for their blades to descend. Instead, he leaped once more, again passing over their hideous heads and landing behind them.

This transpired so rapidly that the swordsmen looked bewildered as they were brought up short by the ape-man's sudden absence.

Hearing him land behind them, they wheeled and charged anew. Their intent was no less murderous.

Seeing that there was no reasoning with the bizarre pair, Tarzan decided to meet them head-on, knowing that upon Mars, his strength and agility far exceeded that of any of its man-like inhabitants.

With one mighty fist, Tarzan blocked the first downward swing, breaking the man's sword arm just in back of the wrist. A weird scream emerged from the bizarre-looking head, and Tarzan seized the falling blade in midair.

Catching the sword by its hilt, the ape-man swung to face his second attacker. The two blades clashed, sparks flew, and Tarzan easily beat back the other, disarming him by the simple expedient of cutting lengthways across his neck.

The awful head rolled off, then it commenced skittering in futile panicked circles, for several of the spidery legs had been sliced off.

The body that formerly had carried the detached head simply dropped to its knees and fell forward, lifeless and inert.

Turning to face his remaining upright foe, Tarzan set the tip of his blade against the other's bare chest, and then pressed forward.

"I am Tarzan of the Apes. Speak truthfully or I will treat you as I did your fellow countryman."

The creature's round, toothy mouth constricted in disapproval. "You undertake a great risk, *Tarzan-ko-do-raku,* but I am Vrok, of Moak."

"I have never heard of Moak. I seek the city of Helium, where John Carter dwells."

"It is far from here."

"What is this place called?"

"This valley is known as Bantoom. Behind you lies the settlement called Moak."

The word Bantoom reminded Tarzan of the name he heard upon the Earth from the lips of the captive Orovar Martian, Gor-Dun-Ree.

"I also am in search of Nulthoom. Do you know it?"

"The name means nothing to me, *Tarzan-ko-do-raku.* Is it a red city?"

"I do not know that it is a city at all. It may be the name of a chief or warlord. But if it means nothing to you, I have no further use for you."

"If you slay me, bronze barbarian, all of Bantoom will descend upon you. Your fate, it will be terrible. For you look like a rykor, but with a head. I am a kaldane. We eat rykors when we grow tired of them for purposes of locomotion."

"I have not decided whether I will slay you or not," replied Tarzan. "Point me in the direction of Helium."

The bipedal creature pointed east, but then he pointed west.

"The city of Helium lies on the other side of Barsoom. Whether you go east or west, the way is almost equally long. It lies below this latitude, far below. Or so I understand. I have never been outside of Bantoom. Why would I? Only lower races live beyond this valley."

Tarzan demanded, "Do you consider yourself a higher race? You who do not have a body of your own, but one you control as if it is a wild beast?"

The kaldane laughed roughly. His voice dripped with sarcasm verging upon contempt when he replied, "The sole aim of my race is to become a brain. A body is necessary for certain tasks, but evolution will soon free us of that unpleasant necessity. After that, the rykor we currently control will be fit only as food or beasts of burden."

"In that case," said Tarzan sternly, "allow me to help your evolution along."

So saying, Tarzan of the Apes drove the point of his blade to the heart of the human form. It toppled backward, landing on the purplish grass, whereupon the weird bodiless head swiftly detached itself and went skittering for the closed gate.

As it ran along, it screeched and whistled in a manner that sounded to the ape-man as a warning.

Almost immediately, the great gate flew open, and out came others of its kind, waving long- and short-swords and shouting dire threats.

Tarzan had no interest in combat for its own sake. He now had a weapon, so he simply turned and leapt away, landing thirty feet distant, then jumping again to disappear into the riotous forest.

Once within its leafy concealment, he climbed to the top of one of the trees and looked about.

A ring of low verdant hills surrounded the valley. He calculated he could reach that natural barrier in half a dozen kangaroo-like hops. So the ape-man sprang out, still clutching the short-sword, and continued leaping until he reached one of the hills.

Poised on its crest, he surveyed the west. Beyond, he could see a seemingly endless expanse. A plain, possibly one of the dead sea bottoms. In contrast to the lush valley, this expanse appeared to be devoid of vegetation.

Nevertheless, Tarzan jumped into it, landing easily, and then proceeded to make his way west.

He leaped for a time but grew tired of the monotony and fell to walking.

Ever alert to all smells and sights, he made his way. The bronzed giant understood that if Helium in truth lay on the other side of the planet, he could not reach it on foot. But he also recalled that Barsoom was marked by ruined cities as well as thriving ones.

So Tarzan remained alert for the smells that might direct him toward habitation. The ruins were often the headquarters of the green tribes, but some had fallen into the hands of the great white apes of Barsoom. The latter would be of no use to him, being but dumb brutes. But the former spoke the universal language of the planet.

Far better, he knew, would be to come to a red city. Those people possessed ships that flew through the air. No doubt they would know the way to Helium. Whether they would assist him was another matter. But Tarzan was confident that he could persuade any civilized Martian of the wisdom of assisting him.

WHEN THE first night came, it was with the suddenness of the tropics. This was the way of Barsoom, as well. The weak sun slipped beneath the horizon and one by one, the two misshapen moons of Mars made their spectral appearance, speeding Thuria and her weaker companion, Cluros.

Tarzan did not become as cold as he expected. From previous experience, he knew the Martian nights could be quite frigid. This one was merely cool.

This told Tarzan that he had landed near the Martian equator. The ape-man studied the emerging stars in the evening sky, familiar but also not quite the same as their earthly arrangement. Long ago he had come to know the blue-black Martian night sky well. Studying it, he reckoned that he was below the equator, not above it. This was helpful to know, for the Empire of Helium lay at the lower latitudes of the southern hemisphere. But this knowledge alone would not get him to his destination.

Tarzan walked or jumped for the entire duration of the Martian night. When dawn came, he saw that he was still traversing an endless expanse. The yellow ochre moss that grew almost everywhere upon the undulating dead sea floors was underfoot now. While this vegetable stuff was inedible, it served as a comfortable spot to sleep.

In the African jungle, sleeping at night was not always a safe thing to do. Many predators prowled after sunset. Here on Barsoom, it was no different. The thick-maned banths of the dead sea bottoms might scent him. But Tarzan was not afraid of them. He was certain he would awaken before one could pounce upon him.

In this case, the bronzed giant's reckoning was that if he must sleep, it was better to do it during the day when a passing flier might spy him and investigate.

This was perhaps a faint hope, given the emptiness of the terrain all about him. And whether friend or foe found him, although naked, he was not unarmed. The short-sword he had confiscated would serve him well in any event.

And so as the sun rose, Tarzan of the Apes lay down and surrendered to sleep, mentally alert but unafraid. He slept well, for the eerie silence of the Barsoomian wastes insured that his ears would warn him of any approaching danger his vigilant nostrils failed to catch.

Chapter 13

THE RED WOMAN

D ISTANTLY, A steady noise reached the sleeping brain
of Tarzan of the Apes.

The day was not far along. The ape-man had slept soundly,
his slumber unbroken until the sound impinged upon his ears.
Snapping awake, he sat up and looked about him.

He was pleased when he realized that the action of suddenly
sitting upright had not caused him to fly off the surface of
Barsoom. Clearly, he was adjusting more rapidly to the changed
gravity than before.

Looking about him, he was able to pinpoint the sound. In
the distance, to the northwest, a Martian flier was sailing along.
It was moving low. The sounds of its motor seemed to sputter
and misfire.

Climbing to his feet with the utmost care, Tarzan oriented
himself toward the aerial conveyance and made his first leap.
Twenty leaps were required to clear the distance and then he
stood looking up at the air boat.

It was flying colors, but he did not recognize them. They
were not the colors of the Empire of Helium, which he knew
by sight. He could not see who piloted the ship, but it was a
small vessel.

There was no point in delaying. With one last exertion, the
ape-man hurtled high into the air and came down on the rear
deck of the vessel, his sword gripped tightly in one bronzed fist.

At the controls, a figure enwrapped in a blue cloak started. The pilot appeared confused as to the direction from which the sudden slap of bare feet had come.

Seeing nothing on either side of the deck, the pilot finally turned about.

It was then that Tarzan of the Apes saw that it was a woman. She was beautiful to behold. Young, with raven hair and dark snapping eyes. She had the coppery red skin of the dominant race of Martians.

This woman was no frail flower of womanhood, however. Upon sight of the naked ape-man, her features became tight and her eyes flashed with anger.

"Who are you?" she demanded without a trace of fear in her voice.

Tarzan lowered his sword and lifted his free hand, saying, "I mean you no harm. I am Tarzan of the Apes."

"I might have guessed that," she replied heartily.

"Do you know me?"

"I know an uncouth ape when I see one," she shot back. "You are as naked as an ape, even though you resemble a man. Although what manner of man you might be, I cannot tell."

"I am a man of Jasoom," said Tarzan simply.

"Yet you wield a sword of the Bantoomian type. Explain yourself."

"Bantoom is where I landed when I arrived on this world. The people there are unlike any I previously encountered on Barsoom."

The woman shuddered visibly. "You were fortunate to escape Bantoom, where the inhabitants you and I would term people are but brainless chattel, to be ridden by the monstrous kaldanes, and eaten by them when their usefulness is at an end. I have never been there, but I have heard accounts from those who have. Of all the races who inhabit Barsoom, the kaldanes are the most unholy."

"Yet they perish like any other foe," stated Tarzan simply.

"They can be slain, it is true. But killing their host bodies accomplishes nothing. It is the hideous head riding the dumb brute of a body that must be slain."

Tarzan nodded. "That was my experience."

The woman's stern expression altered to one of curiosity.

"What is a man born of Jasoom doing upon Barsoom?"

"I have come on an important mission. I seek the Warlord of Barsoom, John Carter, a man who also came from Jasoom."

"Why do you seek John Carter?"

"It is a matter I intend to discuss with John Carter and John Carter alone. But it is urgent. Where are you bound?"

"To my home city, which is Gathol. It lies to the north. If I can but reach it. I am losing altitude. One of the ray tanks is leaking. I fear that I have made a mistake. This is an old-type flier, of a design no longer in use. But it was my favorite ship, and I thought to take it out one last time before consigning it to the scrap heap. Alas, the outdated radio set has a limited range, or else I could signal that I am in need of rescue."

Tarzan nodded in understanding. "I can see that your ship is foundering. Land, and I will help you repair it."

"I do not know that I can trust you," the woman said without insult. Fresh suspicion came into her voice. "How do you know John Carter?"

"I've been on this world before."

"You could not long be on Barsoom," the woman retorted, "naked as you are." She pointed at a locker running beneath the starboard rail and snapped, "Within that locker, you will find an extra cloak. Use this to hide your nakedness. Then we will see about trusting you."

Tarzan went to the locker, knelt, and opened it. Inside was an emerald cloak. It was long enough to cover most of his body. He threw it around his broad shoulders, clasped it in place, and drew it closed in front. It was not entirely to his liking, but it was better than being completely naked before a young woman.

"Now that you are properly dressed for a barbarian," the woman declared, "I must ask you to surrender your sword to me. As you can plainly see, I am armed with only a dagger."

"Since you are a woman and I need your help, I will oblige you," returned the ape-man.

Turning his blade around, Tarzan offered it to the woman. She did not reach out to accept it. Scorn showed on her attractive features.

"I believe you now," she said tartly. "You must be a man from Jasoom. No Barsoomian warrior would surrender his sword so easily."

"You will not accept it?"

"I have a chieftain. I must refuse what to my people is an offer of marriage. Lay your blade down on the deck and step away from it. Only then will I consider the matter settled."

Tarzan did as the woman bade. He knew that he could spring upon the blade before the woman could do him any harm. And no dagger could stab him if he saw it coming in his direction.

Tarzan said then, "You may land wherever you wish."

The woman said, "Not here. There are banths."

"I will protect you from them, if necessary."

The young woman laughed. It was not a laugh of derision, but one of surprise.

"I would prefer not to be protected. There is still buoyancy in the tanks. We will continue until I spy a shelter where it will be safe to set down. You may assist me in the search."

Nodding silently, Tarzan padded his way forward and stood upon the prow of the ship, ahead of the pilothouse. This put him before the woman, which seemed to satisfy her.

Shielding his eyes from the Martian sun, the ape-man conned the way forward.

"How far to Gathol?" he asked.

"Too far for this ship to reach without repair." That was all she would say.

THE SHIP sailed along for some three hours before Tarzan sighted something that he recognized as the broken towers of one of the long-abandoned cities of ancient Barsoom when it was populated by the founding race of seafaring Orovars.

Turning, he asked the woman, "Do you know this city?"

She shook her head. "There are no green hordes known to roam this reach. It is probably deserted."

Pulling back on the throttle, she sent the craft dropping into a shallow path.

"I scent the musk of the great white apes," warned Tarzan.

"I smell no such thing."

"You are not Tarzan."

"In that case, I will not land too close to the center of the city, but on its periphery," assured the woman.

Soon enough, she dropped the craft, which landed with a jar on its flat belly. Tarzan looked about him. They stood in a clearing surrounded by broken masonry, upended columns, and other detritus of an abandoned city.

Tarzan warned, "The ape smell is near."

"I see nothing," the woman said warily.

"If I am to disembark in order to repair this vessel, I would prefer to have my blade in hand."

The woman hesitated. "I will allow this."

Stepping back on deck, Tarzan took up his blade and then went over the side.

The woman stepped over the rail to join him, keeping her distance.

She examined one ray tank, and then went over to the other side and studied its mate. Then she looked up at the bronzed giant. "This one has a long crack. It is very thin. I do not think I carry sufficient patches to mend it."

Driving his blade into the dirt to keep it handy, the ape-man studied the crack.

"Bring what patches you have. I may be able to close the seam."

"I do not see how," said the woman, but she climbed back into the ship while Tarzan grasped the tank in both hands and began applying superhuman pressure. He did this at either end of the crack where it was thinnest. The metal came together, leaving a smaller portion open.

When the woman pilot returned, she saw what Tarzan had done and asked, "How did you accomplish this feat?"

Tarzan replied without boasting, "I am quite strong by nature. On Barsoom, I am even stronger. The metal could not stand up to my pressure."

"So I see," said the woman, kneeling and applying patches of a thin metal to the central crack. A faint hissing ceased when she did so.

She studied her handiwork and said, "This gives us a chance, but only a chance."

As they prepared to climb back aboard, Tarzan's hand flashed for the hilt of his upright sword, but the woman stayed him by saying, "Permit me to board my ship before you regain your blade."

"Do you not trust me?" asked Tarzan.

"I am still learning the wisdom of trusting you. Do me the courtesy of honoring my wishes."

Tarzan withdrew his hand away from the upright hilt and patiently waited for the cloaked woman to board her craft. He showed no expression on his bronze features. He was not insulted in the slightest. He understood the woman and her concerns.

Once she swung her legs over the railing, Tarzan reached for his blade and then a slight sound caught his interest.

It might have been the rattle of a piece of detritus, blown by the soft winds of eerily silent Barsoom. But it caused him to turn and look toward a clump of masonry rubble behind them.

Abruptly, there came a blood-freezing roar, and out from behind the rock pile bounded two great white apes on their lower limbs, their paired upper arms held high.

Seeing them, the woman cried out, "Quickly! Climb aboard. I may be able to rise ahead of them."

"Leave now," called Tarzan. "I will follow!"

"Are you mad?"

"No," said Tarzan, turning to face the great six-armed albino anthropoids, "I am Tarzan of the Apes. I will deal with these Tarmanbolgani bulls."

The woman engaged her controls and the flier rose steadily. She kept one eye on the great white apes as they charged. Fear was in that eye. Fear for the half-naked wild man who called himself *Tarzan-of-the-apes*.

She could not see how one man armed only with a short-sword could stand up against the onslaught of two maddened great white apes.

As they closed, she turned her beautiful face away, not wishing to behold the grisly slaughter she knew was coming.

Chapter 14

TARMANBOLGANI BATTLE

THE RED woman of Barsoom did her best to avert her eyes from the awful sight of combat between a naked man and two great white apes. The apes came on, wielding stone cudgels, which they raised to dash out the brains of their prey. That was the last thing she saw before the battle was joined.

The cries of the apes were terrible. Coming erect, they lifted their intermediate limbs, making fists. They roared their murderous rage and lust for blood.

Their cries were answered by another one, equally terrible. It did not sound as if it could come from a human throat. But the Martian woman at once realized that this was a war cry not vented by the great blundering anthropoids.

"Kreegah! Bundolo!"

Blood-chilling as it was, a human being, not a great white ape, gave voice to that terrifying cry.

Unable to ignore the terrible screams, she settled the craft at a low altitude, raced to the port rail, and looked down.

Two towering beasts with their hairless pale skin and shock of white hair atop their sloping heads attempted to bash their enemy's black-haired skull.

But something about the way he roared back at them caused consternation to grip their expressions. Taken aback, they hesitated.

In that moment of hesitation, she saw the ape-man leap high into the air and decapitate one of his antagonists with a single sideways swipe of his short-sword. A long-sword would have been better for the job, but *Tarzan-of-the-apes* made it look like a simple thing.

His emerald cape flying, he landed behind the second screaming ape as the first toppled over, its head rolling in the dirt. Then he chopped the head off the other great white ape with a single savage cut that cleaved its thick neck.

Leaping from burly shoulders, the brutish head tumbled ahead of a sudden fountain of blood to land atop the crashing corpse, which shuddered once, then fell still.

Landing, Tarzan gathered up their skulls. Using his encrimsoned blade, he scalped them and then knotted the two white-haired scalps together about his loins.

Satisfied with his new attire, he picked up his bloody sword, wiped the gore from his blade against the pale hide of his dead foe, and then leaped for the port rail.

Unsheathing her dagger, the woman recoiled in horror. For she fully imagined that she would be next, so animal-like did this half-feral barbarian appear now.

"You may put down your dagger," said Tarzan without emotion. "I am properly dressed and we might as well be on our way."

"I had not realized I had drawn my blade," she said, returning it to its scabbard.

Gathering her composure, she returned to the controls and sent the flier back into motion. Under her steady-handed throttle pressure, it moved more swiftly now, and she climbed the small vessel experimentally, finding a higher altitude before settling upon it.

In the rear, Tarzan surveyed the surroundings hurtling past him, his open cloak whipping in the wind created by the fast-moving craft.

"How long until we reach Gathol?" he asked after a time.

"Less than a zode now," replied the other.

The ape-man recalled that a zode equalled approximately two Earth hours. "Good. I am growing hungry."

"What were you doing on the dead sea bottom?" she asked.

"Seeking Helium. And John Carter."

The woman laughed in surprise. "It would be a longer walk than humanly possible, even for someone of your superhuman thews."

Tarzan said only, "I have come a long way, and I will not be dissuaded from my mission."

"I will not press you on that point," replied the woman. "For I know you are reluctant to speak. But I believe I can help you reach John Carter."

"Do you know him?"

"Every civilized person on Barsoom knows the Warlord. And many uncivilized ones do, as well."

IN TIME, they reached Gathol, a splendid-looking city of gleaming structures built atop a rugged mountain. It had been constructed on the order of an impregnable fortress, for it was ringed on all sides by a great salt marsh. They settled in a landing bay near the central plaza.

A man in a fine harness, wearing a scarlet cloak and with a gem-encrusted long-sword belted at his side, came up the way as the ship settled in. His skin was not red like the others, but white like an Orovar. His auburn hair was encircled by a complicated arrangement of criss-crossing bands, and his eyes, unlike the dark-eyed red Martians, were a brilliant blue.

"Kaor, my chieftain," called the woman, waving. "I have returned."

"We have been searching for you. You are overdue."

"I experienced mechanical difficulties upon my return from exploring the abandoned city of Exum."

"I see. And who is this man you have brought with you?"

"I beg you to welcome this visitor from Jasoom who calls himself *Tarzan-of-the-apes*. For he has helped repair my ship and in return, I agreed to convey him here."

Tarzan stepped off the ship and said, "I seek John Carter. I am from Jasoom."

Following, the woman interjected, "He would not tell me why, Pan Dan Chee."

"Why not?" asked the auburn-haired man.

"This is between John Carter and myself. It concerns affairs upon Jasoom which involve Barsoom."

"Does it concern John Carter?"

"I will only know that when I lay the problem before him. I see that you are an Orovar man."

"I am. But now I reside in Gathol."

"Do you know the name Nulthoom?"

Pan Dan Chee looked puzzled. "Why do you ask?"

"I understand that it is an Orovar name."

"Yes, it is. And I have heard of it. Nulthoom was the name of an island city of ancient Barsoom. No one alive today knows where it stood. But it is certain that it stands no longer, being now reduced to but a feature on the dried sea floor of Throxeus, formerly the mightiest ocean on Barsoom."

"Perhaps it is the name of an Orovar chieftain," suggested Tarzan.

"I do not think so, but come. Since you have succored my wife, I offer you the hospitality of Gathol."

"I welcome food, then I must be on my way."

"That will not be necessary, *Tarzan-of-the-apes*. If the matter is as urgent as you say, John Carter will fly here as soon as he is able."

"Do you know him personally?"

Pan Dan Chee smiled. "I know him well. As does my wife."

The woman smiled as if revealing a secret. "My name is Llana of Gathol," she said. "The Warlord is my grandfather. Tell to us your story and we will communicate to him by radio."

Tarzan smiled back. "When I left Bantoom, I understood I had the choice of going either east or west in order to reach Helium, the distance being roughly equivalent. I see that I made the correct choice."

Llana of Gathol laughed lightly. "You did indeed."

"But why did you not tell me the truth about who you were?" demanded Tarzan.

"All over Barsoom, there prowl assassins with stealthy ways and sharp and treacherous blades. I could not know that you were not one of those skulkers. If you knew who I was, you might take me hostage as a means to draw John Carter into a snare."

Tarzan nodded. "Your explanation satisfies me," he said simply.

Tarzan was taken to a palace, where he was fed. He ate in silence while Llana of Gathol and Pan Dan Chee discussed him nearby.

"This man slew two great white apes with only a short-sword, and then he scalped them in order to fashion for himself a loincloth. Only a man from Jasoom could leap so high and show such strength, although I believe him to be stronger than John Carter."

Pan Dan Chee said, "I have no doubt that he is a man of Jasoom. His bronzed skin alone tells that story. He could not be an Orovar who lived too long under the sun. His hair is black."

Turning to Tarzan, Pan Dan Chee asked, "What will you have me tell John Carter in order to encourage him to fly here as fast as he is able?"

Tarzan considered his words before speaking. "Warriors of Barsoom have made their way to Jasoom. They sought to establish a colony there. More are coming. From where, I cannot say. I have been given only the name of Nulthoom."

"These are strange tidings, *Tarzan-of-the-apes*. But I will communicate them to John Carter. I am certain once he hears of this development, he will hie here as rapidly as practical. Does John Carter know you?"

"When I last tread the surface of Barsoom, I was known as Ramdar."

Llana of Gathol gasped. "Of course! Ramdar! My grandfather has spoken of you. He says you are a mighty hunter and, although he does not abandon his claim to be the greatest swordsman on two worlds, he has allowed that your mastery of the blade, combined with your great strength, left him doubting his right to be called such."

"I care nothing for such accolades," said Tarzan simply. "I wish only to treat with John Carter. If he will help me, together we will deal with the forces that would despoil Jasoom. If not, I am prepared to accomplish this task myself."

"Never fear," assured Llana of Gathol. "My grandfather has never shirked his responsibility as warlord of warlords. And the tidings you bear convince me that he will take your part."

After Tarzan finished eating, he was shown to his quarters.

"While we are waiting for an answer," advised Pan Dan Chee, "I ask that you make yourself more presentable while you are a guest of Gathol."

In his hands was a leather harness such as those worn by most races on Barsoom. However, the leather was unusually coarse and a pale white, and furthermore lacked the usual trappings of a warrior's harness.

"This harness is made of the tanned hide of a great white ape," explained Pan Dan Chee. "It is ceremonial, not practical. But since you wear a loincloth made from the scalps of great white apes, I thought it appropriate attire for you."

Tarzan accepted the gift in both hands, examined it, then declared, "I understand that this is the custom here. So I will wear this harness out of respect."

"It lacks a device, and therefore marks you as a panthan. I trust you will not mind."

"On Barsoom," returned Tarzan, "I am content with the rank of soldier of fortune."

"Excellent. I will leave you now."

With that, Pan Dan Chee withdrew and permitted Tarzan to don his new raiment. The harness belt came with an empty scabbard. Into this, he placed the short-sword he had seized in Bantoom. The bronzed giant would have much preferred his hunting knife, but he understood that upon Barsoom, a sword was all but indispensable.

He wiped the last of the blood of the great white apes off his blade before he sheathed it. It felt strange to breathe once more the rarified air of the red planet. The ape-man did not care for the peculiar taste of it in his sensitive nostrils.

Not long after, Pan Dan Chee knocked on the door of Tarzan's quarters and opened it at his invitation to enter.

"We have just received a radio-gram from the Warlord. He understands the urgency of the need for a meeting with you. Due to the great distance between Gathol and Helium, John Carter requests that we convey you to the Forest of Lost Men, where he will rendezvous with us. We must leave immediately."

Tarzan buckled on his sword, saying, "I am ready."

Before long, the ape-man found himself once more at the landing stage in the heart of the sprawling city and was taken aboard a medium-sized warship.

Quickly, lines were cast off and she rose into the skies that were growing dusky. The hurtling moons of Barsoom made their appearance, one by one, and the jungle lord stood upon the deck, attired in his ape-skin harness and emerald cloak, thinking that it was fortunate indeed that he had come across Llana of Gathol during his long march in search of the former Virginian, John Carter, Warlord of Mars. Otherwise a great deal of time would have been wasted, and Tarzan of the Apes was of no mind to tarry upon Barsoom any longer than necessary.

Chapter 15

JOHN CARTER'S ACCOUNT BEGINS

MY NAME is John Carter. I am pleased to call myself a son of Virginia, although Virginia was not the state of my birth. Not to the best of my knowledge, I must confess.

Truthfully, I do not know where I was born. My earliest memories are no more. I had formerly lived a very long time on Earth, where I am certain I was born. Beyond that, I can say only that I spent a portion of my earthly existence as a captain in the Confederacy and after the Confederacy fell, I sought my fortunes elsewhere.

It was in an Arizona cave where I laid down my earthly body, having escaped a marauding band of Apaches. I cannot entirely explain what transpired next. But I found myself looking down at my mortal form and, before I could quite comprehend my predicament, I was drawn to the planet Mars, which became my new abode.

A full account of how I ascended from the lowly status of being a mere panthan without harness to rising to the exalted position of Warlord of Barsoom, Jeddak of Jeddaks, and Prince of the House of Tardos Mors can be gotten from previous chronicles of my Barsoomian life.*

Suffice it to say that I have dwelled upon the red planet for more years than I can count, simply because I do not care to count them, for the Martian year is far longer from that of Earth. I do not think that I am immortal. But I am coming to wonder

---

* See A Princess of Mars *by Edgar Rice Burroughs.*

what the actual span of my life might be, for I have not particularly aged upon Mars, a condition that was also true during my life on Jasoom. Inexplicably, I have always managed to look like a man of no more than thirty years.

My participation in the narrative you are reading began after I had been summoned to the atmosphere plant that lies east of the territory of the green men of Thark and west of Zodanga by my comrade, Tars Tarkas, Jeddak of the Tharks.

Tars Tarkas was the first true friend I made upon barren Barsoom. It is a wonder that such different personalities could join in common cause. Tars Tarkas was an olive-skinned nomad, standing approximately ten earthly feet in height and possessing the two sets of upper arms of his barbaric race. Had he managed to reach the Earth, his face would have terrified both man and beast, for it was dominated by a pair of baleful blood-red eyes and white tusks that would have intimidated a wild boar.

It had long been believed among the red race that the green men of Barsoom were incapable of friendship, and largely this was the case. But since our first encounter, so very long ago, this particular green giant and I have been fast friends.

So it was when I received an urgent notification that there was some difficulty at the atmosphere plant, I flew directly there, along with a contingent of warriors and scientists, in the cruiser-of-war, *Xanthron.*

The trouble revolved around the Warhoons, another green horde of nomads, who lived to the south. They had begun encroaching upon the atmosphere plant, threatening the scientists who maintained it.

The Tharks and the Warhoons were long and bitter enemies. And under their Jeddak, Dak Kova, the Warhoons believed that threatening the atmosphere plant would cause the Tharks, who are allies of the Empire of Helium, to come to its aid and rescue.

It was the error of Dak Kova that he set such an obvious trap.

Rather than engage the Warhoons alone, Tars Tarkas summoned me. Together, we made short work of this interloper, producing heaps of maimed green corpses, sending the remnants of its battered and bleeding army south, and preserving the atmosphere plant from serious damage.

This had taken some ten zodes, or one earthly day. After the last skirmish, I made an inspection of the atmosphere plant, Tars Tarkas at my side.

All seemed to be in good working order. This was crucial, for this atmosphere plant was built thousands of years ago by a race that had all but dwindled into nothingness. It had fallen to the red men of Barsoom to maintain the few that remained. Without these massive engines, the thin Martian air would no longer be replenished and all of the myriad races, not to mention the beasts and birds of Barsoom, would similarly go extinct.

As we concluded our rounds, Tars Tarkas and I exited via the massive atmosphere plant portal, and stood outside, where I said to my friend, "It is good that you summoned me, Tars Tarkas. I shudder to think what would have happened if the Warhoons had done damage here. It might be beyond our power to repair it."

"John Carter, I do not think that was Dak Kova's intention. I believe he simply lusted for conquest. The Warhoon tribe has long desired to expand outside of their territory. They could not hope to defeat the cities of Korad or Zodanga, but invading Thark lands tempted him."

"Well, he has learned his lesson."

Tars Tarkas laughed raucously, his great tusks gleaming in the sunlight, his red eyes looking fierce even as merriment leapt into them.

"Since he is defeated, I will not disagree with you, John Carter. Let us see if the chastised jeddak of the Warhoons will now respect what we have done here."

As I prepared to say goodbye to my friend, a crewman with the rank of than came running from the waiting cruiser, which rested on the mossy ground.

"My Warlord, there is an urgent radio aerogram."

"From whom?"

"From Pan Dan Chee in Gathol. He bids us to inform you that the Jasoomian known as Ramdar, also called *Tarzan-of-the-apes,* has returned to Barsoom. He seeks a meeting over a matter of utmost gravity."

"Tarzan has returned to Barsoom?" Turning to Tars Tarkas, I wondered, "Whatever could have motivated him to come back? His time here was difficult and arduous. Only the greatest emergency could compel him to leave Jasoom."

Addressing the soldier, I asked, "Does he state the nature of the emergency?"

Regarding Tars Tarkas, he reported, "This I will only impart to your ears alone. But according to Pan Dan Chee, there is a danger to both Jasoom and Barsoom. And your help is sought."

"In that case, ready the ship. We will depart immediately. Send word to Pan Dan Chee that we will rendezvous on the western verge of the Forest of Lost Men. That will close the distance between us more rapidly than if we flew directly to Gathol."

"This will be done as you command, my prince," returned the than, rushing away.

I looked to my Thark comrade. "I must leave you now, Tars Tarkas."

The green man stared down at me with fiery eyes that would terrify the bravest man of Earth, but in which I beheld only the familiar light of friendship.

"Just as you came when I called, John Carter, I am willing to go with you into this new danger. For whatever threatens Barsoom also endangers Thark."

"I do not know what this new danger might be, Tars Tarkas. But you are welcome to come along if that is your wish."

"I will order my horde to return home. Then I will join you."

Under the mighty Thark's direction, his barbaric troop mounted their wild thoats and turned back toward the dead city of Thark that was their base and headquarters.

WE SOON set off, turning north, flying past the Twin Cities of Helium with their scarlet and yellow towers, and headed for the equator, where the Forest of Lost Men was located.

I gave little thought to the reasons that Ramdar had returned to Barsoom. I would hear them from his own lips. But I cast my mind back to the time, now long ago, when he had first appeared, a warlord without harness. He had assembled a tribe of great white apes who obeyed his command, and whose language he spoke, along with a remnant horde of green men, and commenced marching across the face of Barsoom with unknown intention.

Our first encounter led to a clash of wills, but over time I came to understand who he was and what he desired, which was merely to return to Jasoom. We became allies, and I assisted him in returning to Africa, which he considered his home, even though he was an English lord.

We traveled all night at top speed, eventually reaching the Forest of Lost Men.

There, we found that the ship from Gathol had already beaten us. We set down outside the forest edge and disembarked.

I led a small contingent to the other ship, accompanied only by my aide-de-camp, a padwar by the name of Vor Daj, and Tars Tarkas.

Pan Dan Chee came down the ladder first, and we greeted each other warmly.

"Kaor, John Carter. It is good to see you."

"Kaor, Pan Dan Chee. How is my granddaughter?"

"She thrives. And sends her best wishes."

Tarzan of the Apes did not bother with the ladder, but simply leaped from the starboard rail and padded over.

I pride myself on being an exemplary specimen of manhood, but Tarzan of the Apes was so superbly muscled, standing beside him I felt as if I were his inferior. He was attired in a harness that I recognized to be ape hide and wore a loincloth made from the scalps of two great white apes. The emerald cloak about his shoulders was the only evidence of civilization about him. I was not surprised to see that he walked barefoot, for that was his custom.

I hailed him in English. "Greetings, *Tarzan-of-the-apes*. Or should I call you John Clayton, Lord Greystoke?"

"Tarzan is sufficient," he said frankly. "Thank you for coming. We must talk."

Tarzan came right to the point, which was his way. Despite being a hereditary viscount, he was every inch a man of action. I appreciated that about him, even if he often could be abrupt and seem rough around the edges. I understood that he did not come entirely of his own volition.

"What is the trouble you bring to me?" I asked.

Tarzan said, "It is not trouble I bring to you, it is trouble that Mars has brought to the Earth."

"Tell me."

"An interplanetary ship has landed in Africa carrying white-skinned Martians. They founded a settlement. When I learned of this, I confronted them. They claimed to be colonizers, intent upon making Africa their own. They brought with them certain beasts of Barsoom, which did not belong in my jungle."

Hearing this, I thought back to the scientist Fal Sivas, who had built the first interplanetary ship in Barsoomian history. Fal Sivas had disappeared after running afoul of my blade, and nothing had been heard of him or his extraordinary craft since. *

Now, it seems, he had built another ship. One larger and more powerful than before.

"Two Barsoomian scientists have built the first space-travers-ing ships," I explained. "One, Gar Nal, perished, taking his secrets with him. The other disappeared and is still sought. Now tell me, what transpired between you and this colony?"

"Confronting their utan, I ordered him to leave Africa. But they said their ship was demolished and they could not. More-

---

* *See* Swords of Mars *by Edgar Rice Burroughs.*

over, they refused to do so. They claimed Africa the way English-men and Spaniards once claimed America, by right of landfall, and subsequent occupation."

"These were white Martians, you say?"

"Yes. Orovars. Their hair was fair."

"I do not see how Orovars could have learned to build ships to travel through space unless a red scientist had assisted them. This makes me think of Fal Sivas, who has not been heard of in several years."

"There is more," continued Tarzan. "Before I slew them to the last man, one told me that another ship was coming, much larger than the one that had carried this company. I've come here to enlist you in the search for this enclave. They cannot be allowed to fly to Earth."

"I do not disagree with you, *Tarzan-of-the-apes*. It would be a terrible thing if Barsoomians were to take root in Africa. It would mean conflict. Eventually, war. No good can come of it. Tell me, how were they able to get around? On Jasoom, the heavier gravity would pull them to the ground and hold them there."

"These white men wore armor that counteracted the pull of gravity. Their beasts also wore pieces of this treated metal. And they flew about in great birds constructed of this identi-cal substance."

"Metal birds? I've never heard of such things."

Tarzan explained, "These birds were so large that a warrior could saddle one and fly about, controlling them by mental telepathy acting upon mechanical brains encased in the skulls of these metal steeds."

"Once again, you cause me to recall Fal Sivas. The birds you describe bring to mind malagors. These were the species of giant birds that once inhabited Barsoom. Another scientist, Ras Thavas, found a way to bring the species back to life. He had tamed them to the degree that warriors could ride them about and conduct raids. But Ras Thavas is not a mechanical engineer like Fal Sivas. This would not be his handiwork. It is quite puzzling. Tell me, did any of these Orovar warriors give you intelligence about where they came from?"

"Their leader was an utan named Ro-Dun-Bo. But one of the others said that they had sworn allegiance to Nulthoom. I do not know if that is a person or a place."

I looked to Pan Dan Chee. "I do not recognize that word. Is it an Orovar name?"

Pan Dan Chee nodded. "Yes, I have heard of it. It was the name of an island city in the Throxeus Ocean. No one living knows where it lay."

I considered this. "The Throxeus was the mightiest ocean of ancient Barsoom," I explained to Tarzan. "It covered much of the northern hemisphere. The marshes of Gathol are all that remain of her southernmost reaches. And the Toonolian Marshes, where the malagors dwelled, belong to its eastern edge. This is a wide area. But at least it gives us a direction in which to search."

Tarzan said firmly, "I am ready to go where I must."

I turned to Pan Dan Chee and said, "You may take your ship back to Gathol with my compliments. What must be done must be done stealthily. One cruiser to start with. I have a small crew, as well as Tars Tarkas and this man from Jasoom. You did well to bring him here, Pan Dan Chee. Give my love to my granddaughter, and tell her I will visit Gathol as soon as I am able."

Saluting, Pan Dan Chee took his leave.

I addressed Tarzan and Tars Tarkas. "We will start by seeking Ras Thavas, who currently dwells in Duhor. He may know about the malagors of metal, although I doubt it very much. But it is a starting point, and we must begin somewhere."

Once aboard the *Xanthron*, I gave the order to depart, and we drove northward in the direction of the vast dead sea bottom that was once the greatest ocean of seafaring Barsoom.

"Set course for Duhor," I instructed the helmsman. For I knew that Ras Thavas had taken up residence there after being driven out of his previous outpost in the Great Toonolian Marshes. The renegade scientist was reformed, and was said to have largely retired from his mad experiments with people and animals. Absent any other clues, interrogating him was the only course of action that came to mind, although I put precious little stock in my prospects.

Chapter 16

THE MASTER MIND

FAR INTO the night and well into the next day, the cruiser *Xanthron* carried us ever northward. The air grew cooler and then turned cold after we passed Polodona, the Barsoomian equator. Heavy cloaks of apt fur were brought out of storage, and we donned them to stay warm.

During this passage, I observed Tarzan of the Apes. He was not unfriendly, but he kept to himself a great deal. It was abundantly clear to me that he was a man on a mission, one that was distasteful to him.

Well I remembered those weeks he spent in Helium as my guest while my Lotharian friend Kar Kormak taught him the mental exercises that would permit him, as they did me, to pass from Barsoom back to his natal planet at will.

I knew that Tarzan had missed his wife and family during that time. I do not know how long he had been marooned on Barsoom during that period, the Barsoomian year consisting of an average of 687 days. But it had been several teeans, many Martian months in which he clung to the faintest of hopes that he could someday return to Africa and his beloved forest family.

I never expected to see Tarzan again. I understood that only the direst of necessities had brought him back to Barsoom.

In time, the Artolian Hills with their snowy peaks came into view, and then before them lay the city of Duhor, a city that was now allied with the Empire of Helium. This has not always been the case, but the passage of time brings new perspectives, and the old quarrels were mended and forgotten.

We had wirelessed ahead to await our arrival, so when we dropped into the landing stage that had been set aside for us, we disembarked to a warm welcome.

For no less than Vad Varo was there to greet us. I introduced him to Tarzan, and the two men stared at one another for some time, looking slightly perplexed.

I laughed, saying to Tarzan, "I do not believe I ever told you of this man. During what you call on Earth the First World War, he died a soldier, and found himself transported here. His name was Ulysses Paxton. Now he goes by the Barsoomian name of Vad Varo, Prince of Duhor. *

"Vad Varo, this is *Tarzan-of-the-apes*. Believe it or not, for I scarcely do, he is the son of an English lord who was orphaned in Africa and raised by the wild apes dwelling there. Only upon coming to manhood did he learn of his heritage. His real name is John Clayton, Lord Greystoke, for he is a viscount of English nobility. But he prefers to be known as Tarzan, to be informal about it."

The two men shook hands as Earth-men do, which I found slightly amusing. It was a custom I had half-forgotten.

"His grip is wonderfully strong," Vad Varo told me, with a wincing grin.

"I understand that he wrestled gorillas as a child," I returned.

Tarzan did not partake of this repartee. His face was grim. The seriousness of his demeanor could not be broken by levity.

"Now that we have arrived," I told Vad Varo, "take us to Ras Thavas."

A waiting land flier carried us to the modest home of Ras Thavas, and we were invited in by a husky slave named Yamdor, whom I recognized. It was said that this man was the product of one of the scientist's bizarre experiments. He had transplanted the brain of an unfortunate slave girl into the body of a power-

---

* *See* The Master Mind of Mars *by Edgar Rice Burroughs.*

ful man, thus producing a perfect servant, one possessing the attributes of a bodyguard combined with those of a cultured household servant. Although Ras Thavas had in the past been guilty of performing horrific experiments on human beings, he had put such dubious activities behind him and had devoted his energies to more philanthropic ends, such as reconstructive surgery.

The ancient scientist rose from his chair to greet us. The infamous Master Mind of Mars had not changed appreciably since I had last seen him, a considerable number of ords before, for Barsoomians age very slowly. Although Ras Thavas was more than one thousand Martian years old, he looked no more than forty, for he had prevailed upon Vad Varo, his former assistant, to implant his brain into the head of a strapping young man. The scientist formerly had possessed the largest cranium of a man of his advanced age that I ever encountered. This new body also boasted a skull of formidable size, for Ras Thavas' brain was abnormally developed.

"Kaor, John Carter," he hailed. "What brings you to Duhor?"

"I am investigating reports of giant mechanical birds. Men ride these machines, which are built after the fashion of the malagors you once bred. What do you know of them?"

His dark eyes snapping, Ras Thavas looked puzzled.

"I have never heard of such an invention."

"Malagors were thought to be extinct until you discovered them and bred several specimens," I reminded.

"Yes, I found one in the Toonolian Marshes. So far as I know, none have ever been seen outside of that area."

"Then you cannot help us," I said.

"Not directly. But I recall that one malagor disappeared from its pen, long ago. The lock was broken. It had been stolen in the night and had either flown away or been carried off by a flier."

"How long ago?"

"Perhaps three ords."

Vad Varo suggested, "A clever mechanical engineer might have studied one and built a flying machine that copied its aerodynamic form."

"Such an engineer would have to be extremely clever to accomplish such a feat," noted Ras Thavas. "It is beyond my knowledge, of course. But I suppose it is possible."

"Do you recall other mysterious thefts during that time?" I pressed.

"Yes, two fliers went missing at different times. They were never seen again."

I questioned Ras Thavas at length, but he could impart nothing more of interest. Realizing this, I thanked him and we took our leave.

Once we were outside, we rejoined Tars Tarkas, who, owing to the low ceilings of the humble home, had been obliged to remain on guard outside.

Vad Varo turned to me and remarked, "Peculiar thefts have been reported down through the ords here in Duhor."

"Raiders?"

The man nodded. "Or pirates from the polar regions beyond the ice barrier to our north. Large goods were taken. Fliers. Weapons. Thoats, and even zitidars. In fact, two ords ago, a pair of zitidars disappeared on the same night, from the same enclosure. As you know, we trade with Amhor to the west, whose principal business is breeding zitidars and thoats. They sell them to other city-states such as ours."

Hearing this, Tarzan turned to me and asked, "Are the zitidars of this region shaggy, and do they lack the flexible eye stalks of the zitidars of the southern hemisphere?"

"They do. How do you know that?"

"That was the species of zitidar which the Orovar company brought to Africa. It was entirely unlike the hairless variety I previously encountered."

"This is interesting," I said. "It suggests that Nulthoom may lie in the largely unexplored uninhabited zone between Duhor and the Great Toonolian Marshes. That narrows the search area considerably. Nevertheless, it represents a stupendous expanse of the featureless dead sea bottom."

Addressing Vad Varo, I said, "I believe we will initiate a search to the east. We will use Duhor as our headquarters. I am sure you will see us again soon."

"You are always welcome here, John Carter."

A land flier conveyed us back to the staging area, and without further ado, we set sail. We quickly reached a comfortable altitude, cruising low for better visibility, but also because the air was warmer closer to the ground.

WE WERE soon flying over the snow-encrusted steppes of the former upper Throxeus Ocean. Here the endless ochre moss grew only in the summer. It was now late fall. In the coming weeks, the thin air would grow increasingly frigid and the snow-line would creep farther south than at present.

I conferred with Tarzan. "The type of white-coated zitidar you describe is native to the northernmost reaches, for obvious reasons. We will fly over these latitudes in the hope of discovering something worth investigating."

"Are cities known in these latitudes?" asked Tarzan.

"Very few. All known to me. But a great deal of the upper Throxeus sea bottom is sparsely explored. If a hitherto unknown Orovar enclave exists in these upper regions, it may be well concealed. We can but search and pray for luck."

"Luck is not something in which I place great stock," returned Tarzan of the Apes seriously.

"In that case, I will count on your eyes, which I know to be exceedingly sharp, to keep watch for as long as you are able."

Nodding silently, Tarzan padded forward and went to the prow, where he took a watchful position, his white fur cape blowing in the headwinds. He seemed oblivious to the bitter cold, which I took to be a byproduct of his determination to see out this quest, which had taken him so far from his warm home environment.

I took a strange but reassuring comfort in the knowledge of his presence. I had seen him in battle. Indeed, we had clashed in a sword duel, in which he had gotten the better of me. I had a healthy respect for his physical prowess.

Should we encounter enemies, I knew he would be the first into battle, and no disrespect to Tars Tarkas, or even to myself, Tarzan of the Apes would be the most formidable of our company.

Chapter 17

ACROSS ENDLESS TUNDRA

FAR AND wide, we ranged. The endless steppeland swept beneath our keel. By day we searched, but at night we did not run with our lights or use our searchlights. We did not care to be targets of our unknown quarry, whose capabilities might be formidable.

Three Martian padans passed without incident. Three Martian days in which we covered many hundreds of haads, yet to no avail. We ranged as far east as the Great Toonolian Marshes and circled back in the direction of Duhor.

Except for a few snowy hills here and there, and the long stony ledges that we assumed to be remnants of the vanished Throxeus seacoast, the steppes were largely featureless.

Below the great ice barrier that ringed the northern pole, a range of extinct volcanoes pocked the tundra. None had ever been known to erupt. In ancient times, many of these had been underwater, but some were so tall that no doubt they formed volcanic islands which once lifted over the surging sea that was now a flat plain of emptiness in which not even dead cities could be discovered.

If Nulthoom survived to the present era, it was difficult to imagine where and in what form it could take. Here and there, hidden cities had survived from Mars' seafaring glory days, but the Orovar people who persisted always concealed themselves from their red descendants and were especially fearful of the marauding green nomads who had overrun the ruins of their once-proud cities and seaports.

One night, while standing watch, Tars Tarkas came to my quarters and reported, "Something strange has been sighted ahead."

Summoning Tarzan, we assembled on the forward deck.

In the distance, a red glare burned in the night. It was difficult to make out what it might be, only that it resembled a burning gash running nearly a mile in an east-to-west direction.

Tarzan sniffed the air and said, "Coal."

He used the English word, apparently not knowing the Barsoomian term.

Tars Tarkas spoke up, "I do not recognize that word. What does it mean?"

I explained to Tars Tarkas about anthracite, which was not common on Barsoom. "On Jasoom, coal is burned in furnaces to heat buildings," I concluded.

Soon enough, we overhauled the jagged line of fire.

"Take us lower," requested Tarzan.

I gave the order and we landed. Disembarking, we made our way across the snowy steppe to a long gash gouged in the frozen ground that was burning steadily and causing the thin crust of snow to melt and puddle on either side of it.

Tars Tarkas stared at this with concern written on his olive-green visage.

"I do not understand this."

Tarzan said, "On Jasoom are found seams of underground coal that are sometimes fired by strikes of lightning. They burn themselves out after weeks or months. But some surface coal seams run so deep that they burn for years. Lightning did this."

Having satisfied our curiosity, we got back on shipboard and resumed our search.

During those long hours, I observed Tarzan closely. While he was not aloof in any way, he appeared to be averse to socializing with the crew.

Despite having once commanded a group of green nomads, the bronzed Jasoomian avoided Tars Tarkas without explicitly snubbing him. I recalled from past conversations that in the language of the great apes of Africa, which Tarzan spoke fluently, he considered the green man to be a Hortamangani, which meant roughly, Great-boar-man.

I found this amusing when Tarzan first told me this, but now I realized that the frightful aspect of Tars Tarkas, with his fierce face dominated by porcelain-like tusks, was not something to which Tarzan could easily become accustomed. Or perhaps the towering Thark brought back unpleasant memories of Tarzan's first exile upon Mars.

To all others, Tarzan presented a superficially friendly aspect, but I could still sense a certain remoteness about him. I took this to mean that he did not intend to stay upon Barsoom any longer than absolutely necessary. This was understandable.

Although I possessed the ability to read the mind of almost any human inhabitant of Barsoom, the inner thoughts of this Jasoomian were closed to me, as they had been during our first encounter. I could not fathom why, but since we were allies, it did not matter.

NOT A great deal of time passed when, up ahead, we spied another smoldering spot.

This one was not close to the ground, but was elevated above it. I put my field glass on it, but I could not discern what it could be. It seemed like a massive torch held high over the tundra.

I ordered the helmsman to take us close to it, but not too close, lest the torch draw us into unknown danger.

Carefully, we approached, then circled the looming apparition with appropriate caution.

The greater moon of Thuria came into the sky then, throwing her ever-shifting light about, causing shadows to move as if alive and fleeing the luminous body which cast them.

I saw then what appeared to be a massive mountain encased in rime ice. Yet the top burned in a fiery manner no volcano brimming with lava had ever burned. Curiously, I saw no lava spilling down the sides.

Without benefit of a field glass, Tarzan studied the looming structure.

"This is unnatural," he decided.

"What do you mean?"

"That mountain appears to be a volcano that is active, yet it is sheathed with ice almost to the crater rim. The ice crust is not melting. If the inner chamber brimmed with hot lava, the ice should have turned to water and cascaded down by now."

"If the top is not boiling lava, then what could it be?"

Tarzan turned to me and asked simply, "Can you not smell the air?"

I had not been paying attention to my nostrils, but now I inhaled deeply and this action caused me to cough slightly. I recognize the odor. It was bitter.

"Burning coal," I said. "Apparently this peak is topped by a bed of coal, which lightning has ignited."

"There is more to it than that," said Tarzan.

I studied him. "Please explain."

"The Orovar force who came to Earth wore a symbol on their helmets. It consisted of a white triangle with a red half-moon set over it. This ice mountain pretending to be a volcano reminds me strongly of that insignia. We have found Nulthoom. Let there be no doubt."

I considered the words of Tarzan.

"Could Nulthoom be a mountain?"

"This mountain might simply be a feature marking the spot where Nulthoom may be found," Tarzan pointed out.

"Yes, that is a possibility," I mused. "I am reminded of the red enclave called Ghasta, which is built of volcanic stone in the heart of an extinct crater much smaller and broader than this peak. It lies in the Valley Hohr, very terribly far from here. Pan Dan Chee said that Nulthoom was thought to be an island city. It is conceivable that the island was dominated by a peak such as this one."

I considered the matter. And made a swift decision.

"We will fly onward, as if we do not recognize the significance of this smoldering peak. After daybreak, we will return to reconnoiter."

"That is a sound plan," said Tarzan, going to the rail and stepping onto it. "Look for me in the morning."

"What are you doing?" I asked. "If there is an enclave of Orovars in this area, they will surely hear our motors. We will have lost the element of surprise."

Tensing his muscles as he balanced on the moving rail, Tarzan said simply, "I am the element of surprise."

Then he dropped from sight.

Tars Tarkas joined me at the rail, and we saw dimly the bronze-skinned Jasoomian land on the steppeland, then make his way toward the looming mountain of ice crowned with smoldering coal.

"This Jasoomian is never afraid to plunge into danger blindly," declared the green man.

"He is all but fearless, I agree. We now have no choice in the matter, Tars Tarkas. We will continue on, then circle back once there is sufficient light to conduct a thorough search."

And so the *Xanthron* continued on her course. I went to the stern rail and tried to follow Tarzan's progress through the patches of snow and dark ground.

I thought I caught sight of his white-furred cloak, but then he was gone. His movements were difficult to discern. Overhead, Thuria bathed the barren steppeland in pale light. But she and her more distant companion, Cluros, together made the shadows shift and squirm with their sharply contrasting illumination.

Amid those shifting shadows, I could not separate the stealthy movements of Tarzan of the Apes from the ever-changing patterns of lunar light and shadow. Eventually, we put the burning peak behind us and I gave up. My mind went back to the first time I encountered this remarkable man, and I thought again how much more like an impulsive and headstrong animal he often seemed.

Chapter 18

The Interplanetary Ship

TARZAN OF THE APES landed short of the broad base of the burning mountain of ice. He looked upward. A crimson glow was reflected by the thin scudding clouds above. He sniffed the air but failed to scent man or beast. Coal smoke was the predominant odor, concealing all else.

From a running jump, Tarzan propelled himself halfway up the peak's icy western flank and landed in a craggy crevice, to which he clung.

The way up was too sheer and slippery to safely leap again, so he fell to climbing with hands and feet. The ice crust was hard and slippery. From time to time he was forced to use his short-sword to cut hand and foot holes so that he could continue scaling the towering peak.

This took some time. Eventually, the ape-man reached the lip of the fiery crater. Sheathing his sword, he used both hands to grip the basalt edge and carefully lifted his head in order to see over the craggy rim.

What Tarzan saw did not surprise him. In the center of the wide crater mouth, perhaps eight feet below the gleaming rim, a bed of coal burned steadily. Its harsh warmth washed over his bronzed features.

The coal bed was entirely artificial. This was evidenced by the fact that it was held in place by a circular containment wall perhaps four feet high.

The smoldering fire was encircled by a promenade easily ninety feet in diameter. This, too, was artificial. It consisted of dark stone flags, which were irregular so as to suggest fissures and cracks if seen from a passing flier. But it was obviously man-made.

At the far side of the crater, a pale-skinned man faced the west. He wore a heavy cloak of calot hide, and a helmet covered his hair. He stood with a spear in one hand and was staring in the direction of the departing war cruiser of John Carter. A sentry, no doubt.

While he was distracted, the bronzed giant lifted a muscular leg and hooked it over the crater rim and so slipped over onto the circular stone path, unseen and unheard.

Moving stealthily, Tarzan circumvented the artificial coal bed and came up behind the guard. It would be a simple matter to slay him with his short-sword, but the ape-man did not see him as an enemy. At least, not at the moment.

Using both hands, he took hold of the unaware fellow by the back of his neck, squeezing with great force.

Struggling against the indomitable power of Tarzan of the Apes, the sentry was forced to drop his spear, which clattered to the flags as he attempted to pry irresistible fingers off his neck.

No man born of Barsoom was strong enough to overcome an Earth-man powered by the Martian environment. The sentry lost consciousness and slumped in Tarzan's hands.

The ape-man caught him up and laid him down on the flag-stone circle.

Looking about, he sought a way into the interior of the mountain, for it was evident that there must be such a thing.

His initial search was futile. There was no sign of a door or entry in the crater wall. Once Tarzan had ascertained that fact, he fell to examining the flagstones.

One showed a notch in the seam of its joining. Kneeling, Tarzan attempted to insert his iron fingers into the niche, but it proved too narrow.

Returning to the unconscious sentry, he examined his harness for any signs of a key. He found none. But when the ape-man picked up the fallen spear, he noticed that the spear tip was blunter than it should be. There was no point. Also, the metal showed distress just behind the spear point's flat blade.

Carrying this over to the flagstone, Tarzan inserted the spear point into the notch and levered up the flagstone. This required some effort. The flag was heavy. There was no mechanism involved.

When the ape-man had lifted the flagstone sufficiently high, he took hold of it with his free hand and raised it farther. He saw then that it was set upon massive mechanical hinges.

Tarzan looked down. Below was something he had never seen before on Mars, although it was a familiar sight upon Earth.

A set of steps was cut in the black volcanic rock. These were ancient, for in the center were depressions made by the countless footsteps of innumerable generations.

Leaving the flagstone up, Tarzan went to the insensate guard and donned his helmet. Then he exchanged his cloak for the heavy furred one. The bronzed giant closed this in the front so that his ape-skin harness and white loincloth could not be seen. The helmet concealed Tarzan's black hair, which was a necessity, for the Orovars were all light-haired as well as pale-skinned. In the dark, his gray eyes might not be noticed.

Slipping down the stairs, Tarzan found that it wound to the left, pausing at a landing which connected to a corridor hewn from basalt, also on the left and going deeper into the heart of the mountain. This was deserted. There were no guards inside. No doubt none were required in a camouflaged stronghold such as this. He entered this hallway, which was illuminated at intervals by the glow of radium lamps set into the dark smooth-polished walls.

Padding along silently, Tarzan listened as he searched. The walls on either side were broken by doorways, which were not barred by panels but hung with concealing tapestries.

Carefully pulling aside one of these, he saw a large room used for storage. There are many swords, shields, helmets, and other implements of war. Nothing else.

The ape-man had no need of any of them and therefore no interest. He passed on.

In time, he realized that the corridor was curved and it seemed to follow the curve of the crater walls above. The air was stale but warm. No doubt the coal bed above was transmitting its warmth down into the lower chambers.

Barefoot, Tarzan slipped along silently. In time, he discovered a double door set in the inner wall. This was the first time such a feature had appeared, for the inner wall was previously unbroken. All of the other rooms had been cut in the outer wall.

Tarzan paused at the door, listening. Although muffled, he could hear two men speaking.

"You are working late, Fal Sivas," came a gravelly voice.

"I could not sleep. The new interplanetary ship has fallen behind schedule. If I cannot sleep, I might as well keep working."

Fal Sivas! That was the name of the scientist of which John Carter had spoken, the first Martian ever to build a space-crossing craft.

The voice of Fal Sivas continued.

"Your jeddara has decided that, in addition to a complement of one hundred warriors, some ten eggs and slave women to nurture them must accompany the next expedition. She wishes that a new race take root upon Jasoom as quickly as possible. If the first eggs survive the journey, it will be deemed safe to transfer the rest, which represent the future generations of Nulthoom."

"O-Thuria is very wise," commented the gravel voice. "And no doubt correct. For too many generations, we have abided in this dormant volcano. While it has kept us safe from the other races, especially the marauding green giants, it is a suffocatingly cloistered life and not one fit for the proud descendants of a race of seafarers."

"I am pleased that someone appreciates the work that I do here," returned Fal Sivas. "When I was among my own race, I was not appreciated. Here, I am."

"Have you decided whether you will go to Jasoom on the last ship?"

"I have not. I may build a small interplanetary ship of my own and go elsewhere. Where, I do not know. But since Barsoom is dying, I do not wish to end my days on a barren and nearly waterless planet, any more than you Orovars do."

As he listened, Tarzan placed one eye to the vertical line where the two doors joined. To a limited degree, he could see within.

ILLUMINATED BY glareless radium lamps was a surprisingly large space. It was on the order of a shipyard, but bound by dressed basalt walls and holding only one craft, which sat above the floor cradled in a complicated scaffolding of wood and metal.

This was a stupendous shell, not quite completed, and of a design far beyond any ship of the Earth. Indeed, it was oddly different from the fliers of Barsoom, being entirely enclosed like a gigantic egg.

The design resembled an elongated teardrop. The nose was ellipsoidal in shape and fitted with a pair of forward-facing portholes set with ground crystal lenses that were opaque. It was not possible to see into the craft's interior, nor did it seem as if a pilot could peer out and see where he was traveling. From its head, the ship tapered down to a narrow stem. This was framed by angular projections that appeared to serve as landing legs. There were no signs of propellers, screws, rocket tubes, or any other means of propulsion. Perhaps they had yet to be installed, thought Tarzan.

From what the ape-man could see, this impressive craft was twice the size of the ship that had landed in Africa. Therefore, it would easily accommodate a substantially larger force of men.

How such a ship could escape the confines of this machine shop, Tarzan could not reckon. But here was the object of his quest. He need only destroy it.

Stepping back from the door, the bronzed giant set himself and then charged forward. His great two-handed strength forced both portals to swing wide with such force that one came off its heavy hinge-works.

Tarzan had carried the sentry's spear with him. This he drew back over his right shoulder and then drove it forward.

The blunt tip described a shallow arc and entered an open hatch, producing a clatter followed by the odor of burning electrical elements and the attendant smoke they produced.

The two men reacted to the sudden intrusion.

One was a small red man. He was no threat. But the other was tall, thick-muscled, and wore the white helmet and trappings of an Orovar soldier.

His face broke in shock, but then he recovered. Whipping his sword from its scabbard, he charged Tarzan.

Slipping his own blade from its scabbard, the ape-man rushed to meet this attack.

But the other fellow came up short. "What is this?" he demanded. "I cannot fight a man armed only with a short-sword with my long-sword."

Tarzan's face broke into a fierce grin. "The ways of Barsoom are not the ways of Tarzan of the Apes. Defend yourself or die."

Seeing the fury on the bronzed giant's face, the man decided that this life mattered more than martial custom. Screwing up his courage, he resumed his charge.

With raised sword, the ape-man counterattacked, and their blades met and rebounded. Only the long-sword kept going. So powerful was Tarzan's first blow that it was forced from the grip of its wielder, and it spun back behind him to land with a clangor on the smooth stone floor.

Tarzan's blade point went to the man's throat.

"It is not the length of a man's blade," he said tightly, "but the power of his sword arm which matters."

"I would not have believed this had I not experienced it," grunted the other. "Before you vanquish me, who are you?"

"A man of Jasoom, come to avenge the invasion of my land."

"From Jasoom? How can that be?"

Panting, Fal Sivas spoke up. "He is not the first. John Carter came before him. John Carter, too, is a powerful man. No Barsoomian could stand against him in physical combat."

"So I see." Scorn twisted the soldier's wide features. "Know, man of Jasoom, nothing can stop O-Thuria, Jeddara of Nulthoom, from relocating her people to Jasoom. You may slay me, but you cannot stop the operation. Our jeddara has decreed that our people will once again dwell beside fresh water, build sailing ships, and live as our ancient ancestors did, as proud sailors and merchantmen."

Tarzan would have none of this speech.

"Your first expedition is no more," he hurled back savagely. "The scavengers of Africa have consumed their corpses. The ship is smashed. It will not fly again. Put away all thought and design of conquest. For it is foredoomed."

"What is this?" demanded Fal Sivas in a quaking voice. "The first ship is no more?"

"Damaged upon landing," said Tarzan. "Just as this one now is. Now step aside, I have no need to slay you. It is this ship I must destroy."

"I will not stand aside," snarled the stubborn soldier.

"Very well," stated Tarzan calmly. With the flat of his blade, he delivered a glancing blow to the side of the man's helmet so quickly he did not see it coming and so could not block it. Not that it mattered.

The Orovar warrior fell to the floor, his helmet falling off to reveal blond hair shot with streaks of gray. Tarzan stepped over him and made his way toward the uncompleted interplanetary craft.

"What do you intend to do?" cried Fal Sivas in horror.

"If necessary, I will tear this machine apart with my bare hands."

"In that case," said the scientist meekly, "there is nothing I can do to prevent you from doing so. I am no warrior. And I can always build another."

As soon as those words escaped the scientist's lips, he regretted them. He saw the look that came into the bronze-skinned Jasoomian's eyes and realized that his life was now forfeit.

Fal Sivas stepped back until his legs touched the back of an ersite workbench. He reached behind him, and calloused fingers fumbled for something.

"I will settle with you once I wreck this machine," said Tarzan, stepping onto a narrow steel ramp that led into the spacecraft's interior.

"Before you do," said Fal Sivas, "consider this."

Nearly inside, the ape-man paused and turned.

At that moment, Fal Sivas pulled the trigger of the device in his hand, at the same time closing his eyelids tightly.

The resulting flash of light was like two daggers stabbing into the ape-man's optical nerves. So powerful were they that he was staggered by the sudden assault upon his vision.

"Ha ha!" cried the scientist, chortling. "All men have their weaknesses. I have just blinded you with this welding tool. It will be hours, if not days before you can see clearly again."

Gathering himself, Tarzan stepped off the ramp and made for the sound of the scientist's jubilant voice, the old battle scar on his brow flaming into life.

At the same time, Fal Sivas found a lever and a gonging sound of warning resounded throughout the rock-bound shipyard.

Roused from sleep, Orovar soldiers came surging from beyond the chamber and swept into the room, short-swords at the ready.

Fal Sivas cried to them, "We have an intruder! He has attempted to sabotage the new ship. Slay him if you can."

A swordsman hurled back, "*If* we can? He is only one and we are many."

"He is far stronger than he might appear. Beware his terrible reach."

Tarzan of the Apes did not wait for the swarm of guards to overwhelm him. He turned to the sound of running feet, and with a powerful leap, landed hard on the floor just short of the poised guard.

Bronzed fists rained mighty blows and men fell, their skulls and rib cages breaking under his relentless pummeling. At such close quarters, they could not bring their swords into stabbing positions.

"He is stronger than a great white ape," one man howled.

"I am Tarzan of the Apes!" came the savage response.

It was Fal Sivas who settled the matter. Picking up a hammer from his workbench, he slipped up behind the bronzed giant—who was more than holding his own—and tapped him once behind the right ear.

All the strength went out of the Jasoomian fury at that moment. He collapsed into the arms of his opponents.

They laid him out on the floor, taking stock of their own injuries. None were mortally wounded.

"Take him to the jeddara, Tun-Dun-Lo," ordered Fal Sivas, speaking to the gravel-voiced soldier of the earlier conversation. "She will want to hear his story before slaying the brute."

The dwar of the guard commanded two men to pick up the Jasoomian giant and carry him off, while others of their company took charge of the wounded.

Fal Sivas called after them, "Tell the jeddara that this is a warrior from Jasoom come to avenge the intrusion upon his homeland. He endeavored to sabotage my ship. But I think the damage is not serious. Assure your jeddara that the work will proceed on schedule regardless."

"I will do as you say, Fal Sivas. And I will inform the jeddara of your bravery and resourcefulness. For without you, this man might have overcome us."

With that, Tun-Dun-Lo departed, leaving the scientist to make an assessment of the damage done to his unfinished interplanetary ship.

Chapter 19

EXPLORATIONS

WHEN TARZAN regained consciousness, he could see but little.

At first, the ape-man was not certain that this was due to the darkness of the place in which he had been consigned, or because his optic nerves were still paralyzed as a consequence of the blinding flash of Fal Sivas' welding tool.

Gradually, he knew, his eyes would become adjusted to the darkness. And he would know.

While Tarzan waited for that development, he felt about him and discovered that he lay on a mass of dried vegetation. Standing up, he extended his arms in both directions, discovered nothing, and then moved forward. He soon encountered a rough wall that appeared to be hewn from stone. It was cool to the touch.

With his hand, he followed this until he came to a wall that was composed of metal bars. This is when the ape-man realized he had been placed in a cell somewhere in the confines of the mountain.

There was nothing to the cell except the straw on the floor and the iron-barred door. His nostrils told him that the air was stagnant. The only other odor was that of human perspiration.

Tarzan spoke up. "I am awake."

He expected this to bring a guard. But no guard showed. The sound of sandals slapping the floor of the passage beyond the bars failed to materialize.

Once again, it occurred to Tarzan that there was little need for guards in the fastness of this volcano that no one suspected contained the remnants of an ancient people.

By the time Tarzan understood that his vision was not soon returning, he decided that he would not await further developments.

Taking the cell door in hand, he felt of the bars, seeking to understand their construction, locating the hinges, and feeling for weak points.

There did not seem to be any such spots. So the bronzed giant took firm hold of two adjacent bars and began exerting his tremendous strength. He could feel the bars give under the enormous pressure of his powerful muscles, a might that was greatly amplified on Barsoom.

The iron bars did not surrender so easily as he would have liked, for they were quite thick. But gradually, the ape-man forced them apart. Fortunately, the door-mounted bars consisted of vertical rounds with no intermediate bracing.

By shifting about and exerting pressure from different directions, Tarzan was able to push the bars apart sufficiently to form a narrow gap. This gap would not permit him to step through easily. But by turning his body and expelling all of the air in his lungs in order to flatten his mighty chest, and inserting himself sideways, he was able to work his way through to the other side.

The fact that his lack of vision made him more vulnerable than he would like appeared not to bother the ape-man. He sniffed the air, felt the slightest current of air coming from one direction over the other, and proceeded to walk into the flowing air.

He had lost his short-sword, of course. But his ape-skin harness and borrowed cloak still comprised his raiment.

Tarzan moved along the corridors, using his fingertips, brushing against the stone walls to guide him. He encountered no one.

The stone floor under the bare soles of his feet felt astonishingly warm, and Tarzan wondered if hot magma had pooled beneath the volcanic cone.

Once, he heard a skittering ahead and the moving air brought to his nostrils an unpleasant odor: Ulsio, the many-legged Martian rat which could be found in untenanted ruins all over Barsoom. It retreated as he approached, troubling the bronzed giant not.

His immediate objective was to return to the shipyard high in the volcano's interior summit and finish the task he had begun. The ape-man had no illusions that this would be easy. But he was fatalistic about his prospects. This is what he had come here to do, and he would do it no matter what the cost.

As he moved along, more slowly than he would like, Tarzan heard voices somewhere down the corridor. He paused to listen.

"I did not wish to wake you, my jeddara," said the first voice. Tarzan recognized it as the dwar of the guard he had previously encountered, the gravel-voiced one called Tun-Dun-Lo.

Another voice, feminine but weighted with authority, replied, "There was no need to wake me. Time enough now that it is morning to speak with this interloper."

"He claimed to be from Jasoom. And if I can believe him, our first landing party met its doom at his hands."

"If this is true, then he will pay for it with his life. What did you say his name was?"

"He called himself *Tarzan-of-the-apes*. His strength was terrible, far beyond that of the most powerful warrior we can boast."

"His might will avail him not, trapped behind bars and virtually blind. Once I hear from his own lips his story, we will hurl him from the summit and let the wild apts devour his cadaver. Is that understood?"

"It will be my pleasure, my jeddara."

Tarzan had heard enough. He retreated in the other direction, moving swiftly but taking care to make no sound. He had no clear idea where the corridor led in the other direction, but it would be foolishness to encounter the Jeddara of Nulthoom and the dwar of her guard when he was all but helpless.

The corridor turned and then turned again, and Tarzan began to wonder if it was not similar to the curving hall that ringed the shipyard above. If this were the case, then he was working his way behind the outer wall of the ice mountain itself.

Fortunately, he encountered no opposition.

But behind him, he could hear an abrupt shouting. It was the dwar, Tun-Dun-Lo. No doubt he had discovered the iron bars that had been pried apart and the empty cell within.

The sound of a wooden mallet banging against a gong or bell resounded.

TARZAN INCREASED his pace. No doubt the curved corridor would soon be filling with warriors. Alert to the possibility of doors or passages opening on his right, which might offer escape beyond this volcano fortress, the ape-man was initially disappointed. The first door he happened upon lay on the left.

This, too, was unguarded after the fashion of Nulthoom.

Like the shipyard, the door consisted of two broad panels of steel. Unlike the other doors, this one was locked, but it was closed with a simple bolt, which the ape-man found by touch and unbolted.

Throwing the door wide, he stepped in. And a strange scent filled his nostrils.

Here, he hesitated to enter. The smell suggested life. But what manner of life he could not guess. There were no sounds. The room was unusually warm.

Fortunately for him, it was at this point that his vision began to clear. It was a slow process, but he began to make out shapes before him. Tarzan went to one.

It consisted of a chamber no higher than his shoulders. Over this was a clear dome. And within the dome rested a number of eggs, approximately the size of ostrich eggs.

Moving from one to the other, the ape-man discovered that this room was filled with many similar incubators. Then he remembered that the females of this world were oviparous. They did not give birth to their young the way Earth-women do. They laid eggs, which were carefully incubated until they hatched.

These, Tarzan knew, represented a future generation of Nulthoom. And some portion of these eggs, he understood, was destined to be sent to Earth on the next interplanetary ship capable of escaping the gravity of Barsoom.

To damage them would be unnecessary. While they represented a future threat to the Earth, they were still but eggs. He decided to let them be.

Returning to the corridor, he continued along.

The slap of sandals and the clink of harness trappings drew near. Tarzan continued to search for a way out of his predicament. For if this passage should end in a cul-de-sac, he would be in a position to have to fight his way out against men armed with swords, and he without a single blade.

The ape-man found another set of double doors and opened both. He was surprised to find an extensive garden. How it was irrigated, he could not immediately tell. But it was illuminated by many steady-burning radium lights. The air was steamy.

Entering, Tarzan explored this garden. Fruits and vegetables grew here, chief among them the bland-tasting fruit known as usa that was a staple food among the Martian military class, as well as the poor.

In the center of this profusion of sights and smells stood a spring of bubbling water. Stopping, Tarzan drank his fill. The water was heated, and once more the ape-man wondered if magma flowed beneath his feet. Channels were cut into the volcanic soil of the floor. These carried fresh water to every corner of the fantastic sheltered garden.

After picking one of these fruit and consuming it for refreshment, the bronzed giant moved on, again picking up his pace. No doubt the soldiers of Nulthoom had figured out by now that if they had not encountered him at the other end of the corridor, this is the direction in which he had fled.

It was fortunate that Tarzan's eyes had all but cleared by this point, for when he came to the next door, he was able to recognize its significance.

On Earth, it would have suggested the round door of a massive bank vault, for a cumbersome windlass was set into its face. The door was constructed of the hardwood known as skeel, reinforced by iron and brass.

Inasmuch as it was set into the right side of the passage, the ape-man reasoned that it must lead to the sprawling steppe beyond.

Seizing the windlass, he attempted to turn it. The mechanism resisted his initial effort. It became obvious that this contrivance was not designed to be operated by any single individual, but by several men working in concert. This suggested that its importance was such that it was constructed to defeat the efforts of any one man to open the portal.

One man who is not Tarzan of the Apes, it must be said.

The muscles of Tarzan's broad back, legs, and arms bunched as he applied his fantastic strength. The windlass at first refused to turn, but then it creaked as if it had not been tested in many years.

Inch by inch, the ape-man forced it to revolve. His sinewy hands shifted their mighty grip, taking hold of various handles, seeking fresh leverage as he made slow progress.

Down the corridor, the clatter of approaching men grew nearer, ever nearer....

They would not see him until they rounded the way, for the corridor curved sharply.

There came a groan from the windlass, and it began turning more freely.

Finally, the mechanism was undone, and the ape-man pulled the great skeel door open. There was no time to assess what lay beyond. For the warriors of Nulthoom had finally spilled into view. They spied him at once!

"There! He is at the forbidden door!"

"Stop him!" shouted the dwar of the guard, Tun-Dun-Lo.

As one, the guards charged. Tarzan was more nimble than they. Without regard for unknown dangers on the other side, he leaped into the space beyond, then pivoted, pulling the massive door shut.

There was a windlass on this side, too. Tarzan reached out for two of the handles, and wrenched them in the opposite direction, seeking to lock it.

"He is locking us out!" Tun-Dun-Lo cried out. "Man the windlass. Prevent it from turning all the way back."

Suddenly, the ape-man felt resistance, but he increased his pressure, and little by little, the power of his steely muscles overcame the might of many men attempting to force the issue.

Inexorably, he got the door locked.

From the other side, there was consternation.

"Tun-Dun-Lo, what do we do?"

"There is only one thing left to do! Destroy the windlass so he cannot turn it. It is the only way."

"But it is our only escape route in the event of danger!"

"Danger comes from without, not from within. Remove the windlass so the mechanism can't be foiled."

Tarzan heard the clatter of swords hacking away at the windlass handles.

This did not concern him. He was not interested in being locked out. There were other ways into this strange fortress. And he would find them.

Turning, he began walking through the darkness, which was utterly black. It was as if Tarzan was once again blind. This did not faze him, however.

The floor under his feet was strange. Smooth, yet also ropey in places and ridged with other irregularities. The bronzed giant was not certain of what it consisted.

But when he reached out to the sides, his fingertips encountered the same glassy irregularity. He began to comprehend what he may have discovered. The only question in his mind was where did this passage lead, and what danger might be encountered along it?

If peril greeted him, Tarzan would face it squarely. For he knew there could be no retreat, wherever traversing this tunnel might take him. Whatever lay beyond this end of the passage must take him to freedom, or destruction. There was no other alternative.

Chapter 20

TERRIBLE WHITE ARMS

FOR SOME time, Tarzan of the Apes traversed the long glassy passage. In the darkness, he stepped carefully, for the floor was uneven and in places there were ridges sharp enough to cut into the soles of his feet. Despite that danger, the bronzed Tarmangani proceeded with an utter confidence gained from walking barefoot along stony jungle trails or across thorny arboreal limbs.

The farther along he walked from the mountain, the cooler became the air. His eyes adjusted to the darkness as much as possible. But without any source of light, he saw but little.

As such, the ape-man depended upon his sensitive nostrils to warn him of danger ahead. But there were no smells in this weird tunnel. The furtive scratchings of the rat-like ulsio were not in evidence. It seemed that this tunnel was seldom if ever used by the soldiers of Nulthoom.

Eventually, the passage simply stopped at a blank wall. Tarzan sensed a blockage ahead of him and raised his hands in order to feel the obstruction. His fingertips encountered something new. A cold mass. He tested it and decided it represented frozen subsoil.

There appeared to be no way forward. So he felt around the confines of this terminal space until he encountered a simple rope hanging from the ceiling.

After testing it with a two-handed tug, Tarzan began climbing, using his tremendous strength to pull himself up in monkey fashion.

When his black-haired head encountered a rough ceiling, he paused, and hanging by one hand, groped about until he encountered something that felt like a steel ring. It was not large.

Tarzan tried twisting it and turning it, but it would not budge, so he gave it a downward pull.

The result was startling. A square aperture twice the size of a man dropped down to hang from what must have been a hinge arrangement.

It was still dark, but starlight streamed downward in such profusion that the ape-man's vision was suddenly improved.

Swinging over, he found the lip of the aperture, took hold of it with one hand, then released the rope, quickly catching the cold, crumbling rim with his other hand. Another man would not have succeeded in the feat, but Tarzan's tremendous sinewy strength made it a relatively easy operation.

As he was preparing to lever himself up in order to peer over the edge of what he imagined must be a trapdoor in the snowy steppe above, a strange odor reached his always-alert nostrils.

He paused. For he recognized that the odor was of something alive. And Tarzan knew full well that anything that lived on the bleak tundra must be exceedingly hearty in order to survive. And no doubt dangerous, whether man or beast.

Its musky odor bespoke of a thick-furred beast. It did not smell like zitidar. Nor did its scent suggest a thoat, which he knew to be devoid of fur. If it was a great white ape, it was of a species not in his experience. For they were hairless except for the shock of fur atop their tapering skulls.

Hence, Tarzan was hesitant about lifting his head into view. This was not a consequence of fear, but prudence. One does not blindly enter a lion's den or stick his hand in a viper nest if one does not have to.

The jungle lord understood the value of patience. He could wait until the animal moved on.

However, that luxury was swiftly denied him.

Just as Tarzan was about to release the aperture rim and drop lightly downward, a massive head hove into view.

It was a tremendous, otherworldly sight. It nearly defied description. In general, it suggested to the ape-man Duro, the hippopotamus of Africa. But no hippopotamus possessed eyes such as these. They were massive and ran longitudinally downward from the top of its skull to the corners of its mouth, where a pair of fangs jutted downward.

These eyes reminded Tarzan of the bulging eyes of an enormous insect. They were not compound eyes, he saw, but were composed of numerous individual ocelli that opened and closed in varying patterns as they scrutinized him.

Almost as soon as this monstrosity registered upon his own optic nerves, the ape-man let go of his grip on the aperture's edge, intending to drop back into the passage and race back in the direction he had first come, trusting that the Barsoomian beast was too large to follow.

However, between the time his steely fingers released their grip and before his bare feet could touch the glassy floor, a pair of naked white hands almost as large as his chest reached down, capturing him.

ENORMOUS STRENGTH took hold of Tarzan then. Its fingers were like vises. They pressed the ape-man's wiry arms against his sides as they lifted him skyward.

Virtually helpless and against his will, Tarzan found himself being pulled out of the ground and lifted high so that the thing could scrutinize him in detail.

Flexing his steely muscles, he attempted to break free, but the pressure was too great. He tried again, and the hands that held him fast pushed inward, overcoming his own superhuman strength.

Without a weapon, Tarzan seemed helpless. But the jungle lord is never helpless, even if displaced from the earthly forest over which he held dominion.

Bracing himself, he levered his right foot up, bending his leg at the knee, then gave the monster's right eye a zebra-like kick. The thing reeled back, taking him with it, whereupon Tarzan maneuvered his left foot to attack the other eye.

The thing twisted and thrashed, throwing Tarzan aside as if he were a rag doll. The ape-man landed upon the snowy tundra and scrambled to his feet.

Those two powerful white hands were now pawing at the flat eyepatches whose luminous ocelli winked open and closed in a mad frenzy.

Tarzan could see the beast clearly now, for Thuria was climbing into the night sky, throwing her effulgent light in all directions.

The ape-man could see now that the resemblance to a hippopotamus was confined to the huge head. The thing was a beast well suited for the snowy terrain. It was covered in white fur and stood on two short pairs of hind legs while a pair of powerful hairless forearms grew from its burly shoulders.

With an appropriate blade, Tarzan might have been able to slay the beast, but at present he was unarmed.

But this did not mean he was helpless.

The bronzed giant took a running jump and landed on the other side of the white-furred creature. Once he did so, the thing took down its hands, apparently having recovered from the eye-damaging blows. It began twisting about, looking for its prey, who was no longer in view.

Tarzan leaped again, this time landing on the long back of the creature. Raising one naked foot, he brought it down on the back of the monster's unprotected skull. The thing roared when it felt the impact, then jerked about, endeavoring to throw the bronzed giant off.

Dropping onto his stomach, the ape-man used both arms and took the beast by the throat. The thing snapped futilely. Its fangs were fierce. But it could not bite the man-thing that held it in its powerful grip, for the ape-man's sinewy arms were buried in its furry neck.

The neck was not so thick that Tarzan could not encircle it. His steel-muscled arms constricted tightly, while his right hand grasped the opposite wrist, directly under the trashing thing's open jaw. Then he began squeezing with the muscular power of Histah, the snake. At the same time, Tarzan brought his lower body forward, until he was crouching just back of the jerking head. Now he had gained leverage.

Wrenching backward, the ape-man exerted all of his tremendous might, and the head was drawn backward farther and farther, until there came the muffled sound of snapping neck bones.

With a final grunt and exhalation of fetid air, the brute collapsed into the thin snowy crust. It was dead.

Tarzan did not step off his conquest immediately but gathered himself together after releasing the broken neck.

Standing up, he stood upon the hairy white spine and threw back his head. Once more, the victory cry of the bull ape resounded through the thin atmosphere of Mars as its shining satellites, speedy Thuria and cold Cluros, hurtled overhead, bathing the savage scene in spectral splendor.

Tarzan of the Apes had again conquered. It did not matter to him that he did not know the name of this fallen beast. Nor would the ape-man have cared much to learn that Barsoom called this voracious carnivore of its northern regions an apt. He only regretted that he lacked a tool sharp enough to carve out a steak or claim its thick pelt for a cloak.

Chapter 21

MALAGORS OF METAL

WE PASSED the night in Amhor, Tars Tarkas, Vor Daj, and my company of men.

There, we learned more of the missing zitidars and thoats and it became increasingly clear to me that scavengers and bandits had been preying on the commerce ships of the city. Just as they had apparently raided other outposts of the north steppeland.

In the morning we boarded the *Xanthron* and flew back to the ice-clad mountain that Tarzan of the Apes believed to be Nulthoom.

I did not pass the night worrying about my strange friend from the Earth. I knew how capable he was. I often wondered how he had spent the last hours. If he were wise, he merely would have reconnoitered the mountain, and not called attention to himself. For that is what I would have done. But I am a military man and Tarzan of the Apes is a hunter, at times akin to feral in his behavior, which was often of the instinctual type.

I feared that he would have plunged in at his earliest opportunity. Whether for good or for ill, I could not say. If ever a force of nature took human form, it was he.

Under the morning light, we raced over the steppeland, which was largely barren. Wildlife was not plentiful here. During our flight, I saw nothing that was alive. Once the sunken carcass of a zitidar passed to our port side, its lifeless white fur blowing in an indifferent wind. That was all.

We had no difficulty finding the mountain of ice, although by day its smoldering peak did not present quite so distinct a beacon.

Under my orders, we passed wide of it at first. Two reasons accounted for this. First, not to call attention to ourselves, and secondly, to give the widest possible berth to Nulthoom, lest its soldiers take action against us.

Our initial pass revealed nothing. I ordered the *Xanthron* turned about, and, feeling confident, directed my men to turn their field glasses upon the ground, seeking any sign of Tarzan of the Apes.

We did not spy him. Naturally, this was concerning.

I was in the act of calling for another pass when Vor Daj cried out, "Behold! Off our starboard bow."

I trained my glass in that direction and what I saw all but staggered me.

Rising from the smoldering volcano crater, was one and then two, and finally a third flapping shape.

From this distance, I took them to be long-necked malagors. But as I watched through my field glass, I could see they were formed of metal, with round eyes of crystal, their smooth skulls surmounted by upright metallic feathers whose hues matched their colorful wings. And on their backs balanced white-helmeted Orovar warriors. One clutched a spear. He rode in the lead. Behind him were two who were armed with bows.

They were beating hard in our direction.

I called to Tars Tarkas, towering over the bow. "They will soon be in range of your radium rifle, if you care to employ it."

The green Thark laughed in his semi-savage way and went to fetch his rifle.

The radium rifles of the green men possessed barrels that were exceedingly long. That and the lesser resistance of the thin air of Mars enabled them to strike targets at fabulous distances. Setting himself at the bow, Tars Tarkas lifted his impressive weapon, sighted carefully, and fired but once.

The spearman in the lead bird-scout was knocked off his saddle. He went plunging to the tundra below, his body blown to bits moments into his fall, the radium bullet exploding belatedly. The mechanical steed, bereft of its rider, fell into a flat glide that carried it along at a decreasing altitude until, finally, it plowed into the snowy ground, where one wing was torn off.

By this time, Tars Tarkas had sighted his second target.

The archer saw his peril and quickly fitted an arrow into his bowstring. He released it. But the speeding shaft fell far short.

Not so the Thark's volatile radium bullet. It pierced him in the chest and detonated, hurling his helmeted head and limbs in all directions. Down to the ground, his disassociated corpse tumbled. His bird fell into a slow, spiraling spin until the ground accepted it, completing its destruction.

The third Orovar warrior lost heart at this point. He declined to engage and turned his steed around, beating back toward his base of operations.

"Well done!" I told Tars Tarkas. "I do not think they will send any more."

The tusked Thark laughed again. "If they do, I have bullets for each of them. And it is rare that I miss."

We watched the final metallic bird wing its way back to the volcano's smoldering rim. I wondered how it would safely enter the crater. Since it had emerged from somewhere on the other side of the peak's frozen flank, I knew that there must be a way.

As I watched, the unexpected happened, as it so often does upon Barsoom.

HAD I been watching the ground, I might not have been surprised. As it was, I had difficulty containing my astonishment.

Abruptly, a muscular man in a hairy white loincloth and calot-skin cloak leaped high in the air and managed somehow to land behind the startled rider on his saddle. His surprise must have been complete, but it was also short-lived.

Without ceremony, the interloper swept him off his saddle, hurling him to his doom, then claiming the mechanical steed as his own.

"Only one man could have done that," I said to Tars Tarkas.

"He has stolen his mount, but can he control it?"

That was a question that lingered for several minutes as the mechanical bird continued gliding and flopping toward the crater, and I wondered if that was not Tarzan's intention.

Then, the bird fell into a slow, almost lazy bank, gained altitude, and began beating in our direction.

We watched in a mixture of admiration and disbelief. As the metal malagor drew near, I could see clearly that it was ridden by Tarzan of the Apes. Not that I had any doubt upon that score.

Soon, Tarzan had maneuvered the mechanical mount until it was coursing at our stern, not far behind, its flat crystal orbs regarding us blankly. I saw that its metallic skin was decorated with barbaric orange steaks of paint, suggesting feathers.

We rushed to the stern rail, where I called to him.

"I see you have mastered your new conveyance."

"This bird-machine responds to thoughts. It would not immediately accept mine. But I persisted."

"There is room on the mid-deck to land if you care to attempt it," I offered.

"It is better that I remain in the saddle. I wish to establish complete control over it."

"What have you learned?"

"That you were correct. The scientist Fal Sivas is building a second interplanetary ship, twice as large as the first. It is the plan of their jeddara, O-Thuria, to send one hundred warriors—as well as many eggs and women to raise them—to Earth. I was able to damage the ship, but not so much that it cannot be repaired. Before I could complete the task of destruction, I was overcome. But I escaped. There is a way into the crater. A trapdoor made from a false flagstone. But I found another way out. This was through a lava tube."

"I am not familiar with the term," I admitted.

"Lava moving underground as magma consumes all in its path, leaving behind a passage, sometimes coated in volcanic glass called obsidian. This tube was wide enough to walk through upright. The soldiers of Nulthoom locked the door behind me. No doubt soldiers guard it now. If we are to assault Nulthoom, we must formulate a plan before we dare brave its interior."

I considered this. "You do not think it is prudent to attack now?"

Tarzan shook his head. "I do not know the number of warriors their jeddara commands. But I do know that we have time before the spacecraft is completed, but how much time is unclear. The ship must be repaired before it can be completed."

"In that case," I returned, "it appears that time is on our side. At least for now. We will return to Duhor and discuss the matter. You have done well, *Tarzan-of-the-apes*. You have learned much. And I am eager to hear everything you can tell me. From what I now know, we must lay siege to Nulthoom before the next ship can fly. For that operation, we will need an army."

Tarzan shook his head. "An army would be cut down if it entered the lava tube, which is easily defended. And now that Nulthoom is aware of my existence, they know enough to fortify against a future attack. They will reinforce the crater entrance as well. There may be other ways in and out that we do not know about. But Nulthoom is a stronghold that cannot be taken by numbers. It must be taken by cunning."

"I do not disagree with you, *Tarzan-of-the-apes*, but I am a military man. I will lay plans for the siege of Nulthoom. And you will advise me. Together, we will accomplish our objectives. Between my forces and your intelligence, I believe that we may succeed."

"I refuse to fail," replied Tarzan simply. And I was impressed by the indomitable simplicity of his statement. I remembered that he did not care to live on Barsoom any longer than absolutely necessary. But his words convinced me that he would remain as long as necessary, even if it were to the end of his life.

In that sense, Tarzan and I were opposites. I would not permanently resettle on Earth under any circumstances, for Barsoom I considered to be my home. No change in his fortunes on the red planet could convince this single-minded and determined wildman to entertain the idea of dwelling on Mars, even if he were made Jeddak of Jeddaks.

Chapter 22

War Council

WHEN WE reached the city of Duhor, I ordered the *Xanthron* to set down. Once she had docked, we remained on deck to watch as Tarzan of the Apes attempted to land his mechanical malagor.

He circled an adjoining landing stage, and then the strange lifeless steed began to descend in a slow circle as if wary of alighting. I had noticed during the journey that the bird flapped its wings periodically, but glided with poised outspread wings in between those brief intervals. It was remarkably efficient in that wise.

As the pseudo-malagor alighted to the ground, it pulled up short, arresting its forward motion. Its stiff legs extended downward, and I saw that they were of the telescoping type. Then the claws extended until they were perpendicular to the ground, forming tripods.

When the thing came to a rest, it was with an astonishing lack of noise. The wings folded inward and pivoted until they rested against the metallic body, which appeared to be constructed from forandus, the lightest metal known to Barsoom. Its paint-streaked skin gave it the semblance of a feathered creature.

Tarzan of the Apes dismounted as if it were an ordinary thing. But I could only wonder if I would have been capable of such an expert landing on my first attempt.

Climbing down the ship's ladder, we met him between the two landing stages, and I said, "If you are hungry, we will eat and then talk."

"I am hungry. Let us do both."

I laughed. Tarzan did not care to waste time if that time was being wasted on Barsoom. We found a ground flier to take us to the palace of the jeddak, Kor San. Tars Tarkas and Vor Daj accompanied us. We were soon joined by Vad Varo, to whom I sent word, for I felt his presence would be valuable.

Seated around a large round table, we ate while Tarzan spoke at great length, giving us a full account of his penetration of Nulthoom, and the dangers he faced therein.

At the end of it, he said, "I am convinced that there are only two ways to enter the mountain. From the crater and through the lava tube at the base."

"If there was one lava tube, could there not be two or more?" I asked.

Tarzan replied, "I heard one of the men speak of the lava tube as an emergency escape route. His words suggested that it was the only one."

"And you say it is locked from the inner terminus?" I pressed.

Tarzan nodded. "And the mechanism broken, to block my return."

"But it could be breached."

"Conceivably. But just as I know their intentions, they know mine. They will have fortified the door, no doubt placing guards sufficient to repel any invasion, which must enter in single file, for the tunnel is not wide."

"Then we must enter by the crater."

Tarzan shook his head firmly. "That way, too, is easily defended. Only one man can enter at a time, and the stairs beneath are narrow and curved, forming a bottleneck that will inhibit invasion."

Tars Tarkas interrupted. "I do not know this word, stairs."

I explained, "It surprises me that these Orovar have stairs, which are otherwise all but unknown on Barsoom. On Jasoom, they are common. Think of them as resembling ramps, but cut at regular, closely-spaced intervals so that one cannot race down them wildly. Each step is sufficient for only one sandal at a time."

I do not think that the Thark quite comprehended my description, but we did not dwell on the problem.

Getting back to the matter at hand, I said, "If we cannot breach either of the known entrances, then we must look for another way in."

Tarzan said, "I am willing to scout again. But I do not think there is another suitable entrance. When the malagor scouts emerged from behind the mountain, this pointed to another opening. If another entrance exists, it may not be situated where it can be breached without discovery. And if this other gate lies high on the mountain's flank, it may well be impregnable to attack."

I considered this. I knew Tarzan of the Apes well enough that I respected his judgment.

"Let us assume for the moment that you are correct. What other options exist?"

Vad Varo spoke up. "We could blast the mountain apart with cannon."

"You are correct," I agreed. "No doubt, we could inflict a great deal of damage. But could we accomplish our aim? By that I mean, could we prevent this new spacefaring ship or any future craft from being launched?"

"We can, if we kidnap Fal Sivas. He is the key."

"That is an excellent point," I said. "But we cannot know that the knowledge he possesses is not now in the hands of Orovar scientists."

Vad Varo pointed out, "The Orovar are not known for their science, but the possibility that Fal Sivas has shared his knowledge with the smartest of them cannot be discounted."

At that point, we appeared to reach an impasse. So we fell to eating. Tarzan had insisted that his thoat be served raw. And we watched in wonder as he consumed his steak that way. I was relieved that he used knife and fork, for I understood that he thought them necessary only when in civilized company.

Since the subject had been exhausted for the moment, I turned to Vad Varo and asked, "What news of Jasoom via the Gridley Wave?"

"The great war that consumed half the world has been concluded. America and her allies were victorious. But at tremendous cost."

"And how is your friend, Jason Gridley?"

"He is well. While he would not give me details, Abner Perry built a new and more powerful Iron Mole in order to accomplish a military mission of the war. I understand that he was successful."

"That is good to hear."

"I know Perry and Gridley," said Tarzan unexpectedly.

Vad Varo looked at him half disbelievingly.

"You do? Truly?"

Tarzan put down his fork and said, "I have been to Pellucidar. But I have never seen the Iron Mole, only heard of it. If we had something like that here, we could penetrate the icy crust of Nulthoom unopposed."*

Following Tarzan's casual comment, there was a moment of thoughtful silence.

Vad Varo looked to me and I looked back at him. I could tell that our thoughts were running a parallel course. Before I could speak, an interruption came.

Tars Tarkas asked, "What is a mole?"

I laughed. "A mole is a small creature native to the Earth that burrows into the ground, where it makes its home. In this case, the Iron Mole is a machine fitted with a corkscrew drill at the front and propelled by a motorized mechanism that permits it to dig deep into the ground, carrying passengers. And *Tarzan-of-the-apes* is correct. If we had such a machine, and it was properly armored, the warriors of Nulthoom could not keep us out."

---

* *See* Tarzan at the Earth's Core *by Edgar Rice Burroughs.*

Vad Varo looked thoughtful. "Perhaps Perry could explain how to build one."

I considered this. "Such a device would be a complicated feat of engineering. While it is not possible to transmit blueprints via Gridley Wave, properly instructed, the scientists of Helium might be able to duplicate the mechanism. We would have to use different motors than exist on Jasoom, but I imagine ours would be sufficient to drive such a vehicle. It is worth discussing the matter amongst us. Inasmuch as Fal Sivas' new space-traversing ship remains under construction, we might have ample time to build a Mole suitable for Barsoomian operations."

I looked around the table. There was no dissent. As a plan, it was rather far-fetched. But it appeared to be feasible. If it did not work, there was time yet to devise an alternate course of action.

"Vad Varo, I charge you with the duty of obtaining all the necessary instructions from Abner Perry and conveying them to our scientists for proper evaluation."

"As you wish, John Carter."

THIS WAS done that very day. Vad Varo communicated with Jason Gridley on Earth by Gridley Wave. Once he learned of our predicament, Gridley was pleased to comply. When he was informed that Tarzan of the Apes was on Barsoom, he was initially skeptical but asked that his best wishes be conveyed, which they were.

A convocation of scientists was convened in Helium, and they solemnly listened to Vad Varo's report.

After hearing it, they discussed the matter amongst themselves and came to a tentative conclusion.

"This project is feasible," announced the group's spokesman. "There are some difficulties, but they may be overcome. Substitutions for certain metals and elements will be necessary, as will a change in motive power. The machine will have to be constructed according to engineering specifications that take into account the difference between Jasoomian gravity and our own, of course."

"Excellent," I told them. "Commence work immediately. Time is of great importance. I will see that you have sufficient funds and material to accomplish this tremendous undertaking."

And so it began, the construction of the new Mole machine. Whether it actually would accomplish our objectives, I could not judge in advance. I only knew that it would be better to fight the soldiers of Nulthoom on Barsoom than for Tarzan to return to Earth to interdict them there.

As the work was undertaken, I wondered how Fal Sivas was faring with the rebuilding of his damaged interplanetary ship. We were engaged in a grim race against time, but the renegade scientist had no inkling of that portentous fact.

Chapter 23

The Martian Mole

IN YEARS past, communication between Barsoom and Jasoom via Gridley Wave involved Morse code mechanically imprinted upon a ticker tape. But the mechanism had been improved by Jason Gridley in Tarzana, California, and he had conveyed the means to construct a new transceiver to the scientists of Barsoom. This was soon done, enabling voice communication to take place between the two planets for the first time.

After Vad Varo had explained to Gridley our needs, the man promised to convey them to Abner Perry, the inventor who had built the mechanical prospector dubbed the Iron Mole that had first penetrated Pellucidar, the lost world deep in the center of my natal planet.

In short order, Perry's voice was being reproduced via the Gridley Wave receiver. He was broadcasting from Pellucidar, where he resided.

"It is theoretically possible to build an Iron Mole upon Mars, provided your metalsmiths can fabricate the parts using Martian metals. I understand that you have the means to manufacture steel, which is necessary for the housing, which would otherwise buckle under enormous pressure of tunneling through the frozen tundra. But motive power is another matter."

Vad Varo replied, "The same motors that drive our fliers can be installed to this purpose. I am certain of it."

"Good. I do not pretend to fully understand the differences between the respective gravities of our two planets. You will have to work that

out amongst yourselves. But I will provide the essentials, after which you can improvise your Mole from my plans."

Once cooperation was established, it was agreed that we would relocate to Helium where the construction would commence. Further communication would resume once a Gridley Wave transceiver was properly installed in a construction bay where the scientists of Helium could monitor Perry's instructions and execute them on the spot.

That evening, Tarzan of the Apes and I, along with my company of men, returned to Helium. We set to work without delay.

Apartments were found for Tarzan, and clothing more suitable for city dwelling was provided to him.

Once a Gridley Wave device had been installed in Helium, Tarzan requested that Jason Gridley write a letter to his family in Africa, assuring them that he was alive and well. Gridley promised to send it to Nairobi in care of general delivery, which was the method by which the family received mail. This seemed to lift a burden from Tarzan's mind, although he did not expect a reply, owing to the distance between California and Africa and the uncertainty of the duration of his expected stay upon Barsoom.

And so began the sometimes arduous process of translating Abner Perry's patiently spoken instructions into reality.

It began by placing a substantial engine in the construction garage. Once its capabilities were explained to Perry, he deemed it of sufficient power to drive the Martian Mole, as we called it.

Next came the construction of a corkscrew drill. It was necessary to fix this to the motor first. If it worked, the body of the Mole and its interior cabin could be built with a reasonable confidence that the whole assembly would cooperate toward its objectives.

This naturally took several weeks of more or less continuous endeavor. Not knowing how long it would take for the Orovars of Nulthoom to complete their interplanetary craft, we were in a race against time with no certain deadline. This fact added to our urgency.

Periodically, Vad Varo and Vor Daj scouted the landscape feature we had taken to calling, for want of a better term, Mount Nulthoom. Vad Varo reported no activity other than the cease-less burning of the coal bed contained within its ice-rimed crater.

Tarzan of the Apes often accompanied him, for he had no part to play in the construction of the Mole. Vad Varo reported that Tarzan often reconnoitered the area looking for the terminus of another lava tube, but he failed to find anything of the sort.

Several times, Tarzan launched his mechanical malagor from the deck of the ship around the volcano, seeking to attract attention.

Despite these bold forays, no flying defenders showed themselves. The place from which they emerged proved to be a puzzle without a solution. All sides of the mighty peak were encased in thick ice. While Tarzan suspected that the winged scouts launched from a concealed rookery high upon one side of Mount Nulthoom, inspection by field glass failed to reveal such an opening.

All efforts to draw out the Orovars were abandoned eventu-ally. They appeared to have barricaded themselves completely against the outside world.

No sign that the new ship was preparing to be launched toward Earth was detected. For that matter, the question of how it would be launched, given that it was presumably under construction deep within a hollow volcano, remained an unan-swered one.

When not scouting, Tarzan of the Apes renewed his acquain-tance with some of those he had met before, including Kar Komak of Lothar, the robed bowman who had taught him the mental art of returning to his earthly body.

Inasmuch as Kar Komak played an important role in the events I am relating, I must pause to acquaint the reader about his background and unique nature.

Kar Komak is among the most remarkable individuals I encountered during my life on Barsoom. Long before my advent, during the days when Mars boasted many oceans and the white-skinned Orovars were the masters of this planet, there lived a seaman named Kar Komak, a great mariner who commanded the fleet of Lothar, the greatest ever to sail Barsoom's five salt seas.

The man who walked modern Barsoom was his spitting image, but he was not quite the same man. In truth, Kar Komak was not, strictly speaking, a man at all, but the semblance of one. He was a materialization of the original white-skinned, auburn-haired seamen, and yet he possessed the identical personality of the historical Kar Komak, as well as his memories.

Now I will explain this as best as I am able. In the city of Lothar, the people were of a different order than most of the white-skinned Martians of the ancient days. They were the opposite of materialists. They believed that the mind was all and the body could be conquered by an application of focused will.

The Lotharians proved their theories in many ways, one of which was that they came to a point in their development when they no longer consumed food, believing it to be unnecessary to support their lives. Instead, they imagined themselves sustained without it. And so they were.

Another of the talents the Lotharians developed through generations of mental exercises was the creation of materializations. During the period when the seas were receding and the green men were attempting to overrun the Orovar cities that survived, the people of Lothar discouraged these invasions by mentally conjuring up vast armies of phantom bowmen. These efforts were successful. All green assaults were repelled.

The last Jeddak of Lothar, Tario, chose to create a materialization that was founded upon the legend of Kar Komak, the original, who had been slain during the course of one of the early invasions of the green nomads. During successive green man attacks, Kar Komak was brought back to life to defend Lothar, and then dematerialized once his usefulness was over.

For reasons that are inexplicable, one day Kar Komak failed to dematerialize. And so he discovered that his existence had become a permanent one. To accomplish such a feat had been the tyrannical jeddak's chief ambition. Rather than be a vassal of Tario, however, the once-imaginary Kar Komak struck out on his own and encountered my son, Carthoris. Their adventures, I need not recount. Through him, we became friends.*

When I explained all this to Tarzan on the occasion of his first sojourn on Barsoom, I was amused to observe the dumbfounded expression that came over this bronze-skinned Jasoomian's face. Tarzan had encountered many things that were beyond his earthly experience on Mars, but he was realist enough to shrug them off and cope in his own straightforward way.

Not so the reality of Kar Komak. Although he became comfortable with the man, I suspect Tarzan continues to doubt my story, inasmuch as the former phantom bowman is as substantial as you or I.

These two became unlikely friends after a fashion. But it was inescapable that the ape-man was counting the days until he could complete his task, permitting him to return to his family.

When I suggested that Tarzan return to Earth for a brief period, he rebuffed the idea, pointing out the problematic nature of traversing space, only to have to return to Barsoom.

"When I next leave this world," he said firmly, "it will be for the final time."

Seeing his resolve, I dropped the matter.

Not even the sights and pleasures of Greater Helium entertained Tarzan for very long. When he could, he spent time in our gardens and forest, appearing to be more comfortable in a natural element than in what we would call civilization.

And yet, for all that, he showed great curiosity about Barsoomian life.

---

* *See* Thuvia, Maid of Mars *by Edgar Rice Burroughs.*

When time permitted, we had several long discussions about daily life and culture. During one of these, the subject of slavery came up, for the practice was widespread on the red planet.

"I have come to accept it as a fact that cannot be changed," I explained, "something perhaps easier for me because I once lived in the Antebellum South."

"In Africa," Tarzan told me, "slavers are a scourge. I punish them wherever they thrive."

I laughed without intending insult. "If you were ever to undertake the task of eradicating slavery upon Barsoom, I doubt that you would live long enough to make much of a dent. It represents thousands and thousands of generations of entrenched custom here. I am not sure how far back it goes, or whether the Orovars, who preceded the red and green and other races, practiced it. But I imagine that they did. Unlike on Earth, the slave represents a time-honored social class, as it was in ancient Rome, and not a function of perceived racial superiority or inferiority."

Having dispensed with the subject without argument, I turned to another topic that had rankled me.

"When last you were on Barsoom, you and I battled. Our swords clashed in combat, and I am not in the least embarrassed to admit that you got the better of me."

Without any hint of ego or arrogance, Tarzan pointed out, "On Barsoom, my strength is many times greater than yours simply because on Earth it is more akin to the strength of a great ape than a human being. There is no shame in being defeated by a more powerful opponent."

"I feel no shame," I replied forthrightly. "Up until that point, I had fancied myself the greatest swordsman on two planets. After encountering you in combat, I can no longer make that claim."

Tarzan smiled. "I do not consider myself more than an able swordsman. No doubt you are my superior in terms of experience and technique. No matter your expertise, the overwhelming power of my thews overcame them."

"I propose a friendly contest," I said. "If you will agree to take up a blade, I will in turn select a sword that is its equal and, if you promise not to use your strength to its fullest, we will have at it."

Tarzan's gray eyes narrowed. "Do you challenge me to a duel?"

I nodded in a friendly fashion. "A duel involving swordsmanship and not brute force."

Tarzan's smile grew warm. I believe he understood my sentiments perfectly.

"I am willing to indulge you, John Carter."

THE DUEL took place that afternoon. In a large courtyard, where many gathered to watch, for the word went out, spreading quickly.

Since it was not a fight to the death, and certainly not a duel intended to injure, the rules were set forth clearly.

"The first man to touch the other's bare skin with his blade will be declared the winner," I stated. "He need not draw blood."

"In the heat of combat," Tarzan pointed out, "that will be difficult to avoid."

"I am neither afraid of drawing blood or shedding my own in the course of a fair contest," I asserted.

And so with that, we drew our blades and engaged.

I had not forgotten the power of this man who was raised by wild apes. But when I felt his sword smash against my own blade, my respect for his physical prowess was renewed. It was formidable.

We stood toe to toe, our swords contending, our faces set.

The battle went on for some ten xat, or half an Earth hour. I will not describe it in minute detail, inasmuch as it was as much a contest of wills as it was of martial skill.

Back-and-forth we battered, shifting our feet, and, as well-honed as my reflexes were, which ever enabled me to evade his searching blade point, this man of Africa possessed reflexes that reminded me of a bobcat of Old Virginia.

My blade was of the finest steel. Tarzan had been given his choice of weapons, which was only fair under the circumstances. Such was his confidence, he had chosen rather carelessly. I thought that rather arrogant of him, but soon realized that his confidence lay in his mighty sword arm, not in the weapon it gripped. Try as I might, I could not break it with my own blade.

There was no getting past his guard. Yet I held my own. Ten xat wore on, and then we fought for ten more.

At length, we began to tire. I perhaps more than Tarzan, whose steely muscles seemed indomitable.

When it became clear that neither one was able to score a hit or take the advantage, through clenched teeth I suggested, "I had not anticipated a battle of this duration. Perhaps we might call it a draw."

I doubt my words were the cause of what resulted next. I suspected another reason. But for a moment, after he heard my suggestion, Tarzan paused slightly, but pointedly did not agree.

"I am not yet tired," he said, as if taunting me. "And I do not believe that you are ready to surrender your claim to be the greatest swordsman on Barsoom, deserved or not."

In spite of myself, I felt a flash of anger. In that moment, I saw my opening.

Sweeping around, my blade touched his right elbow, but without drawing blood. Swiftly, I withdrew.

Lowering his sword, Tarzan said with a tight-lipped smile, "I yield to your superior skill."

"And I accept your surrender with what I hope is equal graciousness."

To the cheers and applause of our previously-rapt audience, we placed our hands on one another's right shoulder in the customary Barsoomian way. But I saw something in Tarzan's gray eyes, a hint of humor, that made me wonder if my suggestion had caused my friendly foe to provide me with an opening in order to assuage my wounded pride.

I was too much of a gentleman to suggest this possibility. To all outward appearances, I had won the duel. But as we walked back to my palace, I could not shake the nagging feeling that Tarzan of the Apes had permitted me to score rather than leave the matter unresolved.

I considered the matter settled, but in my heart of hearts, I was left wondering. For although I could easily read the mind of most inhabitants of Barsoom, for some undiscoverable reason, the innermost thoughts of this remarkable ape-man were forever barred to me.

After that interlude, we turned our attention back to the increasingly desperate race to build a burrowing machine capable of penetrating Mount Nulthoom.

Chapter 24

CRAWLING UNDER THE CRUST

AFTER NEARLY two teeans, which is the approximate equivalent of two Earth months, the Martian Mole was at last completed.

Like its earthly counterpart, it consisted of one hundred feet of jointed steel. At the forward end jutted the tremendous drill, looking like a steel corkscrew with broad, curving flanges. The interior was fitted with four staggered seats mounted on transverse bars whose orientation pivoted depending on the angle of inclination at which the Mole traveled.

The four seats were designed for Tarzan of the Apes, Vad Varo, Tars Tarkas, and myself. I would have preferred a larger complement, but I felt that we had a sufficient force for the task at hand.

As we inspected the impressive machine, I asked one of the engineers for a demonstration. Of course, we were not going to drill through the floor of the workshop. I merely wanted to see how the mechanism operated at rest.

The Mole sat on a platform designed to keep the drill nose poised horizontally and unobstructed. An engineer entered the device through a dorsal hatch, took the driver's seat, and started manipulating the controls. The great electric engine crackled into life, and its sound soon achieved the state of a constant whine. The fellow listened to it for some time before finding it to be satisfactory, then he reached for the lever that engaged the drill mechanism. This commenced revolving, and before it had completed three revolutions, the drill was spinning powerfully.

We all watched as the drill revolved until it became a metallic blur. The Martian Mole vibrated slightly, but seemed otherwise sturdy.

When we were satisfied, the brake was applied and the drill immediately seized up, whereupon the driver shut off the engine. All became quiet.

"All that remains," I said, "is to hoist this into the hold of a warship and convey it to Mount Nulthoom."

"Give the order, O prince, and it will be accomplished," replied the engineer, climbing out of the mechanism.

I turned to Tars Tarkas and asked, "What do you think, my friend?"

"If it will carry us to our enemies, I will endure being confined in this weird machine for however long it takes to reach our objective."

"Well said," I exclaimed. "Let us waste no more time. For the enemy is surely wasting none of his."

THAT NIGHT, the Martian Mole was conveyed by transport flier onto the deck of the dreadnought *Dejah Thoris*, which was the pride of the Navy of Helium, and lowered into her hold.

The plan had been formulated and gone over many times in the weeks that led up to this moment. I did not expect any dissension, so I was surprised when Tarzan of the Apes turned to me and said, "I will fly with you to Nulthoom, but when we reach our destination, I will go my own way."

"Why is that?"

"No doubt the enemy will become aware of us as we approach," he replied. "Though you travel underground and unseen, the noise and vibration of this machine will carry. They will launch their metal scout-malagors from their hangars. Once they do so, those hangars will remain open to receive them again. I propose to enter one of those portals, flying my own malagor."

I considered this. As a military man, I was reluctant to change plans at the eleventh hour. But Tarzan's suggestion would open up a third line of attack. Also, it would vacate a seat in the Martian Mole for an additional warrior.

"I agree to your amendment of the plan, Tarzan. It is a sound strategy. And of all of us, you may be the best one to take them by surprise. If they are looking for us at the base of the volcano, they will not expect you to come in from another angle."

Tarzan smiled. "I prefer to exploit the element of surprise whenever possible."

I laughed. "My friend, I consider you to be the very embodiment of the element of surprise."

"Let me suggest that Kar Komak take my empty seat. I understand that he has volunteered to join the crew of your ship."

"That is a splendid idea. He will be a capable addition to my band."

With that, preparations were made to crew Helium's mightiest warship for the planned assault.

WE SET sail that evening, flying the proud colors of the Heliumatic Empire, the greatest on all of Barsoom.

When Tarzan boarded the *Dejah Thoris,* he had changed clothing. He was once again attired in his ape-fur loincloth and the harness of ape-skin leather that had been gifted him. In a scabbard at his side was the elaborate Orovar sword which he had wielded during his previous sojourn on Barsoom. I had presented it to him in a solemn ceremony. He accepted it with gratitude, but without unnecessary words. The blade had been forged from a fallen meteor and was composed of a bluish metal unknown to Barsoom. It was superior to steel. I had dared not duel with him against such a weapon, and so had reserved it for war.

Tarzan's only concession to civilized raiment had been to don a cloak of snow-white apt fur, which flapped and waved behind him as he strode the deck, showing once more his impatience to get on with the task at hand.

We flew directly northward, toward the steppe where Mount Nulthoom reared up west of the fiery gash of the infernal coal seam that pointed toward it.

En route, Vad Varo joined us, arriving in his personal flier. After his ship was taken aboard, he greeted us on the deck, saying, "I have long awaited this day."

Clasping the former Ulysses Paxton by one shoulder, I greeted him, saying, "In that case, you are certain to be disappointed, for we will not attack until after dark."

Vad Varo laughed. "This is acceptable to me."

I explained to him the new arrangement of the battle plan, and he agreed that Tarzan's idea was exemplary. The plan was to discharge the Martian Mole at a great enough distance from Mount Nulthoom so that by night the operation would not be seen. This would be done during the interval when both of Barsoom's moons had finished their first transits of the night sky.

Once that was accomplished, the Mole machine would burrow into the ground at a shallow angle and then, thanks to its jointed steel body, level itself off and continue in the horizontal position just far enough below the ground that it could angle up easily once the volcano's base was penetrated.

This would take some time. While we pushed toward our objective, the *Dejah Thoris* would swing about, and at a prearranged time she would commence firing her cannon, in order to create a diversion on the opposite flank of the mountain peak.

With his orange-streaked malagor at the ready, Tarzan would be waiting for the opening of the hangar doors, an eventuality not entirely certain.

We spoke about this.

"What if they do not send their scouts to repel you?" I asked him.

"Then I will attempt to enter by the crater trapdoor."

"The element of surprise will be lost."

Tarzan seemed unconcerned. "If it is lost, I will do my best to overcome that handicap."

THE MARTIAN dusk is so brief that it almost does not exist. One moment, the sun was setting, and then it was absolutely black. I gave the signal to land.

The *Dejah Thoris* set her flat keel on the snowy steppeland, a hatch was opened in her hull, and the Martian Mole was extracted using a draft zitidar pulling it on a wheeled platform.

Once all six of its wheels were on the ground, men attacked the wooden platform with tools and axes, quickly disassembling the forward portion, leaving the Mole lying on the ground at a shallow angle that would permit the monstrous drill to bite into the frozen ground.

Vad Varo, Kar Komak, Tars Tarkas, and I stood about the machine as the *Dejah Thoris* lifted off and turned to the east. Tarzan had remained on board, along with his malagor steed, which had been hoisted onto the deck from an upper hatch.

During this operation, one after the other, Thuria and Cluros, the effulgent moons of Barsoom, showed themselves. I looked east and spied the smoldering peak of Nulthoom, whose icy flanks seemed to squirm under the spectral rays of the hurtling moons and their ever-shifting light.

There is a romantic myth that held that bright Thuria was the female pursuer of her cold and distant lover, Cluros, perpetually chasing him across the Barsoomian night sky, never catching him, but forever in ardent pursuit. This was a futile ritual repeated several times a night, for the misshapen moons of Mars came and went in a schedule quite different than Earth's majestic lunar orb, which rose and fell only once each night.

Their contrasting illumination presented no issue for our subterranean assault, but the *Dejah Thoris* would have to travel at an altitude close to the tundra, rising to attack, if our timing was accurate, only after one or more of these speeding satellites dropped below the undulating horizon.

In any event, we were presently too far away to be seen, but time was of the essence. With alacrity, we four climbed inside, closed and dogged the hatch. I engaged the great engine, and the corkscrew drill began to turn. As it revolved, it picked up speed, and as its revolutions increased, it began to gouge the uneven terrain ahead of us.

The construction of the drill was, as I previously said, like a stupendous corkscrew, and so its spinning flanges, in catching the hard turf, pulled us forward and, as we lurched ahead, it began to gouge a trench in the hard snowy ground, the long flanges scooping up and flinging aside clumps of soil.

All was proceeding satisfactorily. The only question was one that we could not test in advance in similar soil: Whether the drill would carry us through the frozen ground without seizing up. There had not been time to test the vehicle under this or any other ground conditions. Hence, we were risking much. But all parties had agreed that this risk was preferable to the prospect of the Orovar super-ship escaping Barsoom's gravity while we field-tested the Martian Mole.

There was another consideration, one we could not avoid. Tarzan had reported that a hot spring lay under Mount Nulthoom. Was it a pool of underground water, or a river? There was no telling. But should we encounter it, it might prove disastrous.

Worse still, Tarzan believed the spring was heated by subterranean magma. Thus, we dared not drill too deeply lest we plunge into its unforgiving caldron. And so we had plotted a comparatively shallow course in the hope that we could avoid the worst of these deadly obstacles.

We traveled for some distance, but all we accomplished was to gouge a great furrow in the tundra. We had counted upon the fact that the flat terrain sloped upward as it approached Mount Nulthoom to carry us under the surface. But our engineers' calculations failed to account for the machine's more stubborn characteristics.

"The machine is not working, John Carter," rumbled Tars Tarkas.

"So I see," I said dryly.

Then I conceived of an idea. This machine had a reversal gear for the eventuality of reversing out of a hole.

I shut down the drill, gave it time to cease revolving, then geared it into full reverse. The drill pushed us backward, much more slowly than forward of course, but we were soon reversing course. Fortunately, the rear of the shell had been designed for such an eventually. It tapered to a fine point. This pushed into the mass of loose debris that had been deposited in our stony wake, forcing it to part. But soon enough, the accumulating conglomeration became too compacted to be moved aside.

Once I reached that impassible point, I threw the machine into the forward gear again. And the drill dragged us deeper into the trench we had created.

Back and forth, I jockeyed the Mole until it was half sunk into the frozen soil. Then I pushed it forward again, and it began to bite and dig as I turned the control wheels that made the jointed sections deform on command, improving the angle of attack, making it more acute without plunging us downward through the planet's crust. Well did I know the story of Abner Perry's Iron Mole. Through a miscalculation, Perry and David Innes had lost control of their machine, and ended up penetrating some five hundred miles deep, stopped only after they broke through to Pellucidar, the hollow world in the interior of the Earth.*

It took much longer than I would have liked, but at last the Mole was burrowing under the steppeland crust. The upheaving soil swallowed us, and we were enveloped in darkness.

I switched on an interior light. But it was of limited use. Visibility outside the machine's interior was naturally nonexistent. Through certain inspection ports set dorsally and ventrally along the hull, we could see the crumbling dirt as we bored through it. But of the way ahead, and our objective, we could discern nothing.

---

* *See* At the Earth's Core *by Edgar Rice Burroughs.*

Onward, we burrowed, and I wondered if, like an earthly mole, our progress was visible from above ground in the form of the tundra heaving and separating in a straight line.

There was nothing we could do about that possibility. To go too deeply risked passing beneath Mount Nulthoom at a depth that missed penetrating the weird habitation and possibly plunge us into boiling water—or worse.

On and on, we traveled, as blind as moles are reputed to be, determined to reach our objective unobstructed. On occasion, I perceived through an inspection port an ancient relic of the lost Throxeus Ocean, a fragment of fossilized bone of a long-extinct ocean creature or the broken shell of a bivalve not known to modern Barsoom.

My only concern was how long it would take to reach our objective. It was imperative to penetrate Mount Nulthoom while it was still dark. My thoughts went to the *Dejah Thoris* and how her crew was faring.

The Martian Mole had been equipped with a wireless set. But I did not call prematurely, lest Fal Sivas possess a wireless set of his own and might overhear. Our set was reserved for emergency use. But for the present, no emergency existed.

Chapter 25

THE DREAM OF JOR

FAL SIVAS was worried. The Martian scientist had been toiling every waking hour since he had been attacked by the strange yet powerful Jasoomian who called himself *Tarzan-of-the-apes*.

The jeddara had ordered him to accelerate the construction of the new interplanetary ship after this man of Jasoom had managed to escape his cell by bending the iron bars apart, a feat considered impossible.

Fal Sivas had come to believe that his servitude to the jeddara was drawing to a close. When first he had fallen into the hands of her warriors, after fleeing his native city of Zodanga to the south, he had been received as an honored guest.

For the people of this hollow mountain had lived apart from all other nations on Barsoom by remaining hidden, venturing out only to scavenge what they could from the trade between the civilized cities of the northern hemisphere. They were very interested in the knowledge that Fal Sivas had brought of the cities of the southern hemisphere, a place they knew of only by inference. No warrior of Nulthoom had ever ventured as far south as Polodona, much less below it.

When Fal Sivas had explained that he was a scientist and spoke of his accomplishments, the jeddara O-Thuria became very interested. She offered him sanctuary in return for his efforts toward improving their lot.

Initially, this consisted of constructing mechanical duplicates of a malagor they had captured so that their warriors could skim across the steppeland during their raids, and to evade capture.

He built radium rifles to arm them. And other devices, principally a camera-telescope which permitted the jeddara and her advisors to study other planets. When the ruler's instruments fell upon Jasoom with her many oceans, she became passionate about living upon such a world, a planet whose oceans were mightier than the greatest of ancient Barsoom, all teeming with exotic fish whose flesh no Orovar had ever tasted. Indeed, no one in Nulthoom had seen a fish in many generations.

For teeans, O-Thuria had studied the watery planet, with its multitude of minor seas and vast oceans, some greater than the extinct Throxeus, over which this volcanic stronghold had once towered as part of the island state known as Nulthoom. In time, she became fixated upon one continent, which she called Jor, because it resembled in profile the skull of the legendary horned man-ape named Jor, whom an ancient sect of Ovorars had worshipped, and whom O-Thuria considered an ancestor. West of the horn stood a large lake, which the jeddara fancied to be the living blue eye of Jor. She further realized that this was a freshwater lake, which would supply unlimited drinking water, as well as the means to irrigate vast tracts of farmland. Most of this weirdly-configured continent was bound by vast oceans. The jeddara imagined erecting a magnificent city on the shore of the great lake of Jor, and a sister port city upon the horn, from which mighty sailing ships could be launched in order to explore the other continents of Jasoom.

These dreams had taken root not long after Fal Sivas came to find himself a castaway from Barsoomian civilization, and had taken refuge when his greatest invention, a space-faring flier, had encountered mechanical trouble in these northern wastes. They had been the wholly impractical fantasies of a ruler whose people lacked modern inventions, and were forced to pilfer and scavenge from distant red cities to acquire basic tools, just as they had claimed Fal Sivas and his wrecked ship as tundra salvage.

When O-Thuria had learned that the country-less scientist had constructed a space-faring ship capable of traveling to other planets, she became inflamed with ambition. For she saw in the horned continental outline a sign and a summons from the great long-dead warrior, Jor.

She asked Fal Sivas to build such a machine, but he had replied it was possible only if the raw materials could be collected in order to repair and enlarge his damaged craft. No time or effort was spared and this was done in a series of raids over a number of years.

The reconstructed interplanetary ship was necessarily limited in size. But it had succeeded in reaching Jasoom. For Fal Sivas had tracked the vessel across the black void until it had fallen toward the continent which they called Jor.

Because the telescopic camera could record images only at intervals, it was assumed that the Jor had landed successfully. That is, until the powerful Jasoomian calling himself *Tarzan-of-the-apes* had brought the terrible news of the colony's destruction.

This news only inflamed the passions of the jeddara. And she had ordered Fal Sivas to work night and day, for she had changed her mind about the second expedition. Previously, it was meant to carry a second group of warriors. But now she decided that she would go on the next ship and bring with her the eggs she had laid, which represented the future generations of Nulthoom.

And so Fal Sivas toiled tirelessly. But he was an aging man. And not growing any more robust in captivity, although he could expect to live a few more centuries by Martian reckoning.

The scientist had begun to see his role gradually change from that of an exalted guest to one of desperate servitude. The jeddara and her dwar drove him day and night to complete the second ship, which O-Thuria had named the *Jasoom*. Since the first incursion, the pair had become increasingly desperate.

She feared the return of *Tarzan-of-the-apes*, but Fal Sivas feared even more the Warlord of Warlords, John Carter, once the latter discovered his present whereabouts.

Should John Carter learn of Nulthoom, Fal Sivas knew he would be lucky to trade one form of servitude for another. If the Warlord permitted him to live, that is.

Now that the *Jasoom* was all but completed, the scientist hesitated to convey this to Tun-Dun-Lo, dwar of the guard. For once the jeddara and her eggs departed for Jasoom, they might decide that they no longer had need of him. Perhaps worse, they might bring him along. Fal Sivas did not want to go to Jasoom. Although he had invented the ray-treated armor that permitted them to move about on the watery planet in defiance of its greater gravity, he did not share their interest in living beside great lakes and mighty oceans.

On Jasoom, he would have no place that he could see in the new colony, other than as a vassal. He was not an Orovar, nor a Jasoomian. He worried that they might slay him once his usefulness was at the end. And if he remained useful, then that only would extend his servitude.

Fal Sivas saw no advantage in completing the *Jasoom* any sooner than he needed to, and yet it was now ready. It had been ready for padans. He had pretended otherwise.

So the scientist worked and worried, feeling his situation growing ever more hopeless.

Had Fal Sivas been a warrior, perhaps there might be a place for him. But it would be an inferior place, for the Orovars of Nulthoom saw all other Martian races as beneath them. The jeddara valued only the youngest, most strapping of men. Not only as warriors but as lovers, carefully selected so that the eggs she produced would be of the highest order.

It was a strange colony, this dormant volcano fortress. The women were few and reduced to the status of domestic servants. Only one woman was free. But O-Thuria had never married, yet mated with whomever she wished.

During the years of Fal Sivas' time in this grim redoubt, several times a warrior rose up to challenge the existing consort, and they fought for the privilege of being the favored one with whom the jeddara mated, the Cluros to her Thuria.

By this strict method, the population was sufficiently suppressed to remain contained within the basalt chambers of Mount Nulthoom. Any who sought to flee were ruthlessly executed. This prevented its discovery by the other races.

After the jedarra had ordered her most recent consort, Ro-Dun-Bo, to lead the first expedition to Jasoom, it was widely seen by many that O-Thuria had tired of the man and would soon be seeking a new suitor. None so far had stepped forth, but this was seen as only a matter of time. Now that it was known that the utan had perished along with the crew of the *Jor*, long-simmering rivalries were certain to explode.

AS HE worked, Fal Sivas heard the march of men outside the closed workshop doors and there came an exchange between the dwar of the guard and the guardsmen posted as sentry there.

"Open the doors!" commanded Tun-Dun-Lo gruffly.

The doors were pulled open and Fal Sivas crawled out of the innards of the great teardrop-shaped craft to meet with the dwar.

"Fal Sivas, the spacefaring ship must be ready as soon as possible," said Tun-Dun-Lo. "A great cruiser has been sighted within the last few minutes. It passed to the south of Nulthoom, running without lights. That by itself was suspicious."

"Perhaps it was a smuggling ship."

Tun-Dun-Lo shook his head vigorously. "The ship was extremely large, conceivably a battleship of one of the red cities. Something of this size has never before been seen."

Hearing this, the Martian scientist quailed inwardly. This sounded like a warship of the Heliumatic Empire, perhaps commanded by John Carter himself. But he did not mention this possibility.

"The *Jasoom* is not quite ready," he returned. "But she is very close to completion."

"Make all haste. The jeddara has commanded it. Do not sleep until it is accomplished. Do you understand?"

"I do," replied Fal Sivas woodenly. He knew he had no choice now. He could pretend only a little while longer.

And so he returned to the interior of the interplanetary craft and resumed his futile tinkering. Previously, it had been useful to extend his life. But now he would not delay any longer than absolutely necessary. He did not wish to fall into the stern hands of the Warlord of Barsoom, who would almost certainly slay him on sight.

Chapter 26

BALKED

ALTHOUGH THE Martian Mole made steady progress tunneling through the frozen tundra, I could not help but feel that our pace was agonizingly slow. No doubt our inability to see the way ahead and gauge the remaining distance to Mount Nulthoom's broad base preyed upon my mind.

Fortunately, Vad Varo, seated immediately behind me, had assumed the role of navigator. Using the surveying tools of Barsoom, he had plotted our best course and by the simple expedient of watching the pulverized soil and other debris crawl past our inspection windows, he was able to gauge our progress.

"We are approximately one haad from our objective," he called out.

I glanced at my wrist chronometer. "I would judge that we are perhaps eight xats from the mountain's base."

Vad Varo shook his head slowly. "I would put the time-distance ratio closer to ten xats."

This intelligence did not please me, but I trusted my fellow Jasoomian. If Vad Varo thought we were 30 Earth minutes from our objective, I would be foolhardy indeed to doubt him.

My nerves were steadily becoming keyed up. In battle, I never feel such pangs. But we were not in battle, only drawing inexorably closer to the fight we knew we must initiate.

I had not been prepared for the awful racket that the Martian Mole made as it ground up tundra and dispersed it from our path. It was a relentless cacophony. Many times I wished I could plug my ears with something thick to keep out the worst of the noise.

At one point, the sound changed to an alarming grinding, and we briefly slowed as the engine labored in a queer way. Finally, the Mole lurched ahead, and we regained our forward momentum.

Glancing out our inspection ports, Vad Varo and I saw chunks of what appeared to be black basalt swimming by, mixed in with clumps of tundra subsoil.

"We seem to have encountered a stony conglomeration," I stated.

"Fortunately," returned Vad Varo, "it was not large. Otherwise we might have stalled. The drill head is powerful enough to penetrate basalt, but not for long. The engine would surely overheat and seize up."

After that, I almost welcomed the relentless racket of the burrowing machine. Silence would have been infinitely worse, for it would have meant that we had failed in our mission.

Perhaps ten more Martian minutes passed before a new concern presented itself.

Once again, it was Vad Varo who perceived the problem before it was fully apparent. I silently thanked my ancestors that I had brought him along.

"John Carter, look!"

I glanced back, followed the direction of Vad Varo's pointing finger and saw that the dry shreds of tundra slipping past the inspection windows on his side were beginning to smear and discolor the glass.

"What does this mean?" I asked before my brain caught up with my perceptions and supplied the answer that came from Vad Varo's own mouth.

"We are entering a zone of muck."

I did not doubt it. And instinctively I reached for the arrestor control, slamming the motor to a dead stop.

From the rearmost position, Tars Tarkas demanded, "John Carter, what is happening?"

"We have penetrated a pocket of underground mud. This means we are approaching the hot springs Tarzan warned us about."

"Dare we proceed?"

Instead of responding to the green man, I directed my attention back to Vad Varo. I have always known him to possess sound judgment in scientific and mechanical matters.

"I await your evaluation, Vad Varo," I said calmly.

The man was not long in responding. But he took a few moments to compose his thoughts.

"The muck surely means that we are approaching the subsurface hot spring. But does that mean that it is in our path, or does it lie beyond it?"

Knowing that there was no certain answer to his question, I said, "We dare not dive more deeply and risk blundering into a bed of hot magma which would surely cook us alive. Yet if we angle the nose of the Mole upward, we will perforce become visible on the surface and also lose much of the powerful forward traction the drill provides."

Again, Vad Varo considered the alternatives.

Finally, he said, "Let us plunge ahead. If the soil becomes more watery, we will drive upward in the hopes of avoiding it."

"I agree," I said, reengaging the Martian Mole's engine.

The nose drill resumed revolving. As it picked up speed, the machine lurched ahead, and we were once again in motion.

We had not gone very far when the sound of the drill biting through the hard tundra ahead changed radically in character, now sounding like the churning of butter, but on a greatly magnified scale. We slowed perceptibly.

Inspection ports became smeared with semi-liquid mud, and I knew that I had no choice but to reorient the Martian Mole to drive us closer to the surface. Here and there, water began seeping into the machine. The steel hull had not been designed to be watertight. And that proved to be a nearly fatal flaw. Warm water commenced pooling on the floor.

I adjusted the wheels and levers that canted the flexible forward section of the Mole so that its busy nose pointed increasingly upward. I did this with extreme caution for I did not want to break the surface, whether at a shallow or an acute angle.

We did not have all night. And I did not care to lose the element of surprise created by the combined forces poised to attack our objective.

The Mole responded. The forward section slowly tilted upward as it dug blindly. Water continued to seep into the machine, and I feared for the worst.

Behind me, Vad Varo spoke up. "John Carter, if the water reaches the electrical connections, it will cause a short circuit and this machine will become our mutual coffin."

I threw off my cloak and tossed it on the floor where it would soak up pooling water, Vad Varo and Kar Komak did the same, and finally Tars Tarkas added his heavy cloak to the effort. The great Thark got down on hands and knees and swished the cloaks around in an effort to sop up as much water as possible.

"Our cloaks are not sufficient, John Carter," he said at last.

Vad Varo and I exchanged glances, and we could see no other option. Silently, I once again shut off the great motor.

The mechanical Mole ground to a halt. This would only serve to protect the electrical equipment from water damage, but we would have to engage the motor once more if we hoped to escape the tubular machine alive.

I turned to Vad Varo and said, "Give the order to attack. Do not communicate our predicament."

Switching on the radio set at his right hand, Vad Varo instructed the *Dejah Thoris* to commence firing at once.

The voice of a radioman came crackling back. *"At once, John Carter."*

Once the communication was acknowledged, we four sat in morose silence, contemplating our future, which was bleak.

Chapter 27

Extinguished Fires

THE DREADNOUGHT *Dejah Thoris* flew south of the fiery ice peak of Mount Nulthoom, running lights extinguished, her colors furled, taking care to avoid the westernmost end of the burning coal seam which illuminated the dormant volcano's eastern approach.

The beat of her mighty engines, however, could not be baffled. This sound was assumed to carry to the fortress formed from an ice volcano. This was expected. In fact, it was considered to be desirable.

In command of the ship was Kantos Kan, Overlord of the Heliumatic Navy. His orders were to pass below the altitude of the volcano's crater and then swing around to come up upon its eastern flank. This maneuver was presently in the course of being executed.

In the wheelhouse, Kantos Kan watched the way ahead, beside him was his son, Djor Kantos, who held the rank of teedwar, commanding one thousand men.

So many haads distant, Mount Nulthoom's truncated summit smoldered. This was the beacon by which they steered their midnight course.

Turning to his son, Kantos Kan said, "What the Orovars of Nulthoom must consider to be a warning to steer clear of their volcanic habitation is instead the lighthouse that guides us to our objective."

"Do you think they heard us passing?"

"It does not matter whether they did or not. They will hear our next approach. And they will respond to it. Ready all guns."

Djor Kantos wheeled and went off to convey the Overlord's orders.

Closer and closer, the *Dejah Thoris* beat toward Mount Nulthoom in the fortunate darkness, for the moons of Barsoom had vanished from the starry sky in the course of their irregular orbits, which causes them to rise and set repeatedly each night. It was cold on the exposed decks of the battleship. Men went about their duties with their cloaks tightly clasped, trusting this to keep warm the hilts of their swords, which they expected to soon draw.

There was one exception: The bronzed Jasoomian who called himself *Tarzan-of-the-apes*. He patrolled the carborundum aluminum decks, his snowy cloak flying from his shoulders, his Orovar sword strapped to his side. The bracing cold did not seem to bother him.

Below deck, his malagor mount sat quiescent, an inert machine whose mechanical brain would come alive only when the ape-man's thoughts roused it.

Tarzan was growing eager to commence the attack. But he would not hurl himself into battle until the battleship had initiated its attack. That assault would not commence until they received the signal from the Martian Mole that its great revolving drill had pierced the ice-covered basalt base.

Tarzan stood close to the radio room, where he would be among the first to hear of John Carter's success.

AS THE night wore on, that success seemed to be slow in coming. No one could predict how long it would take the tunneling machine to pierce the outer walls and breach the lowermost level of the volcanic redoubt. Precious hours were passing.

As Vad Varo had explained, once the drill broke through, it was not certain that the Martian Mole would possess sufficient momentum to penetrate the secret stronghold of Nulthoom permitting the machine's hatch to open so that its four-man fighting complement could be disgorged.

If blocked by soil or defenders, John Carter, Vad Varo, Tars Tarkas, and Kar Komak would have to batter a path through if they could. Either way, a brutal battle was in the offing.

It would be up to the *Dejah Thoris* to create a diversion before that assault could properly commence, or the greater force of Orovar defenders would rush to meet the subterranean attack.

Dawn was quickly approaching. With the rising of the sun, the element of surprise would be drastically reduced. Moreover, the enemy contingent would be awake and not asleep in their beds. Should the breach take place after the people of Nulthoom had risen from their sleeping mats, their defense would be that much more fierce.

As Tarzan watched, the smoldering crown of Mount Nulthoom loomed larger and larger beyond the battleship's majestic prow.

Then something happened that made the threat of dawn seem immaterial.

Unexpectedly, mysteriously, the fires of Mount Nulthoom vanished from view, to be replaced by a climbing cloud of vapor that squirmed under the hellish light emanating from the ground fissure of incandescent coal beneath their keel.

This brought Tarzan pelting to the wheelhouse.

"What is happening?" he demanded.

Instead of replying, Kantos Kan brought his field glass to his eye and stared at the blackness that was now all but unrelieved.

"I can see nothing," he exclaimed. "Somehow they have banked the coal fires."

"They hear our approach," said Tarzan.

"No doubt. But I had not expected this development. Our gunners were counting on opening fire upon the illuminated peak. Now it has gone dark."

"You have searchlights," suggested Tarzan.

"And I will use them if necessary. But I would rather not betray our exact position in the dark."

While they were considering the consequences of this new development, a radioman came running from the radio cubicle and reported, "Kantos Kan, Vad Varo sends word from John Carter. He has given the command to commence firing!"

The Overlord relayed the command to his son, Djor Kantos. Without waiting for more intelligence, Tarzan of the Apes rushed down into the hold, where he claimed his metallic steed.

Climbing into the ornate saddle, he trained his mind upon the mechanical brain encased in its metallic skull.

The silent command was direct: *Return to your hangar.*

The pseudo-bird unfolded its wide, paint-streaked wings and prepared to sweep forward while, at a signal, a crewman opened a hatch in the side of the mighty ship.

With a tremendous flexing of forandus-metal wings, the mechanical malagor propelled itself out into the cold darkness of the steppe.

Chapter 28

SOUNDS OF WARNING

F AL SIVAS decided that he would announce the completion of his newest interplanetary vehicle once the sun rose.

There was no point in doing it any sooner, for the jeddara
always awoke with the dawn, even though the interior of Mount
Nulthoom was artificially illuminated by radium lamps. These
were not turned on in her quarters until the master chronometer
coincided with the rising of the sun.

The people of Nulthoom were as regimented as a military
garrison. They needed to be in order to function as a soci-
ety, which they had for literally thousands of years since they
regretfully abandoned their island city when the Throxeus had
retreated.

Those who survived relocated to the hollow interior of this
dead volcano, which they then carved out into floors and chambers, creating a mighty fortalice against both the cold and any of
the new warring nations that were rising in the aftermath of the
collapse of the Orovar civilization, which had previously been
the dominant race upon Barsoom.

All of this had been explained to Fal Sivas. In the beginning,
jeddaks had ruled, and men were allowed to marry women. But
the population over the first generations exceeded the capac-
ity of the hollow mountain to contain their numbers. Food was
perpetually scarce, and therefore strictly rationed.

A program of eugenics was instituted in which the majority
of female infants were not allowed to survive their hatching.

Those permitted to live were made slaves and nurses. Over time, the last jeddak gave way to the first jeddara, and so it had been down through the generations.

The word of the jeddara, O-Thuria, was absolute law. She had no rivals of her own sex. The men of Nulthoom had been raised to worship and revere her as the embodiment of the moon after which she had been named. For O-Thuria was the source of all life, every egg, and so represented the only opportunity any of them had to mate and conceive offspring.

It was a hard system, but through it the last of the Nulthoom people were perpetuated in peace and rigid security.

Now they were prepared to relocate wholly to a new and better world. A watery planet that more resembled the world of their ancestors than it did the Barsoom of today.

Unexpectedly, the two great doors were thrown open and Tun-Dun-Lo, dwar of the guard, barged in, saying, "Fal Sivas, you are needed urgently."

"I am almost finished here," he said peevishly.

"Come with me. A more important matter has arisen now."

Reluctantly, Fal Sivas followed the dwar down the ever-winding staircase that took him past the various levels that had been hewn from the empty magma chamber of Mount Nulthoom and to the broad base of the volcano.

Before he had reached the bottom floor, the scientist detected a strange sound. It was a ground-grinding noise, deep and resonant.

"What is that clatter?" he demanded of Tun-Dun-Lo.

"We do not know," the other said tightly. "That is why you are needed. Inasmuch as you know machinery of the outside world, you must tell us."

Showing increasing reluctance, Fal Sivas was brought to the lowermost level of Mount Nulthoom. Here, the jeddara's eggs were incubated, live animals were kept, and food was grown. Most of it was held in storage. No one lived here. Except for the unfortunates who were consigned to the few dungeon cells that were maintained for the recalcitrant.

Reaching the bottom, the pair moved along the circular corridor, toward the sound. Doing so, they went past the sealed skeel portal leading to the lava tube that ran to the west. This was still firmly in place, the scientist saw, its windlass removed.

Eventually, they came to the spot where the sound was loudest.

The noise was a continual grinding, a particularly annoying sound. Mixed in was the clatter of stones being caught up in some mechanical operation. It sounded as if the perpetually-frozen tundra was being pulverized.

Fal Sivas felt of the walls with his hands, then knelt on one knee and placed an ear to the lowermost wall, which was of basalt.

"The sound is coming from the west and it appears to be emanating below the level of the ground," he reported.

"What does it portend, Fal Sivas?"

"I do not know what it portends, Tun-Dun-Lo. But it sounds as if a great machine comes burrowing through the ground."

"It is not an animal?"

Rising to his feet, Fal Sivas shook his head definitely. "No, it is not an unknown beast. At least no animal I have ever heard of. The sounds are mechanical. Something being driven by a motor is creating them because they do not pause. It operates without changing speed. And whatever it is, it is growing nearer."

"Will it pass beneath us?"

"I cannot tell, for I do not know how large it is. But one fact is certain: Through its mechanical exertions, it is coming ever closer."

Tun-Dun-Lo's voice grew terse. "I will awaken the jeddara. She must know of this. For this can only be a threat."

Fal Sivas responded frankly, "I cannot conceive that it is other than a threat."

"You must hasten to finish the spacefaring ship. We may have to flee as early as today."

Fal Sivas suppressed a smile of cunning. "You have my word that the craft will be ready to launch when it is needed."

"Then return to your task. I will awaken the jeddara."

Now even more worried than he was before, Fal Sivas climbed the towering circular stone staircase that wound around the inner circumference of the dormant volcano to the uppermost level, and his workshop. The moment of truth was fast approaching. The ship was ready. It could be launched within a few brief zodes. The only question was: What fate would befall him once it did?

Fal Sivas was not a brave man, only a cunning one. To delay any further would be futile. It would be postponing the inevitable. Mentally, he steeled himself for come what may. Even if he, in his heart of hearts, did not care to encounter it.

Chapter 29

"So Say We All."

I DID not know how long we four sat in the narrow confines of the Martian Mole. I did not glance at my chronometer, and neither did Vad Varo.

The water continued to seep in, and its steamy heat made the atmosphere humid. I felt helpless. I could not see a way out of our predicament and looking toward Vad Varo, I could see that he was equally flummoxed.

Finally, I declared, "We will have to chance it and break for the surface. It is the only way. Tarzan and the crew of the *Dejah Thoris* must carry the attack without us."

From the furthermost rear seat, the deep voice of Tars Tarkas spoke. "Are these the words of John Carter that smite my ears? Does the Warlord of Barsoom give up while he still breathes?"

"While I still live," I returned stiffly, "I will never give up, Tars Tarkas. But we cannot penetrate Mount Nulthoom in this wretched machine. All appears to be hopeless. At least if the Mole can reach the surface, we can rush to the aid of our allies if the marching distance is not too great."

Tars Tarkas accepted these words in silence. But before long, a throaty laugh rumbled from his thick throat, filling the narrow steel tube that was the mechanical Mole.

I heard the swish of his great sword as it left its leather scabbard. Turning, I saw him lift the hilt to the level of his tusked face, holding it with the broad blade pointing downward.

With a wordless grunt, he drove that point through the floor of the machine.

Immediately, pooled water started draining from the floor plates.

"I do not give up so easily as you, John Carter," he said firmly. And he forcefully brought his sword-point down on another spot.

Realizing the efficacy of the green man's solution, Vad Varo and I drew our blades and copied the great Thark's thrusts. In a trice, all three of us were piercing the floor with our swords. We cut sufficient vents that the pooled water drained rapidly, and the situation was swiftly saved. Kar Komak, who carried no blade in his robes, employed his hatchet to assist in our efforts.

"Thank you, Tars Tarkas," I said sincerely. "I sometimes forget that brawn may show a path that brain fails to grasp."

"It is nothing, John Carter. After all, I am preserving my own life as well as those of you and your friends."

I laughed at that blunt remark and once again thanked my ancestors that I had these unique men as my companions.

Re-engaging the motor, I sent the Martian Mole driving forward, and it soon dug its circular snout into the swampy tundra, dragging us forward and upward.

Necessity forced us to break the surface of the crust above, but by manipulating the controls, I managed to keep the mighty machine traveling two-thirds beneath the crust. The night sky was now visible through the top portions of our dorsal inspection ports, and I could spy Thuria and Cluros once more making their futile rounds.

If a sentry should be looking down from the crater's rim, no doubt he would spy our approach. But it was equally true that the defenders would soon enough hear us, for the grinding power of the mechanical Mole was again chewing through hard frozen ground with a relentless and remorseless force that made me once more wish that I could plug my ears so I could block it.

Despite that, the commotion was one for which I was grate-ful.

"What say you now, John Carter?" rumbled Tars Tarkas from the rear of the machine.

"I say what I always say, my friend. I still live."

"So say we all," added Kar Komak.

Once more, Tars Tarkas' rumbling laughter filled the Mole's interior as it pressed onward, ever onward, devouring rock and tundra, pulling us inexorably toward the base of our objective, Mount Nulthoom.

I no longer had any doubts that we would achieve that desired objective.

Chapter 30

THE BREAKTHROUGH

O-THURIA, JEDDARA OF NULTHOOM, awoke before the dwar of the guard, Tun-Dun-Lo, could reach the heavy doors of her bed chambers, which were hung with tapestries depicting a legendary warrior-god who resembled a cross between a primitive Orovar soldier and a great white ape. This worthy was further distinguished by a solitary horn which grew from its wide forehead, and was remembered under the heroic name of Jor, which meant Horned One.

She woke unexpectedly, before her usual hour. This was a consequence of an unsettling vibration in the walls of her apartments that were decorated with maritime scenes of ancient Barsoom during the era when Nulthoom was an important trading island in the Throxeus. This vibration caused her sleeping platform, which was a small boat once built by a distant ancestor, to shake.

Throwing off her sleeping furs, she slipped into a silken cloak and fastened it about her womanly form, then moved on bare feet to the chamber door. The vibrations coming up through the soles of her feet were disquieting.

O-Thuria was a beautiful woman of indeterminate age, no longer a girl, but still youthful and vital. Her hair, however, was not the blonde of her race, but a platinum hue that shone nearly metallic in the artificial light. It was held in place by a fillet of gold adorned with the metal of Nulthoom, a curious white triangle surmounted by a red half-moon.

Throwing open the chamber doors, she saw Tun-Dun-Lo rushing toward her and demanded, "What is this vibration? Is the ground quaking?"

"No, my jeddara. The ground is not quaking, at least not from natural causes. There is a disturbance beneath the tundra that Fal Sivas insists is mechanical. And I agree with him. Something is burrowing through the ground in our direction."

"A machine?"

"It could be nothing else."

"It must be the work of enemies!" she insisted.

"Enemies or interlopers," returned Tun-Dun-Lo, "they are one and the same. We must prepare for an imminent onslaught. For if the sound of its operation is any indication, it is large in size and must perforce carry warriors."

"Have my sacred eggs conveyed to Fal Sivas' interplanetary ship without delay."

"As you command, my jeddara. Fal Sivas assures me that it is almost ready to depart."

"Then we will depart at once. Order the fires banked. Have engineers man the controls governing the great skyward hatch."

"This, too, will be done," said Tun-Dun-Lo, departing in haste.

The jeddara raced to the lowermost floor where she rushed to the enclosed hatchery. The sound here was terrible and growing stronger with every passing moment. It filled the great corridor which ran around the outer circumference of Mount Nulthoom.

She did not bring with her the key to the hatchery but only stood waiting for the caretakers to arrive, which they did in short order.

"Convey every egg to the *Jasoom's* cargo bay," she commanded. "Set every available man to this task. Let no egg be damaged, lest the clumsy calot responsible lose his head in punishment."

The work began as O-Thuria made her winding way up to the uppermost level. Along the way, she collected her personal guard, consisting of two young men who were currently under consideration to be her next consort. They did not yet know that. Nor did they suspect that she would pit them against one another for the privilege.

"Accompany me," she commanded. "Make haste."

When they reached the uppermost level, she rushed into the workshop and cried out, "Fal Sivas, how long until departure is possible?"

Fal Sivas turned from his work and said gravely, "You may commence preparations. The ship is ready now."

"Excellent. For your good works, you will be rewarded handsomely."

Fal Sivas looked relieved. "Might I inquire what my reward will be?"

"Previously, I had considered your usefulness at an end. But now I offer you the opportunity to accompany us to Jasoom."

"This intrigues me," returned the scientist. "But if I do not care to go with you to live on Jasoom, what will you permit me to do?"

"You may fall on your sword, if that is your decision."

Fal Sivas looked momentarily perplexed. "But I do not own a sword, my jeddara."

"I am quite certain that one can be found that will be suitable," she said coldly, then swept from the room without another word.

Fal Sivas felt his knees turn to water. Now he knew his fate. He could follow this cruel, imperious woman to another world, or he could perish here. He was not sure which destiny he preferred. So he turned about and continued making the interplanetary ship ready for its impending departure.

THE FIRST eggs began arriving and were loaded into bays that had been designed to hold them safely.

"The more of these that you load," the scientist warned the dwar of the guard, "the fewer accommodations will remain for our soldiers."

"Sacrifices must be made," returned Tun-Dun-Lo. "Do not interfere. I shall return."

At that moment, a stumbling sentry came down from the crater, dragging his spear.

"My dwar, the sun is coming up. And I have sighted something to the west."

"Show me."

Tun-Dun-Lo followed the sentry to the crater hatch and lifted the flagstone. The fires had already been banked. There was little light up here, only what trickled down from the star fields above. But the sun was rising.

"Behold," proclaimed the sentry. With his spear, he pointed over the crater rim and to the west. Tun-Dun-Lo saw in the growing gray light an elongated furrow in the snowy steppeland. It was moving, splitting and fracturing the tundra as it progressed.

It appeared that something was borrowing just under the ground, and its progress was causing the hard crust of the snow-dusted steppe to lift and crack with its approach. This line of disturbance stretched out as far as the eye could see, although it was difficult to discern beyond a few haads, due to the insufficient light.

Taking hold of the crater rim, Tun-Dun-Lo stared downward and saw to his horror that the disturbance was steadily approaching the base of Mount Nulthoom, directly below.

"It is almost upon us!" he cried, turning to race for the open hatch.

In doing so, his eyes caught sight of something that was just catching the rays of the rising sun.

It was a battleship. It was standing off not very far from them, in the direction of the east, its steely hull ablaze with reflected light from the coal seam burning like an inflamed wound in the ground. And it was approaching steadily.

His mouth fell open, and his eyes started. Before the dwar could react, the ship swung about majestically, turning its starboard side to him, and her guns commenced to make themselves heard.

The first shell struck the eastern flank of Mount Nulthoom, fracturing its icy sheath, and causing huge pieces to crack, break off, and clatter down, revealing its black basalt face.

"Follow me!" the dwar told the sentry. "We are under attack!"

Rushing down the steps, Tun-Dun-Lo raced past the men carrying the incubators that contained the jeddara's precious eggs, knowing he must inform O-Thuria at the earliest moment.

Struggling with his load, one gasped out, "The disturbance is very loud on the first level now."

"I will investigate," he said, rushing on.

Encountering the jeddara on the circular staircase, Tun-Dun-Lo reported, "A battleship is opening fire from our eastern flank. It appears to be manned by red men."

"Dispatch the malagor scouts," O-Thuria commanded.

"But it is a mighty battleship, against which we have no comparable forces."

"Send them anyway. Tell them to fight to the death. Harry them long enough to give us time to depart. Time is of the essence!"

"At once, my jeddara."

Turning, Tun-Dun-Lo fled to the middle levels, where a squad of mechanical malagor scouts sat in a quiescent rank in their dressed-stone hangar, their armed riders posted close by.

Addressing them, he directed, "You are hereby ordered to attack the battleship approaching from the east. Sweep its deck of gunners. Fend it off at all costs. Do not return while it is still shelling us."

One warrior saluted and said, "We will fight to the death."

"Your jeddara expects that," returned Tun-Dun-Lo stiffly, "and she asked me to convey to you her eternal gratitude."

Blindly compliant, archers mounted their long-necked steeds and prepared to depart. The mindless malodors obediently extended their paint-streaked wings.

Confident that they would do their utmost and, if necessary, give their last breath to the cause, Tun-Dun-Lo returned to the lowermost level. He raced along the curving corridor until he came to the spot where the grinding noise of unknown machinery was loudest.

The racket was so terrible that the dwar could not tell if it was emanating from beyond the mountain wall, beneath his feet, or both. He was forced to clap his hands over both ears to keep out the worst of it.

Turning back, Tun-Dun-Lo checked on the sacred eggs of the jeddara. The hatchery was almost empty. Only two incubators remained.

"Finish up here," he told the workers. "If we are going to be breached, it will be soon."

"What is attacking us?" asked one warrior. Terror of the unknown was inscribed upon his pale features.

"Not even Fal Sivas knows," the dwar replied curtly. "Once you have conveyed the last egg to safety, return with as many men as you can muster. The battle is about to be joined."

And he rushed back to the sound of the commotion, his sword sliding out of its scabbard, although he had no idea what conceivable use it would be against something that sounded as if it was powerful enough to pulverize the entirety of Mount Nulthoom.

Watching the zone of greatest intensity, Tun-Dun-Lo stood ready to meet the threat like a true soldier of Nulthoom.

There came a thump from the opposite side of the mountain, and he knew that another shell had struck its eastern face. Yet he waited tensely as, one by one, warriors returned to take up defensive positions behind him.

The sound was by now almost indescribable. The relentless cacophony penetrated their helmets, making their eardrums ring.

Finally, even though they expected it to happen, something broke through, striking terror into their hearts with its mad ferocity.

Close to the floor, the basalt wall cracked, and pieces flew out, rebounding off the inner walls of the passage.

To a man, the soldiers of Nulthoom stepped back, swords gripped tightly, as a great spinning contrivance pushed its way into view. It was massive, easily as large as a zitidar. It sent pieces of the broken basalt clattering in all directions, bombarding them and driving them backward.

Retreating around the curve of the corridor, they halted on command. Cautiously, Tun-Dun-Lo stuck his helmeted head out and saw to his horror the great convoluted drill-point of a thing break into view, revolving madly and hurling debris everywhere. Detritus clattered off the walls and bounced to the floor, which the awestruck dwar saw had cracked wide open, an unbelievable thing.

Then, abruptly, it ceased operating. And a strange silence fell over the corridor, one that left the frightened guard gaping in awe.

Turning to his men, Tun-Dun-Lo said, "When I give the word, we will attack."

"But what is that we are attacking?" whispered a warrior.

The dwar hesitated. Finally, he admitted. "I do not know, but it is fierce and terrible. But we must hold it off until the jeddara is safely away."

The soldiers of Nulthoom looked to one another as they realized that they were deemed expendable. This came as no great shock to them. But it caused their hearts to sink, even as their hands gripped their weapons more firmly in defiant resolve.

Chapter 31

"No Quarter!"

INASMUCH AS we were traveling blind, Tars Tarkas, Vad Varo, Kar Komak, and I did not know precisely when the Martian Mole would penetrate the base of Mount Nulthoom. Only when the sound of its burrowing changed from a steady and ceaseless grinding to a noisy clatter—as fragments of basalt and clod were hurled about and the steady racketing of machinery to which we had become accustomed abruptly ceased—did we know that success was at hand.

Vad Varo informed the *Dejah Thoris* that we had at last penetrated our objective. That the wireless communication was received was promptly acknowledged.

Almost as soon as this was accomplished, I realized that we had been premature in our jubilation. The drill-head, having penetrated an empty chamber, ceased to drag the Martian Mole along after it. All positive forward movement had stopped.

I turned in my seat, "Tars Tarkas, open the hatch."

The Thark rose out of his oversized chair, undogged the hatch above his head, then threw it to one side with a clanging that made the Mole ring like a struck bell. Reaching up, he poked his hairless olive-green head above the broken tundra, and reported, "The machine is stuck in the mountain's base. The way remains blocked."

I switched off the now-useless drill.

"Is there a break through which we could pass?"

"None that I can see, John Carter."

Vad Varo spoke up, "John Carter, reverse the drill."

"Excellent idea," I exclaimed, re-engaging the motor and listening as the drill-bit spun with increasing rapidity. Once it was turning at its maximum revolutions per minute, I engaged the reversing gear, causing the elongated machine to jolt backward. There came a clatter, as of settling rocky debris, as the drill extracted itself from the basalt base.

From above, Tars Tarkas shouted, "The way is now clear!"

Batting aside a conglomeration of detritus with his swords, the green man lumbered out of the machine, ran half its dorsal length, and leaped off its side. As I shut down the drill, I could hear him give vent to a savage battle cry.

Vad Varo, Kar Komak, and I duly followed, charging across the long surface fissure the Mole had gouged over the tundra until we reached the broken base of Mount Nulthoom.

The breach was large enough for the huge Thark, once he ducked his tusked head, and we all clambered over loose debris until we found ourselves in a dim corridor that curved in both directions.

I found myself only momentarily stymied as to which direction to take. For, with a raucous shouting, helmeted Orovar soldiers came charging from our left.

Here, I took charge.

"No quarter!" I shouted, leaping ahead to meet the oncoming foe.

My blade came purring out of its leather scabbard to meet the steel of a man I presumed to be a dwar.

Clashing, our blades rang and resounded, and for all that, while the man was a capable swordsman and his Orovar sword a superlative blade, I quickly beat him back, disarming him with a cross stroke as I did so. Before I could finish the fellow, he fell back, ordering his men to protect him.

His company appeared to be without fear. They swarmed us, and for several minutes our blades licked out and drew blood.

Soon, we were outnumbered. However, my greater-than-Martian strength and Tars Tarkas' mighty arms decisively demonstrated that their force was less than potent.

Vad Varo, employing his rather scientific swordsmanship, more than held his own.

For his part, Kar Komak the bowman preferred to loose arrows where he could. Alas for him, we so thickly choked the corridor that he achieved only one clear shot. It went into the right eye of a helmeted defender, and he twisted to his knees, expiring there as his comrades tasted our thirsty steel.

I will spare the reader detailed accounts of the gory dismemberment and decapitation that followed. But suffice it to say that this initial resistance was quickly cut down.

Two of these men, seeing their fellows overwhelmed so handily, broke and retreated back in the direction from which they had come.

We followed, hard on their heels.

Eventually, they found a niche that led to a set of stone steps leading upward. Even though Tarzan had warned me of this feature, I was rather taken aback by the prospect. Stairs were so rare on Barsoom, and I had not encountered them in so long, I hesitated.

"Tread carefully," I called back to the others. "You will become used to planting your feet one at a time."

Vad Varo, Kar Komak, and I mounted the lower steps. We gave pursuit, gaining confidence with every leap and bound.

Behind us, Tars Tarkas struggled, for the art of climbing stairs was something he had never had to master, being a nomad of the dead sea bottoms. Also, his great girth and longsword proved to be handicaps in the narrow winding passage.

Sheathing his blade, the giant Thark dropped to all six muscular limbs and made his way in the manner a four-legged dog mounts steps. He soon fell behind.

During our difficult ascent, we periodically came to breaks in the winding staircase, which opened onto landings. Here, we found doors, evidently leading to passages carved into the magma chamber. I had no doubt rooms had also been excavated in the interior. But the clatter of the routed defenders we pursued told us that none had taken advantage of any of them. They were continuing their climb, and we charged after them, our bloody blades in hand.

Our quarry reached a point I judged to be one-third of the way up the mountain interior, where they found an open door and disappeared behind it. This they barricaded in some fashion so that when we drove our bodies against it, the heavy wooden portal scarcely gave.

"Shall we continue to the summit?" asked Vad Varo.

"Yes, make for the hangar holding Fal Sivas' new ship. That is our ultimate objective." I looked down the curved stairs, which I imagined followed the outer wall and was carved from it, and Tars Tarkas soon lumbered up, lifted his powerful torso in becoming erect, then used his upper arms to help him navigate the cramped and narrow passage.

"Why do you stop, John Carter?" he asked, red eyes burning.

"Our enemies have disappeared behind this barricaded door. We are going on ahead to the interplanetary ship. Attempt to breach this portal while we do so."

"I will do my best, John Carter."

As we continued the long upward climb, we could hear the Thark's mighty fist pounding against the door. I had no doubt that if he continued his assault, the door eventually would surrender and the guards behind it would be overcome quickly.

Before we could gain the summit, the satisfying sound of splintering hardwood drifted up, and I smiled in the certain knowledge that Tars Tarkas, Jeddack of Thark, would not be long at his task, and would soon rejoin us.

Chapter 32

TARZAN THE AVENGER

TARZAN OF THE APES directed his mechanical malagor straight toward the dark flat summit of Mount Nulthoom as, behind him, illuminated by the fiery gash of burning coal that was the only visible surface feature surrounding the Orovar stronghold, the *Dejah Thoris* opened up with her mighty starboard cannon battery.

His keen eyes were watchful. The enemy malagor scouts must soon appear. But from where had yet to be made clear.

A wave of warmth touched his sun-bronzed body, and he was soon enveloped in a cloud of steam that carried the bitter tang of coal smoke.

It was obvious what had happened. The coals perpetually burning in the volcano's crater had been doused by water, banking their fire.

As the ape-man watched, he saw that the still-smoking coal bed was rising and separating into two sections, hurling its contents aside, whereupon the smoking nuggets tumbled down the mountain's icy flanks. This drew his suspicion.

Mentally directing his flapping steed to climb higher, Tarzan saw in the rising rays of the sun a clearer picture of the crater.

The coal bed had been arrayed on an ersite-flanged platform. This was lifting and separating in its center, exposing a large dark space below. Yet no mounted malagors rose up to give challenge.

Then, from the other side of the mountain, the first aerial defender swept into view, its agile and exceedingly light forandus wings catching the morning rays.

Tarzan directed his steed toward it. Out from its scabbard came his Orovar sword. The ape-man was practiced with the bluish blade. On Earth, he had fought other swordsmen on horseback. This was a very different prospect. To be unhorsed at this altitude would be to fall to his death. And the widespread wings of each opponent's steed inevitably would interfere with attacking his foemen.

Yet the advantage remained with Tarzan. He had the greater altitude.

The ape-man swept down, commanding his own unliving mount to execute a spiral around the other, confusing the helmeted warrior, whose lifted sword shifted wildly about in his attempt to parry a lethal thrust that seemed as if it might come from any direction at any moment.

It did. The Orovar continually shifted and banked, attempting to keep his foe in sight while also controlling his malagor, when he was caught unawares.

Swooping down, Tarzan knocked the blade away with a backhand swipe, and the other rider was nearly precipitated from his saddle with surprise.

While the stunned warrior watched in horror as his sword fell to the ground, Tarzan casually removed his head. It tumbled to the ground, mouth agape.

No longer under telepathic control, the metallic malagor flapped on unwittingly.

Turning his attention back to Mount Nulthoom, Tarzan saw that the others had hung back to observe the skirmish. They now knew his tactics.

Tarzan did not care about that. Tactics could be changed. It was strategy that mattered. These fools did not know that.

Together, the two new enemies rose up and started circling him, as if to confuse the bronzed giant in the same way that he had baffled their headless fellow.

"Who are you?" one of them shouted. "You are not Orovar!"

"I am Tarzan the avenger," the ape-man replied in their language.

The other enemy demanded, "What are you avenging?"

"Africa, my home."

This appeared not to impress these riders, for they continued their sweeping and swooping maneuvers.

One of them had a spear attached to leather loops in his saddle, and this he took up.

Tarzan was not afraid of their swords, for he could parry and avoid them easily. But a spear was another matter. So he kept a wary eye on the circling spearman.

The fellow launched his weapon at Tarzan. Gauging its trajectory, the giant Jasoomian lifted in his saddle and caught the thick shaft as it passed over his head.

The spearman's jaw was all but dislocated in surprise.

While he gawked, Tarzan reversed the spear and returned it with all the strength of his mighty right arm. The man was impaled by his own weapon and went tumbling backward, his malagor flying on, brainlessly unaware of the loss.

The sight of this feat of physical skill duly impressed the third malagor rider. Sheathing his sword, he took up his bow, which he quickly fitted with an arrow.

This was an even greater threat than the spear, Tarzan knew. For one arrow could be followed swiftly by another and then by a third.

Directing his steed to climb upward, Tarzan gained sufficient altitude so that, as he swooped around, the bowman struggled to maintain his aim.

Finally, in a combination of frustration and desperation, the archer let fly.

The arrow struck Tarzan's spiraling steed on the upright orange-metal feather sticking up from its forandus-sheathed skull like an antenna, breaking it off.

The consequence threw the mechanical thing into confusion. No longer able to receive thought-commands from its rider, it commenced flopping about the sky, aimless and ungovernable.

Confident of victory, the enemy bowman swooped in to finish the job, a cruel cry of triumph on his lips.

In return, a laugh of contempt emerged from Tarzan of the Apes before he sprang from his mount to land atop his enemy, ripping him from the saddle, and throwing him aside as if he were a rag doll.

Trailing an incomprehensible cry of despair, the man fell to his death.

As Tarzan's first steed flopped about, sinking toward the steppe, the ape-man settled into the vacated saddle and exerted mental control over his new mount.

Although this steed was fresh, the command was the same: *Return to your hangar.*

OBEDIENTLY, THE flapping machine turned its crystal orbs toward Mount Nulthoom and skimmed toward it. As Tarzan's gray eyes fell upon the summit, he saw to his surprise something lifting up from the open aperture that formerly had been a bed of hot coals. It was a steely nose like that of an earthly dirigible, but dominated by a set of crystal lenses that gave the impression of blank, insectoid orbs.

Tarzan knew at once that the *Jasoom* was preparing to depart! Here was the explanation of how the previous ship had been launched from the innards of an inactive volcano.

The ape-man commanded his wheeling steed to hasten, and its metal wings started beating with an alarming and frantic rhythm. Circling the ice-clad volcano, it gathered its wings together, preparatory to landing.

Tarzan could spy no opening large enough to admit them, but he knew there had to be such a thing, for he could feel its talon-tipped legs extending in preparation for landing.

With a last spasmodic flapping, the malagor tucked its broad wings close to its sides and swept toward the forbidding icy mountainside where there seemed to be no hollow at all.

Assuming the flying machine and its mechanical brain to be infallible, the ape-man clamped his saddle with steel-muscled legs and placed one bronzed hand upon the hilt of his sheathed sword, so that it would not be dislodged if he should be in error.

Death seemed all but inevitable.

Yet, at the last possible minute, when it seemed to the ape-man's eyes that he was about to slam into a wall of ice, some instinct caused him to draw his great sword and use it to strike at the obstruction. Instead of encountering ice, the blade swept away a curtain of what appeared to be spun glass that was like icy diamonds woven into a net.

The malagor skidded to an ungainly halt, and Tarzan found himself in a horizontal space in which other mechanical steeds stood about. Dismounting, he saw one guard, who had been slain by a sword thrust to his belly.

At the other end of the great rectangular space loomed Tars Tarkas, a long-sword gripped in two of his upper hands. The giant green man was methodically decapitating the immobile malagors, which were waiting for soldiers who would never ride them again.

Striding over to him, Tarzan demanded, "Tars Tarkas, where is John Carter?"

"He is climbing toward the peak where the Orovar ship stands ready to depart."

"It is about to launch," returned Tarzan sharply. "We must join him if we are to stop it. Leave off your work until later."

With a backhand swipe, Tars Tarkas removed the head of one last malagor, grunting, "I will finish this task later."

Together, they raced for the stairs, stepping over the twitch-ing bodies of fallen Orovar warriors that the mighty Thark had forcefully dispatched when he came upon them.

Chapter 33

The Hour

THE DREADED hour had come.

Fal Sivas watched as the great oval aperture in the crater pit was opened. It split into two matched sections, which separated, sending the smoking coal nuggets cascading down the flank of the mountain. This was accomplished by engineers working worm-gear support mechanisms that lifted the cooling coal-bed halves, which then stood upright like twin shields resembling half moons, leaving the ceiling of the interplanetary ship's workshop-hangar exposed to the lightening morning sky.

The jeddara had assembled the cream of her warriors. With her was the wily dwar of the guard, Tun-Dun-Lo, who had abandoned his routed soldiers and fled for the workshop-hangar, knowing that he had no future unless he was among the select company destined to depart Mount Nulthoom for the bountiful planet Jasoom.

"Not all of you may come," she said imperiously.

Consternation overtook the assembled warriors. They looked to their ruler, and then at one another.

"But," objected a man, "we were all hand-picked for this lofty purpose."

"The outsiders have forced my hand. I had not planned to accompany you on this trip, but necessity requires that I do so, and further, that all of my eggs are preserved by removing them from Barsoom forthwith."

"How will you decide who is to accompany you and who is to remain behind?" asked another man.

"There is no time for such difficult decisions," declared O-Thuria. "You must sort this out among yourselves. The ship is ready to leave Nulthoom. The men who are left standing and are whole of limb may accompany me. Do you understand?"

As loyalists who had in the past, or expected in the future, to vie for the favors of their jeddara, the soldiers of Nulthoom understood perfectly and without delay.

"You heard your jeddara," shouted Tun-Dun-Lo, drawing his own blade. "Fall to it."

"Not you," O-Thuria told him. "I look with favor upon you, most loyal of my chosen company. Board the ship."

His thick features alight with a mixture of relief and joy, the dwar turned away and walked up the steel ramp that led into the imposing ship, sheathing his sword as he did so.

Knowing the way of it, the remaining troops turned on one another. Bright swords flashed and contended, and quickly the floor became slippery with blood as O-Thuria turned to Fal Sivas and asked, "What is your decision?"

Fal Sivas did not hesitate. "If it is your desire that I accompany you, my jeddara, this is what I shall do."

"This meets with my favor," O-Thuria returned crisply. "Board the *Jasoom*. I must choose among the survivors once combat has ceased."

Fal Sivas entered the craft as the noise of battle rose in a cacophony of clanging blades and shouting men. The hot scent of blood soon filled the entire space, rising through the oval aperture to climb into the open sky above.

As he did so, the red scientist backed into Tun-Dun-Lo.

"Ready the ship," barked the dwar.

"It is ready, Tun-Dun-Lo. I await only the jeddara's order."

Glancing out over the slaughter spilling all around the great teardrop vessel, the dwar growled, "It will come soon enough, never fear."

Both men could see that O-Thuria, Jeddara of Nulthoom, was enjoying the sight of her followers butchering one another in order to be among the select who abandoned barren Barsoom for a better existence.

Fal Sivas thought to himself that the jeddara was well-named. The lunar orb called Thuria was often termed the "mad queen of heaven." O-Thuria was no less insane in her singleminded zealotry to lord over her subjects. The wily scientist promised himself that he would escape her cold mastery at his first opportunity, whether on Barsoom or Jasoom.

As O-Thuria watched, her azure eyes cold and yet fascinated by the sight of so many strapping warriors battling to brave the new world in her company, the slap of sandaled feet came from beyond the workshop.

So it was not unexpected when three foreign men, swords in hand, appeared in the open doorway.

O-Thuria turned at the intrusion.

"Intruders!" she cried out. "Assassins! Break off fighting one another and fend them off. Your jeddara commands this! Great will be the rewards of those who slay them. For any one of you may one day rise to become my chosen Cluros."

Over the din of battle, her words penetrated. And men who were prepared to lay down their lives on her behalf whirled almost as one, breaking off their mortal combat to meet the new foe as they entered the vast space.

From the open hatch of the waiting ship, Tun-Dun-Lo thrust out his helmeted head. His anxious eyes sought O-Thuria, who represented life itself.

"My jeddara," he called out, "I am prepared to enter the battle, if such is your command."

"It is my command that you, of all my followers, not perish, for I shall need you once we reach blessed Jasoom."

"I do not care to be called a coward," he asserted.

"No man who stands so high in my esteem can ever be accused of cowardice, Tun-Dun-Lo. And any who dare make such an accusation will suffer my displeasure. I will take a new mate once we arrive at the placid shores of Lake Jor. Know that you stand high on my list of favored ones."

Conflicted yet pleased, Tun-Dun-Lo retreated to the safety of the interplanetary ship that would soon ascend into the sky of Barsoom for the first and final time.

Outside, his guards rushed to meet the challenge of the fool-hardy intruders. Swiftly, the harsh clatter and clang of close-quarter swordplay filled the great workshop, punctuated by the death cries of the mortally wounded. This brought a wolfish grin to the dwar's lips. The assassins were greatly outnumbered. He had utter confidence in their defeat.

Chapter 34

THWARTED

UP AND up we charged, unchallenged, Vad Varo and Kar Komak hard at my heels, our accoutrements clanking and slapping against our leather harnesses.

"Where are the other defenders?" wondered Vad Varo.

I had been asking myself the same question with each turn of the winding basalt stairway. Periodically, we passed barred doors, and my gaze went to them, half expecting one to fly open and soldiers burst out. But such an ambush failed to happen.

This did not make us any less wary of the possibility.

I imagined that we were fully three-quarters of the way to the crater when below us a door did burst open, and out flooded a rush of movement.

I turned and saw that the door was disgorging angry defenders wielding short-swords. I called to the others, "Hold! Turn and meet the foe."

But just as Vad Varo and Kar Komak halted in their climb, another door, one higher above, was thrown open, and another squad leapt into view, blocking our way.

We were caught between two groups of foemen!

Our enemies converged on us, and we took up positions, standing back to back, prepared to sell our lives dearly. But even more determined not to surrender them to the shouting soldiers of Nulthoom.

As we stood our ground, perched atop basalt steps upon which only I was comfortable fighting, I saw to my right that Kar Komak was lowering his great bow.

He closed his eyes, and over his handsome face came an expression of deep concentration. I was at first puzzled by the lowering of the bow, but when I saw my comrade fall into a kind of trance, I was not surprised by what next transpired.

Above and below came into existence two groups of robed Lotharian bowmen. They snapped into reality with a suddenness that was startling. Even though I half expected it, this multiple materialization momentarily took my breath away.

The soldiers swarming above us loosed their arrows, and our raised swords flashed, intercepting and knocking aside those that did not miss entirely.

Simultaneously, the phantom archers created by Kar Komak's powerful mind unleashed their own shafts, and our enemies fell almost as one. Many went tumbling down the unforgiving stone steps.

It was all over in three breaths, possibly less. But when I looked about me, I saw that Kar Komak had dropped his own bow and was holding the side of his head, which was bleeding.

At once I saw what had happened. With his eyes closed, he was unable to defend himself and a speeding shaft had grazed his scalp. I examined the wound. It was superficial.

"It is nothing," I said.

Nodding, Kar Komak looked about and saw that his bowmen had vanished. He looked puzzled.

"I did not dematerialize them," he muttered, picking up his fallen bow.

"No doubt the sudden wound broke your concentration," I said. "It doesn't matter now. The enemy has been vanquished. We will continue our ascent."

We ignored the wounded soldiers below us and charged up again, taking care to finish off any of the foe who had not already succumbed to the arrows of the phantom archers who, being not mortal men, had been unerring in their marksmanship.

The way was now clear, and we continued mounting seemingly endless steps carved into the interior wall of the dormant volcano.

ONCE WE gained the top level, Vad Varo, Kar Komak, and I found ourselves in a radium-lit corridor at the far end of which we could hear the ringing clangor of clashing swords.

We could not imagine what it portended, but where there was combat, I knew that was where we belonged.

"You must be prepared for anything," I told my comrades-in-arms.

"Lead the way, John Carter," Vad Varo exclaimed.

We raced along, finally coming to an open set of double doors. Within, I beheld a gleaming teardrop-shaped craft, much larger than I imagined it to be, but constructed along lines of the ship designed by Fal Sivas years previous, on which I ventured to Thuria, the nearer moon.

It rested in a cradle-like scaffolding. At the blunt head gaped a matched pair of huge crystal eyes, giving it the appearance of a stupendous steel insect. I swiftly recalled that these lenses were the interplanetary craft's "eyes," which were attached to the mechanical brain set immediately behind them in the control cabin. These false portholes enabled the spherical brain to "see" and navigate in response to telepathic commands received from the pilot.

A majestic woman with hair the hue of platinum stood before the ship. I knew this must be the Jeddara of Nulthoom. She took notice of us, and her face convulsed in anger without losing its mature beauty.

Pointing to us standing at the threshold, she commanded a group of men who were fighting amongst themselves to redirect their wrath upon us.

"Defend your jedara!" she cried out. "Repel all intruders!"

This they did with an alacrity that was so swift that it was breathtaking. Breaking off, they disengaged from one another, turned as one force, and from their throats came a resounding battle cry that bespoke of their deeply ingrained military discipline.

They rushed us, and we advanced to meet their charge.

With my greater strength, I disarmed the first two men who dared to attempt to penetrate my guard. At my side and only slightly to the rear, Vad Varo, a capable but not superlative swordsman, took on two others.

From the doorway, where he had room to employ his bow, Kar Komak commenced unleashing his arrows with impunity. They rarely missed their targets.

And so the battle was joined, we three against overpowering numbers.

Vad Varo and I smashed our way in. But—although we made a good account of ourselves—the numbers were not in our favor. These defenders of Nulthoom were consumed with some powerful emotion. Loyalty to their jeddara, no doubt. They would not yield to our blades.

Slowly but inexorably, we were forced back out into the corridor. And there we made our stand.

I turned to Kar Komak, who had retreated with us. "How many arrows remain?"

"Five, John Carter."

"Use them well then."

Grinning fiercely, Kar Komak took up a kneeling position at one side of a yawning door, a shaft fixed in his bowstring.

The first Orovar to step out was transfixed by that very shaft. It entered his jugular and stopped, its fletched end sticking out. The man quivered after he fell, his life's blood gushing out without cease.

Two more defenders jumped out after him, undeterred. When one spied the Lotharian hastily drawing another arrow from his pouch, he swept in, bringing his blade slicing down.

The sword's keen edge bisected the bow and would have taken Kar Komak's left hand off at the wrist, but his reflexes saved him, even if they did not preserve his weapon.

Coming to his feet, the Lotharian drew his hatchet, the sight of which brought a derisive laugh from the lips of the swordsman, who advanced with the clear intention of disarming Kar Komak by removing the hand that wielded the hatchet.

Vad Varo and I swiftly came to his defense, our blades striking as one, mine piercing the man's vitals, while Vad Varo's sword sliced his sword arm off at the shoulder. He fell, cursing his fate.

Thus distracted, we spun about, only to discover that the corridor was filling with Orovar foemen.

What next would have happened, I do not know. I do not care to contemplate it. These Orovars were able swordsmen, individually. Taken one at a time, I conceivably could have bested the cream of them. And no doubt Vad Varo would have more than stood his own ground. But these men of ancient Mars were bereft of honor. They did not care to take us on one at a time. In a human wave thorned with steel, they swarmed us.

And so we found ourselves hard pressed. Especially Kar Komak, who had only his long-hafted hatchet.

I dispatched two before Vad Varo could engage one foe. But his conquest fell on the heels of the pair I vanquished. Their open wounds made the cold stone floor of the passage slippery with gore, which in turn complicated our defense. Again, forced back in the face of overwhelming numbers, we took up a fresh line of defense, and attempted to hold it.

My heart sank when I heard a sudden grunt coming from Vad Varo. Keeping my guard up, I stole a glance and saw that his sword arm had been laid open by an Orovar blade. He shifted the hilt to his other hand, but in that brief but perilous interval, his foe lunged, striving to strike his groin.

Kar Komak plunged in, burying his hatchet into the man's helmeted head. When he withdrew the blade, it was crimson.

With his free hand, the Lotharian relieved the faltering foeman of his sword.

Now we three were all properly armed. But still overmatched. Matters looked increasingly bleak. But we were prepared to sell our lives as dearly as possible.

Half under my breath, I asked, "Kar Komak, can you summon up reinforcements?"

"I regret to say that I cannot, John Carter."

"How do you know unless you try?" I shot back.

"I have been trying since we gained this level," he answered dispiritedly. "But to no avail. My head wound has stunned my senses. I cannot concentrate, except to defend myself."

"Under the circumstances," I replied. "I can ask for no more."

Our prospects appeared as bleak as the steppeland to which we had come. But I knew that I was in no finer company in which to make a final stand in life.

Once more, we took up defensive positions, standing back to back, our weapons poised to deal merciless death.

SUCCOR CAME in the form of Tarzan of the Apes and Tars Tarkas, who appeared suddenly in the corridor behind us, and swiftly took our part.

Turning to Tarzan, I saluted him with my sword, saying, "Once again, my friend, you prove yourself to be the personification of the element of surprise. But in this instance, you are also exceedingly welcome."

"I see that you are outnumbered," he stated firmly. "But no longer."

I laughed at the bronzed giant's unshakable confidence in his physical prowess. For it reminded me of my own.

Now we were five, standing in a human wall, facing a larger mass of warriors.

Once more, steel met steel, and the din of close-quarter battle filled the corridor.

Here, the powerful blades of the new arrivals turned the tide. Tarzan savagely smashed his way into the thick of them, disarming enemies with the flat of the blade and then disdaining to finish them. These hapless ones he left to Vad Varo, Kar Komak, and I.

I do not know whether these hermit Orovar soldiers had ever laid eyes upon a green nomad before. But from the looks upon their faces, the sight of the towering four-armed Thark was a terrifying one.

With a sword in each upper arm and a stabbing dagger in one lower fist, Tars Tarkas fell among them, and the carnage he inflicted was unstoppable.

Steadily, inexorably, we forced the survivors back into the spacecraft workshop, stepping over the dead and groaning wounded alike in order to do so.

The jeddara, seeing the tide turning against her cohort, cried out, "Those still sound of limb, retreat! Come aboard. We leave for Jasoom at once!"

Some of the less scrupulous soldiers took advantage of this command and pushed their compatriots into our blades in order to block any effort to interdict their own escape.

Several men rushed for the open hatch, and most of them threw themselves in. Before we could reach it, the hatch sealed shut, locking some bewailing Orovar warriors out. Their cries were pitiful. The damned could not have sounded more lost.

We made short work of them. For once they realized that their beloved jeddara had abandoned them, they lost hearts, and were easily overcome.

I knew, based on past experience, that the wonder-ships of Fal Sivas were controlled by a mechanical brain. All that was necessary to send them aloft was the proper mental message.

I assumed that Fal Sivas was on board. But I did not ever see him.

Before we could reach the craft, it silently lifted upward off its cradle, cocked its crystal eyes skyward, and began ascending. This process was initially a slow one, for the ship was not propelled by rocket motors, but flew thanks to an anti-gravity principle I did not understand. This delay allowed Tarzan of the Apes and I to reach the hull after repelling the last stubborn defenders.

In rising, the ship quickly cleared the crater rim, Tarzan and I clinging to various vents, cleats, and flanges along its gleaming hull. Had it not been for my precarious position and the rush of air threatening to tear me from my perch, I might have endeavored to capture one of the metal projections with a steel ring or grappling hook hanging from my harness, but I dared not release either grip.

I did not see that I could accomplish much, so I shouted to Tarzan beside me, "I cannot long hold on! Can you reach the hatch?"

Tarzan did not reply. Using his greater strength and agility, he commenced climbing upward along the ship's surface, which was marked with narrow apertures intended to permit access when the craft stood upright on its flat, angular legs. I knew that his animal strength was far greater than mine. If there was any hope in inhibiting the ship's escape from the Barsoomian atmosphere, it lay with this Earth-man who rightfully boasted the muscular strength equal to that of the great white apes of Barsoom.

Higher and higher rose the ship, and when I looked down, I saw that if I did not swiftly release my grip, I would fall from an altitude too high to land safely upon the ground.

Thus I was forced to let go, trusting that my leg muscles would cushion my fall, for I was falling from a height no greater than I could successfully leap of my own volition.

As I tumbled downward, I threw my gaze upward and saw the sun-bronzed form of Tarzan of the Apes, working his way up the interplanetary ship's gleaming side with a stupendous strength and fierce-faced determination that I could only envy....

Chapter 35

THE FALL OF TARZAN

H IS APT-FUR cloak whipping wildly, Tarzan of the Apes used the steely strength in his fingers to climb higher and higher as the interplanetary ship rose with increasing speed toward the upper atmosphere of Barsoom. He did not pay attention to the ground below. His entire attention was on the hatch door, which he intended to tear open and thus disable the escaping craft.

But when at last he reached the hatch, the bronzed giant found that there was no handle or catch that he could take hold of. Clinging to an indented notch with one powerful hand, he used his other fist to smash at the door, and although it dented slightly, he could not dislodge it.

By now, the air was growing thin.

Tarzan was forced to look down, and he could see that he had ridden the rising craft higher than he had anticipated.

Certain destruction awaited him if he fell now. But an equally certain death would result should the ape-man cling to the fast-traveling ship any longer.

With a fatalistic expression on his features, he let go, then began tumbling downward.

Tarzan did not fear death. Death was an ever-present companion in the African jungle. It was no different on Mars. He understood that when he revisited this planet, it entailed the risk that he might not return to Africa alive.

So as he fell, his snowy cloak flapping and snapping from his sun-bronzed shoulders. No twinge of fear crossed his features. The only outward evidence of his inner turmoil could be seen on his brow. The old battle scar he had collected in his youth now flamed to life again. It was the scar that had inspired his original Martian name when he had first arrived on Barsoom. Ramdar, which meant Red Scar.

The bronzed giant's eyes went to the open crater. Between the raised half-moon shields that had formerly been the circular coal bed, he could see into the topmost chamber where Tars Tarkas towered over Vad Varo and Kar Komak. Heads thrown back, their faces upturned, they watched in anticipation and no little trepidation. At some distance from the volcano, John Carter stood upon a snow-covered upthrust of volcanic rock where he had landed, also staring upward.

All three men were helpless, as was the *Dejah Thoris,* which floated in the near distance and out of useful range. For they could see clearly, as could Tarzan, that the giant Jasoomian was falling unerringly toward the great flaming scar that was the burning coal seam that creased the tundra to the east of Mount Nulthoom.

The smoldering ground rose up to meet Tarzan of the Apes. It seemed that nothing could save him. He closed his eyes as if to prepare for his inevitable, fiery end.

Then, out from the far side of Mount Nulthoom, a solitary malagor swept up and about on majestic metallic wings, then fell to beating madly in his direction.

Tarzan's expression relaxed at the sight. For the elaborate saddle was empty. No warrior was coursing up to dispatch him. This particular malagor was responding to the thought-commands Tarzan was transmitting to it. He smiled at the memory that he had interrupted Tars Tarkas in the act of dismembering the last specimen of these mechanical steeds.

When the malagor achieved the altitude desired, it swept in so that Tarzan could reach out with both mighty arms to capture its elongated neck. He was successful, and so was carried along by the coursing machine. It was a challenge to maintain control over the mechanical brain while simultaneously clinging to its neck as he strove to hook his right leg over the saddle. But at last, he accomplished this.

After that, it was just a matter of positioning his body so that the ape-man could ride the metal bird back to the open crater mouth.

At the last moment, he changed course to collect John Carter, who smiled when he alighted.

"I had believed you to be lost forever, Tarzan of the Apes."

There was no joy in Tarzan's face. He said only, "We have failed in our objective."

"I will not argue the point. We strove our utmost, but it wasn't sufficient. Let us rejoin the others."

After John Carter settled behind him, Tarzan commanded the malagor to leap back into the air. It beat its wings skyward, topping Mount Nulthoom as the ape-man directed the bird-scout's mechanical brain to drop them down into the open crater.

But the machine refused to obey.

"It will not go where I tell it to," Tarzan called back to John Carter.

"Fal Sivas may have installed mental blocks in its brain," suggested the Warlord. "Perhaps to prevent it from landing amid the crater fires and destroying itself inadvertently."

Tarzan nodded. "I will tell it to take us back to its hangar."

The malagor redirected its sweeping flight, and soon it swooped through the ragged diamond-like curtain and settled on its extended talons at the place from which it had launched itself.

Tarzan and John Carter dismounted, drew their blades in anticipation of battle, and rushed for the interior stairs. They started up, making for the open crater, only to encounter Tars Tarkas, Kar Komak, and Vad Varo, who were coming down.

"We have slain the wounded," announced the mighty Thark.

"Was it necessary?" John Carter asked.

"They begged to be dispatched. They told us that without their jeddara, they had nothing left to live for. The only women dwelling in this place are slaves, and forbidden to them."

"There may be other survivors," said John Carter. "We will seek them out."

But the only survivors the quartet found were slave women, who huddled in their common chambers on a lower level. They had been locked in. But Tarzan shattered the lock with one blow of his Orovar sword.

These milky-skinned blonde women fell to their knees, begging for their lives.

John Carter told them, "We have no quarrel with you. But your men have all departed. We will provide you safe passage to Helium, for you cannot live here any longer."

The women were only too happy to accept this, although they showed every sign of being anxious as to their ultimate fate.

Tarzan and John Carter reconnoitered the entire hollow mountain, and discovered that there were no other survivors. Nor were there any children to be found.

"The entirety of the surviving male population of Nulthoom is hurtling toward the Earth," John Carter exclaimed.

Going from level to level and chamber to chamber, they discovered that Nulthoom was essentially a self-contained city in miniature. They grew their own food and slaughtered their own animals. For water, they used snowmelt piped in during the warm weather months, storing it in two reservoirs, on upper and lower levels for the convenience of transport.

That the Orovars of Nulthoom were scavengers was self-evident when they discovered many storerooms containing items pilfered from the outer world.

Vad Varo remarked, "It is amazing that they were able to steal so much, entirely unsuspected."

John Carter replied, "They did this over many generations, knowing that no one would question the fate of any merchant flier that had gone down in the endless tundra, and that a search would be futile in the little-explored vastness of this steppe."

After exhausting their search, they retreated to the workshop hangar with its heaped dead Orovar soldiers arrayed around the now-empty scaffolding cradle. None moved.

Leaping upward so that he landed on the flagstoned prome-nade rimming the open crater, John Carter took up a position so that he was visible in the space between the great lifted shields. With a raised sword that gleamed with fresh gore, he signaled the *Dejah Thoris* to approach, heave to, and take them aboard. Then he dropped back into the hangar workshop.

"It appears that Fal Sivas is also on his way to Earth," John Carter declared.

Tarzan put up a hand, signaling for silence. His nostrils were distended.

Without warning, he moved toward a corner of the work-shop where was piled numerous pieces of assorted equipment. Reaching into this, he took hold of something, and the sound of a man squawking in surprise resounded.

Out from the assemblage of equipment was dragged Fal Sivas, the scientist.

Lifting the captive by his harness, Tarzan marched him over to John Carter and set the scientist down on his feet. Fal Sivas was trembling in fear.

John Carter stared at the quivering wretch. "Fal Sivas, we had thought you had departed for Jasoom."

"That is what the jeddara thought as well. She commanded me to board the ship. But I fooled her. I had built a secret escape hatch in the rear. Before the *Jasoom* launched itself, I slipped out, unsuspected."

"Who is piloting the ship then?"

"The mechanical brain I devised. It is an improved version. Once I gave it the mental command to depart for Jasoom, I locked the controls so that no other brain could interfere with it. So powerful is its anti-gravity engine, that it will reach Jasoom in approximately one teean. Nothing can cause it to swerve from its course."

Tarzan said, "In that case, I must return to Earth to meet them."

John Carter replied, "Of course. But first, you will be my honored guest in Helium, before you must leave us."

Tarzan did not acknowledge the invitation. "What is to be done with this man?"

"Fal Sivas is guilty of grave crimes. He will come with us, and a just punishment will be meted out."

The scientist did not look as abashed as he otherwise might have been.

"I would rather face punishment in Helium than be a slave of the Jeddara O-Thuria on Jasoom," he stated. "I would not call her entirely mad. But she has convinced her warriors that she and only she is the only worthy woman with whom they could mate. They are constantly challenging one another to duels for the right to be the next fertilizer of her womb. It is perpetual madness."

"Well," said John Carter, "it is a madness that has been transferred to Jasoom. Come, let us gather up the slave women and we will be on our way."

The *Dejah Thoris* warped alongside the crater rim, and climbing ropes and ladders were dropped.

The frightened but compliant Orovar slave women were assisted to the main deck and shown to quarters. Tarzan, John Carter, and the others climbed aboard, then the Warlord of Mars gave instructions to set a course for the Twin Cities of Helium.

"What of the Mole?" asked Vad Varo. "Considerable time and expense went into its construction."

John Carter said, "No doubt Tarzan of the Apes is anxious to return to Africa. We will salvage it another time. It has served us well. Perhaps it will become useful again in the future. For now, there is no one left to disturb it."

Before long, the *Dejah Thoris* turned south and beat her way toward the equator, her colors unfurled and flapping in the thin, cold air.

Behind them, Mount Nulthoom loomed, an empty monument to a lost people, its icy mantle cracked and broken, revealing its dead black walls of basalt. Only the great jagged coal seam still burned, a perpetual flame marking what had been a last survival of the long-dry Throxeus sea floor.

Chapter 36

FAREWELL TO BARSOOM

D URING OUR journey, I held conference with Tarzan of the Apes.

"According to Fal Sivas, the jeddara travels with the entourage of only twenty warriors. Far fewer than she planned on, owing to the necessity of bringing all of her eggs with her. I possess the ability to transfer myself to Earth. I am prepared to go with you to meet the *Jasoom* when it lands. Of course, there is no necessity of my doing so for another month. And I am certain that you do not care to tarry on Barsoom any longer than necessary."

Tarzan nodded in assent. "It will be good to be home again. I do not think I will need your help, but I am grateful for the offer."

"Nevertheless, I would like to know how the matter is resolved. If you are able to, perhaps you can have Jason Gridley convey the outcome to us via Gridley Wave."

"If I am able to do so, I will," said Tarzan with the simplicity that made his word his ironclad bond.

I left him to his thoughts, for I could see that he craved solitude.

HELIUM LAY south-southwest of Mount Nulthoom. Half a day passed until we transited the equator.

As we neared Helium, I went in search of Tarzan and found him interrogating Fal Sivas, who had been consigned to the brig.

"There you are," I declared. "I thought you had gone over-board to hunt a thoat. You seem to have acquired quite a taste for thoat meat during your time here."

"I have learned all I need from this man," Tarzan said, turn-ing to me. "It is time that I return home."

"Please do not be in such a hurry," I implored. "All of Helium is awaiting us. There will be a banquet in your honor. Surely you can stay a few days longer as my honored guest."

Tarzan shook his head firmly.

"I am grateful to you for your help, but I have dwelt on Barsoom longer than I cared to. I am ready to depart."

I could see that this man's mind was made up. I did not attempt to change it. I could see that it would be of no use.

"Do you believe you can effectuate the transition without assistance?" I asked.

"I do not know," replied Tarzan frankly.

"I'm sure Kar Komak will be willing to assist you, as he did before."

"Let us not delay in finding him," returned Tarzan.

We found Kar Komak in his quarters and explained the situ-ation to him. The Lotharian was only too willing to oblige.

"I would be pleased to assist my friend Tarzan to return to his rightful home," he said graciously.

"Very well then," said I. "If you wish privacy, you may use the wardroom."

"Thank you," stated Tarzan. And there was a moment of confusion when I put my hand upon his bronzed shoulder in the Barsoomian way and he reached out to shake my hand in the manner of men of Earth.

We laughed and did both.

"Here on my adopted world," I said gravely, "I have risen to the exalted rank of Warlord of Barsoom. I wish you to know that I consider Tarzan of the Apes to be my equal, the unac-knowledged Warlord of Jasoom."

Tarzan nodded in acknowledgement of my compliment. "You will always have a friend in me," he said. What his inner thoughts were, I could not tell. His gray eyes were unreadable. It felt to me that his mind was already focused upon Africa.

I escorted Tarzan and Kar Komak to the wardroom, and the door closed behind them.

I waited outside some ten xats. When the door again opened, Kar Komak emerged alone. He held the ape-skin harness and blue-bladed Orovar sword, whose scabbard was buckled to it.

"He is gone, my Warlord."

I nodded. "I wonder if we will ever see him again?"

"It is my impression," stated the Lotharian solemnly, "that if *Tarzan-of-the-apes* has any say in the matter, we will not."

"Well, it was interesting to see him again. While the trouble he brought to us did not directly concern Helium, it resulted in the capture of Fal Sivas. This was important by itself."

"What will be done with the scoundrel?"

"Fal Sivas is the only man alive who understands the theory and methods of devising an anti-gravity craft capable of conveying explorers beyond Barsoom's atmosphere. I do not know whether that is a good thing or not. But this knowledge should not perish with him. Fal Sivas will probably be spared and his secrets extracted, willingly or not. After that, who can foretell what will become of his scientific wisdom? I do not think it practical for the people of Barsoom to escape this dying world by going to Earth. Our cultures would not mix. Earth's scientific advances are fast exceeding our own. Perhaps, if Barsoom's atmosphere should entirely fail, another habitable world just as suitable as the Earth might be located. If so, the interplanetary ships of Fal Sivas will take the survivors to that as-yet-undiscovered planet."

"That is a good plan," agreed Kar Komak.

Together, we went out to the deck, there to join Tars Tarkas and Vad Varo, where we discussed the question at great length. We did not resolve it, for it did not require immediate resolution.

Zodes later, the scarlet and yellow towers of Greater and Lesser Helium showed ahead.

I gave the order to Kantos Kan. "Prepare to land."

The majestic *Dejah Thoris* settled into her elaborate berth, and, trailed by her crew, we four strode up to the moss-covered Avenue of Ancestors to the roaring acclaim of the citizenry.

My wife, the incomparable Dejah Thoris, Princess of Helium, was waiting for us at the Temple of Reward. I could imagine no more beautiful mate in all the universe. It was good to be home again. For Helium is my true home.

I thought back to Tarzan of the Apes and regretted that he chose not to join us. I further hoped that he was feeling the identical emotions that filled my breast, a mixture of pride and satisfaction.

I firmly believe that, of all of us, he deserved it most.

Chapter 37

SECOND HOMECOMING

AS HE had many years before, and under similar circumstances, Jad-bal-ja the golden lion stood sentinel over the temporary resting place of his master, Tarzan of the Apes, Lord of the Jungle.

Weeks went by. The blazing African sun rose and set in silence. In between, the afternoon rains came. Even during the most torrential of downpours, the loyal lion patiently waited, stretched out like a living sphinx, his only concession to the inconvenience of daily precipitation the fact that he withdrew to the shelter of a shady sumac tree.

How much Jad-bal-ja understood could never be known. During the previous ordeal, he had dug a man-sized trench and carefully buried Tarzan in the dirt, protecting his still-warm body from jungle predators. He had refused to leave the grave until the day the ape-man unexpectedly came back to life and with his powerful arms broke through the clay that covered him.

Here and now, his master had been sealed in a small chamber, into which he had gone willingly. Jad-bal-ja did not display outward signs of mourning. Only one who knew him well could tell that his feline spirits were depressed. It was noticed that he slept more often than usual.

Jad-bal-ja was fed daily by his mistress, Lady Jane, and sometimes by Korak. Occasionally, he vanished into the woods to hunt for himself. But always he returned to his master's resting place.

Night came again, and Jad-bal-ja lay his head between his mighty paws and slept, his ever-alert ears lifted in anticipation of what even he did not know.

JUST BEFORE dawn, something stirred within the raised vault of teak, and this faint sound reached Jad-bal-ja's tufted ears. His green eyes snapped awake with the immediacy of a jungle carnivore who instinctively understood that he who was slowest to react was quickest to die.

The stirring caused the golden lion to rise up on all four paws and lift his wrinkling snout to sniff the cool night air.

Did some familiar scent reach his widening nostrils? Or was it the sound of movement within the box containing his master's body that caused him to rear up and pad forward, slowly at first, but with increasing alacrity?

There came a stirring, followed by the snap of a bolt being drawn, and out from the chamber emerged Tarzan of the Apes, attired only in a loincloth of antelope skin.

The ape-man stepped onto the ground. Moonlight and starlight painted his magnificent bronze figure, etching his muscles into sharp relief. His head turned and eyes fell upon the familiar golden coat as, with a friendly growl, Jad-bal-ja leaped to his side.

Tarzan had to brace himself to keep from being bowled over by the tremendous weight of his ever-faithful lion.

"I see that you have been keeping watch, Jad-bal-ja," greeted Tarzan. Then he stopped and sniffed the air. The familiar smells of the African jungle stirred his senses. It was good to smell the myriad odors of a planet that was still teeming with life.

Jad-bal-ja stepped back, lifted his head, and gave out a tremendous roar of welcome.

This roused everyone on the estate. Lady Jane, son Jack, Jack's wife Meriem, and others came rushing out to hear what the commotion was about.

"John!" Lady Jane cried. "You have returned at last!"

They rushed into each other's arms and embraced warmly.

Smiling with relief, Jack said, "We received a letter from Jason Gridley in America only last month, but nothing since. You have succeeded in your mission, I hope."

Tarzan smiled in return, but then the smile hardened.

"I have half succeeded. Another Orovar company is coming. It will not arrive for one month. We must make ready to meet it."

Old Muviro came up at that point and, hearing these words, said joyfully, "If we have four weeks to prepare, then we have two days to hold another feast in honor of your return, B'wana."

"I have not eaten the sweet fruit of the Earth in many weeks, Muviro. I give you permission to undertake preparations for a feast. And while you do so, I will hunt meat for the celebration."

Lady Jane complained, "John, but you have only just returned."

"And my body has been lying inert and unused since you saw me last. It is my wish to plunge into the jungle that I love so well and become a hunter of meat once more. On Mars, I was a warrior. And I have spent the last few years being a soldier of the Crown. Now I want to be myself. And I wish to remain Tarzan of the Apes until the day this body is laid to rest in earnest."

Jane laughed good-naturedly. "In that case, I understand. I won't stop you. But hurry back. I want to hear all about your adventures on Mars."

"I would just as soon forget them," said Tarzan frankly. "But while we feast, I will speak of it. After that, it is best forgotten."

With that, the ape-man felt for the hunting knife at his hip, found that it rested firmly in its sheath, and turned away to disappear into the jungle while it was yet dark. Jad-bal-ja followed on his naked heels, and little Nkima—who had been slow to awaken from his roost on a high tree—chattering excitedly as he tried to keep up.

The others returned to the bungalow, where Lady Jane blew out the olive-oil lantern that had been burning a steady vigil since the strange departure of her mate, but which was now no longer needed.

AN HOUR later, the victory cry of the great bull apes resounded, blending with the savage yet familiar roar of a lion, and everyone in the Greystoke estate knew that Tarzan had made the first kill of his return to Africa.

They would feast well that day....

Chapter 38

SHIPWRECK

THREE WEEKS passed, during which the family of John Clayton, Lord Greystoke, gradually returned to the routine of life on the estate.

Tarzan was pleasantly surprised to discover his P-40B Tomahawk warplane parked at one end of the dirt airstrip, its fixed shark grin undiminished.

"In your absence," explained Jack, "we carried fuel north, and I was able to get her off the grass. But it was a difficult undertaking."

"The aircraft may come in handy in the future," agreed Tarzan.

Periodically, Tarzan would disappear into the forest to hunt and bring back game. He often spent more time doing this than was necessary, but his family understood that after the rigors of so many weeks on the desiccated red planet, the lush green rainforest in which he was reared was like a tonic to the jungle lord's soul.

After he had recounted his adventures on Barsoom, Tarzan began laying plans to intercept the Martian interplanetary craft that was even now hurtling through the trackless void toward Africa.

Holding council with old Muviro and Korak, Tarzan explained, "Even with a reduced complement of warriors, these Orovars must not be underestimated. We cannot know the exact hour of their arrival. Even the day is not certain. So we will march on Victoria Lake in advance, to prepare an ambush."

237

Muviro asked, "Do we take prisoners?"

Tarzan considered that question thoughtfully. "It is not my desire to kill unnecessarily, but these people do not belong on this planet. If they could be persuaded to turn around and return to their own world, it will not be necessary to slay them."

Korak asked, "Do you really think they can be talked into going back to Mars after journeying all this way?"

Tarzan shook his head firmly. "No, I do not believe so. But if they will listen, we can try to reason with them."

"And if they won't listen to reason?"

"Then we fight. And the outcome will be what it will be."

"Will you not scout with the Tomahawk first?"

Tarzan had already considered this point. "If fuel was unlimited, yes. Under the circumstances, I do not care to risk the airplane in a matter best settled on the ground. The *Kala* will be available if an emergency warrants its use."

So they set out, Tarzan, Korak, and Muviro on horseback, with a force of Waziri spearmen and bowmen following on foot.

For days, they marched for Lake Victoria and when they reached its muddy shore, they made camp near the deserted huts that had been erected with metal sections of the first space ship from Mars.

On the first night, sitting around the campfire, Jack asked, "They could land anywhere along the lake shore for hundreds of miles in either direction."

Tarzan nodded. "This is where they landed before. This is where we will wait for them."

And that was that. The matter was settled.

WHEN THE *Jasoom* arrived, it made no sound. Not in passing through the atmosphere, nor in landing. No one in the scouting party heard the sound of its passing or witnessed it land. This took place in the middle of the night, further defeating discovery.

After several days, by Tarzan's reckoning four days after the Martian vehicle should have arrived upon the Earth, he made a decision.

Speaking with Korak, he said, "We form two search parties. One will go north and the other south."

"Good hunting, Father," said Jack.

Tarzan gave the order to Muviro to divide his Waziri into four groups, consisting of two squads of bowmen and two spearmen. "Half of each will come with me, and the others will go with Korak the Killer."

Without waiting for the headman to relay his instructions, the jungle lord took to the trees and struck north.

Knowing that the Waziri would stick to the shore, Tarzan used his ability to move freely through the treetops to achieve a superior vantage point.

For half a day, the ape-man ranged north, pausing to allow the Waziri warriors to catch up, and in order to share in the hunt for food.

The metallic scent of blood reached Tarzan's sensitive nostrils in mid-afternoon of the second day of the search. Now the ape-man knew the smell of blood well. The blood of a giraffe and the blood of the antelope smelled quite unalike one another. And both smell different than that of European men or African natives.

What Tarzan scented was the spoor of men, but not of the black or white race. This was Martian blood. He was certain of it.

Dropping from the treetops, he found his Waziri contingent, which was led by the trusted warrior named Warinji.

"The ones we seek are not far from this place," Tarzan told Warinji. "Their blood has been spilled. I will go ahead. Advance with caution. Retreat if you are not commanded by me to do otherwise."

Warinji nodded. "Of course, B'wana. But we are not afraid. We will not retreat."

"Do not rush into danger unless you know what the danger is and are prepared to meet it with equal or superior force," warned the ape-man.

With that admonition, Tarzan of the Apes returned to the trees.

He moved unerringly through the upper terraces, racing from crown to crown and along the interlacing boughs, often swinging from one tree to another wherever the space was too great to otherwise clear by one of the prodigious ape-like leaps for which he was renowned.

Tarzan found the great interplanetary ship from Mars lying on its gleaming belly in a freshly-created trench. It had landed roughly, gouging the ground for a short distance. Crouching in the top of a tree, he peered downward and saw that the main hatch stood open. And out of it wafted the bitter tang of Martian blood.

The ape-man did not know what to make of this, so he did not investigate immediately. Carefully, he sniffed the air, but no other smells reached his sensitive nostrils. The odor of blood was overpowering. It suggested that many men had died.

As he watched, something emerged from the open hatch.

It was a crocodile. The reptile was backing up. And fixed in its long jaws was the body of a white Martian. The man was dead. His corpse was ensanguined with gore.

The bull crocodile struggled to pull the limp corpse through the hatch, but when he at last succeeded, he dragged it to the shore and then disappeared into the water, there to enjoy his meal, no doubt.

Tarzan waited some time before he dropped out of the trees and then slipped over to the *Jasoom*.

With appropriate caution, he entered the commodious interior and found other bodies. They were covered in blood. The walls also were smeared with gore.

Going among these dead men, he discovered many had died of stab wounds. Some had been dead for some time. Others appeared to have been slain more recently.

In the hands of several were clenched the swords of the Orovar race in tight death grips.

It became evident to the jungle lord that many of these men had slain one another. Had there been a mutiny? It would seem so.

Investigating further, he went to a rear compartment of the ship and found the incubators holding the eggs of O-Thuria racked neatly on either side of the hull. A few had been damaged, but the rest were missing. Had the crew been forced to consume them during the long voyage? No broken shell fragments were visible. And many were the empty racks that previously had held incubators.

Tarzan frowned. These missing eggs represented the next generation of citizen-soldiers of Nulthoom. He would have to do something about locating them.

There was no sign of the imperious jeddara, O-Thuria. Tarzan counted the dead and was surprised the number was more than fifteen. With the one taken by the crocodile, that accounted for nearly every passenger except the jeddara and two others.

Exiting the machine, the ape-man went in search of them.

Chapter 39

FINALE

TARZAN TRACKED his quarry along the forest trails that led to the verge of Lake Victoria. His jungle skills told him that three persons had traveled down to the water's edge, often heavily laden. One pair of sandaled footprints suggested a woman bearing only her own weight. The other two were larger and sunk more deeply into the ground. The awkwardness of their tread proclaimed that they shared a heavy burden between them.

These signs alone told a story. Warriors had carried an unknown number of surviving incubators away from the wreckage of the ship. From the overlapping tracks, the ape-man could discern that they had made several trips. This explained the missing incubators and eggs.

Tarzan knew that it was the way of Barsoom for certain tribes to place their eggs in locations where they would receive abundant sunshine, but also be sheltered from the elements. The elements of Barsoom and those of the Earth were quite different, of course. Rain on Mars was not plentiful. Storms tended to be more akin to dust storms than tornados.

As he approached the water, which was sheltered by a fringe of palm trees, the ape-man could hear voices.

O-Thuria the jeddara was speaking.

"You men have done well. Now we must guard my eggs against the beasts that swim in the water and any others that walk by land."

"Very well," relied one man. "We will do this. And after these eggs hatch, you will have to make your choice between us."

This was the gravelly voice of Tun-Dun-Lo, the dwar of the jeddara's personal guard. Tarzan of the Apes recognized it.

Another male voice lifted, saying, "The eggs will not hatch for many weeks. We should settle this now."

"No," returned O-Thuria. "Not now. I will not abide in the strange new world with only one male companion. Perhaps instead of choosing between you, I will direct that both suitors share my company."

Tun-Dun-Lo objected. "This is not the custom. The Jeddara of Nulthoom is permitted one lover at a time."

"We are no longer in Nulthoom, but on Jasoom. I hereby decree a new custom, one necessary in order that we Orovar populate this world of water and plenty."

The other man growled, "I object. I do not care to share your favors with any other man."

"The subject is closed," proclaimed the jeddara imperiously. "We will revisit it once the eggs hatch."

By this time, Tarzan surreptitiously had climbed the bole of one of the palm trees, to hang unseen and unsuspected beneath the shelter of its leafy fronds. He was looking down upon the tableau below.

O-Thuria, Tun-Dun-Lo and another man stood facing one another. All wore the white-metal helmets and armor which assisted in counteracting Earth's powerful gravity. Over her panoply, the jeddara wore a regal silk cloak woven of some metallic material that matched her long, half-concealed tresses. Framed by the helmet, O-Thuria's features were severe and not feminine.

Along the muddy shoreline, numerous incubators had been placed. They were half buried in the mud so that only their glass domes poked into view. The hot sun beat down upon them, presumably hastening the day of their hatching.

As Tarzan watched, the taller of the two men stepped back from the woman and her guard, and his sword came sliding out of its scabbard. His muscles tensed in anticipation of battle.

"I challenge you, Tun-Dun-Lo, to a duel over the future ruler of Jor."

Tun-Dun-Lo hesitated. Tarzan could read upon his wide face the tension of a man torn between his duty to his ruler and his own ambitions.

"I do not care to fight you at this time, So-Dun-Jo," he said, but his hand went to the hilt of his sword.

"The time is not of your choosing, Tun-Dun-Lo," the other responded, lifting his blade so that the sun made it resemble a large thorn of molten metal.

"Stop!" the jeddara commanded. "I will not have this!"

But nothing she could say would sway the man who sought her favor. Taking a step forward, So-Dun-Jo advanced upon his burly rival.

Looking to his ruler, Tun-Dun-Lo said helplessly, "I have no choice in the matter, my jeddara. I cannot let him run me through without a fight."

Something leapt into the eyes of the woman. It was a kind of fire. Although she clearly detested the thought that her commandments were not being obeyed, the ape-man could see the prospect of a duel inflamed her passions.

"If I cannot stop you, therefore I withdraw my objections," she conceded, stepping back and letting them square off against one another.

"Prepare to die," said the challenger, as the other drew forth his blade.

These two did not waste time in preliminaries. They did not touch swords in salute or circle one another, looking for an opening. They simply charged and met in a clash of ringing blades that flashed in the African sun.

Sparks flew as the swords met, rebounded from one another, and crossed again. A harsh clanging rang out. These men hacked and chopped at one another with a ferocity that promised swift death and dismemberment to the loser.

They rarely broke contact. The blades smashed continually against one another as each soldier sought to wear down his opponent sufficiently to land a killing stroke.

The limbs of both duelists were encased in the ray-treated armor that enabled their limbs to operate unobstructed on Earth's gravity. These unconnected elements turned all but the most serious blows. Still, Tarzan could see that the heaviness of their arms prevented them from doing their best to defeat the other.

Birds roosting in nearby trees rose and fled amid the cacophony of ringing steel. Observing from his perch, Tarzan decided to let matters take their course.

The jeddara watched with the heat of her own passion flushing her pale face as she shouted encouragement without selecting a favorite.

"Fight on! Fight on! For only one of you will be the Cluros to my Thuria. Only one will enjoy the warmth of my arms and become the father to my next hatchling, blessed to fertilize as many eggs as needed to populate this world according to the old Orovar way."

If the duelists heard O-Thuria over the din of battle, they paid her words no heed. Circling and smashing, and clashing again, they battled on.

So-Dun-Jo the challenger appeared to be somewhat of a hothead. Relying simply on his brute strength and the power of his sword arm, he smashed again and again, but could not break through the other's guard.

Tun-Dun-Lo, however, showed deep knowledge of swordsmanship. While he smashed back with equal fierceness, he employed the dancing and darting point of his sword to loosen the other man's armor. He succeeded in prying loose with a quick swipe the armor guarding his opponent's free hand. That proved to be a handicap, for So-Dun-Jo's arm soon became heavy with unsupportable weight.

The dwar did this again and again until he found an opening that enabled him to knock pieces of armor off the other's sword arm. Over and over, that arm faltered as So-Dun-Jo could not easily wield his sword. That became clear when Tun-Dun-Lo brought his blade up over and around, removing the exposed sword arm itself at the joint of its armor.

After giving out a long groan of shock, So-Dun-Jo toppled forward, thereupon Tun-Dun-Lo drove the point of his blade into the back of the other's neck, in the opening between his helmet and back plate, severing the challenger's spine once and for all.

Removing the encrimsoned point, the victor turned and laid his sword at O-Thuria's feet. With bowed head, Tun-Dun-Lo addressed his silver-haired jeddara.

"I have achieved victory. I claim my right to be your consort."

The jeddara smiled. It was a smile of approval. Bending, she picked up the blade and returned it to him.

"You are no longer the first among my dwars, but my jedwar. Know, my loyal subject, that you will be my consort until the first males who have yet to hatch reach their maturity."

This seemed to strike Tun-Dun-Lo not in the way his ruler intended.

"I think not, my jeddara."

"No? What do you mean?"

"I think that we lack the numbers to establish more than a modest colony. I do not wish to share you with anyone else, now or in the future. I intend to go among the eggs and plunge my sword into those whose tint promises a male hatchling. The females we will nurture together. And when the time comes, I may claim one of them as your successor."

"What are you saying, Tun-Dun-Lo?" she shrieked. "I am your jeddara. I am the ruler of Nulthoom."

"We will co-rule New Nulthoom, but it will not be like the old one. I will be jeddak and you will be my jeddara. We will rule together, but I will be first among equals. Is that clear to you?"

"It is clear that you talk treachery!" O-Thuria flared.

"Treachery or not, I wield the red sword of victory. My word will henceforth be law."

Looking down, Tarzan could see the various expressions marching upon the woman's face, from rage to indignation, and finally to a kind of surly resignation.

Proud shoulders fell, and O-Thuria intoned only, "It will be as you say so long as you are able to say it."

"We are in agreement then?"

"I cannot balk your will. Therefore, I succumb to it. You are my jeddak and I am your jeddara. But the eggs must be allowed to hatch. All of them. Grant me this wish, and I will deny you nothing else."

Tun-Dun-Lo seemed to consider that at length. Finally, he said only, "We will let the eggs hatch and sort matters out then. I promise nothing beyond that."

"Then I am forced to accept your conditions."

Having heard all this, the ape-man decided to intervene.

Dropping out of the palm tree in which he had concealed himself, Tarzan landed in a dry spot and then showed himself.

Hearing the sound of his arrival, Tun-Dun-Lo whirled about, his gory blade releasing drops of blood in all directions.

"You!" he cried.

"Tarzan of the Apes welcomes you to his world."

The jeddara spoke up, demanding, "How did you get here, Jasoomian?"

Tarzan did not deign to reply. Instead, he declared, "You made a grave error coming to my world. Your eggs will not be permitted to hatch. They belong on Barsoom. You will load them back into the ship, and I will send you on your way."

"Never!" cried the jeddara. "Slay him, my jeddak."

"Gladly," said Tun-Dun-Lo, striding forward, his weapon lifting.

Tarzan's right hand went to the horn handle of his hunting knife and this he withdrew.

"You draw a sword against a foe wielding only a knife?" the ape-man asked. "That is not in accordance with Barsoomian custom."

A disdainful leer split Tun-Dun-Lo's broad features. "We are not upon Barsoom, but in Jor."

"No, you stand on Africa, where you will perish for your temerity."

"I will cut off your hand, and take your knife for my own," he retorted, stepping forward.

The ape-man permitted the Orovar to get within striking distance, and when he brought his blade up in both of his hands with the clear intention of cleaving his half-naked challenger as he had his last foe, Tarzan rushed him, knocked the blade aside with an ease that stunned the other, and drove his knife into the man's neck, breaking it.

Tun-Dun-Lo fell into the mud, gurgling his final words, which were not articulate. His eyes slowly closed to bitter slits.

Striding past him, Tarzan went to the woman and said tersely, "You and your eggs must return to Barsoom. I will hear no other argument."

Shock made the woman's face far paler than it was normally. Her sensuous lips moved, attempting to form words, but nothing came out initially.

Finally, she forced a smile that she thought was seductive, but was in fact a caricature of a smile.

"Perhaps I can persuade you otherwise, Jasoomian. I am presently in need of a consort. And you appear to be a superior specimen of this world. Would you consent to be my lover?"

"I have a mate," Tarzan replied simply.

"Am I not more beautiful than she?" she appealed. "When I was born, I was blessed with hair this silvery color. Its luster caused my parents to name me O-Thuria. There is no other hair like it on Barsoom. Perhaps not on Jasoom."

"I have no interest in your hair," said Tarzan with veiled contempt. He seized the woman by one arm and said, "I will take you to your ship."

"What about my precious eggs?"

"I will carry one for you, but only one. The rest must be buried where they cannot ever hatch."

Her blue eyes flared in indignation. "I forbid it!"

"You can forbid nothing on Earth. You are in Africa. I am Tarzan, lord of this forest. Here, my word is law."

O-Thuria seemed to shrink into herself, and there came the beginning of tears in her stricken eyes. She suppressed them by an effort of will.

Finally, she said, "Permit me to pick the best of my layings."

"I give you that permission," said Tarzan sternly. "But make haste. I do not care to suffer you to be on my world any longer than necessary."

After he released her arm, Tarzan watched as O-Thuria went among the incubators that were half-buried in the mud, examining them closely, seeming to take care in selecting one above all others.

She pointed to one. "This is a male. I want this one."

Tarzan went to the incubator. Kneeling, he dug it out of the mud and prepared to lift it.

Before he could do so, the jeddara turned away and, throwing off her metallic cloak, made a sudden dash for the waters sparkling behind them. She plunged into the smooth blue lake and waded out with a speed that was almost mad.

"Fleeing is pointless," Tarzan called out.

Turning a helmeted head framed by silvery tresses, O-Thuria hurled back, "I have traveled millions of haads over thousands of zodes to dwell by this body of water. Before I depart, I wish to swim in the sacred eye of Jor, even if only for a few minutes."

"There are crocodiles," warned Tarzan.

"I do not know that word," she flung back, then pushed out farther into the lake.

Standing up, Tarzan moved toward the water, for it occurred to him that a woman who had been raised in a place where natural bodies of water did not exist could not be expected to understand what she was attempting.

Without warning, O-Thuria threw herself forward in an effort to swim.

Suddenly, her head disappeared beneath the wrinkled blue surface. It popped up again. She shrieked once, as she splashed about wildly.

"What is happening?"

Tarzan did not take the time to reply. He could see plainly what was happening. The woman did not know how to swim and was floundering about in the unfamiliar environment. Her armor, too heavy for her body's natural buoyancy to overcome, was pulling her down, its gravity-defeating properties insufficient to keep her afloat.

The ape-man plunged into the lake, striking out for her frantic-limbed figure. He arrowed swiftly through the cool water, but not swiftly enough, for Gimla the crocodile proved to be swifter still in his instinctive reactions.

Tarzan saw the reptile's half-submerged ridged head moving toward its confused prey, green eyes fixed. As it lunged, the great jaws lifted upward, to clamp down upon the last jeddara of Nulthoom, who gave out a final ripping shriek of horror before being taken from view when the crocodile carried her beneath the choppy surface.

Tarzan's knife came out as he dived. Swimming hard, the blade clenched between his set teeth, he closed the distance.

By the time he reached Gimla, the blue waters around the reptile were a crimson cloud, and the bronzed giant knew that he was too late.

Nevertheless, he took the knife from his mouth, wrapped his steely arms around the reptile's twisting neck, and stabbed repeatedly until it was no more alive than a floating log. Turning over on its ridged belly, the crocodile sank.

Tarzan pulled the woman from its distended jaws and brought her to the surface. There, he held her head above the water. O-Thuria's eyes were wide open. But there was no life in them.

Reluctantly, Tarzan released the body and permitted it to float away. Let the crocodiles finish her then. There was no point in burying the half-devoured remains.

Chapter 40

"The Enemy Has Been Defeated"

RETURNING TO shore, Tarzan found himself amid the many incubators which were all that remained of the failed colony of Jor.

The ape-man regarded these eggs in silence for a time and considered placing them back in the interplanetary ship and giving it a mental command to return to Barsoom. But who was left to receive them? He knew of no other Orovar cities.

Lifting his voice, he gave the victory cry of the bull ape, which resounded throughout the immediate veldt. Before long, a contingent of Waziri warriors trotted into view.

"What has transpired here?" asked Waranji.

"The enemy has been defeated. All that remains are their unhatched eggs."

"What is to be done with them, B'wana?"

Tarzan considered this for some minutes. He was usually a decisive person, but in this instance, the ape-man was torn between two alternatives.

Finally, he said, "Carry them back to the interplanetary ship that brought them to Earth. We will send them back to Mars. Let John Carter dispose of them as he wishes."

This task was done, although it took several hours, with the Waziri acting as porters, carrying each egg balanced upon his head. None were damaged during the operation.

The dead bodies strewn about the ship were first dragged out and buried in a common pit. This took much of the night.

By this time, Muviro and his troop had arrived, along with Korak.

Once the ship was cleared of corpses and the eggs replaced in their padded berths, Korak asked, "How do you know that you can give the ship the correct mental commands that will guide it back to Mars?"

Tarzan declared, "I can only try."

Once everything was in place, Tarzan went to the control room and regarded the sphere that was the brain of the interplanetary craft. It was only slightly larger than a coconut. He stared at it, mentally commanding the artificial brain to depart the Earth for the Empire of Helium on Barsoom.

Having done this, Tarzan sprinted for the hatch and jumped out as the teardrop-shaped vehicle began to hum. Actuated by automatic machinery, the hatch closed of its own volition. The bronzed giant and his companions stepped clear and watched as the ship commenced to levitate into the night air, and then tilt its blank crystal eyes upward, and speed off into the wheeling African stars.

Korak said, "It seems to have worked."

Tarzan nodded. "I will endeavor to get word to John Carter via Gridley Wave to expect its return. What he does with these eggs is entirely up to him. But they represent innocent lives. Destroying them was not necessary."

With that, Tarzan of the Apes gave the order to strike out toward the south, back in the direction of the Greystoke estate.

It was a long march, but they did not falter. The Waziri helped keep cadence by singing the old war songs that proclaimed Tarzan of the Apes to be the war chieftain of the tribe. Their voices carried far and wide. By the time they reached home, a feast of welcome already had been laid out for them.

Epilogue

I WAS enjoying a period of peace and relative tranquility in Helium when my aide-de-camp, Vor Daj, entered my apartments, reporting, "John Carter, there is a message from Jasoom. It is from Jason Gridley."

I rushed to the room where the Gridley Wave machine was maintained.

Taking the microphone in hand, I spoke. "Jason Gridley, I bid you greetings from the Empire of Helium."

"And I greet you from Tarzana, California. I have received a letter addressed to you in care of me. It is postmarked Nairobi, Africa. I will now read it to you.

" 'Dear John Carter,

" 'I have been successful in vanquishing the surviving forces of Nulthoom. They will trouble neither of our planets any longer. The details are unimportant. Their jeddara is no more. It was not necessary to slay her. In her zeal, she became the architect of her own undoing.

" 'The interplanetary ship is returning to your world. It has been instructed to land in Greater Helium. It is unmanned but carries a cargo of interest. This comprises the surviving eggs of O-Thuria, Jeddara of Nulthoom. Do with them what you will. I wash my hands of this matter.

" 'Please accept my sincere regards.' "

Jason Gridley concluded by saying, *"The letter is signed in a peculiar way, John Carter."*

"What do you mean?"

"The signature reads: Tarzan of the Apes, Warlord of Jasoom."

Hearing this, I could only laugh.

"Inform the Warlord of Jasoom that his counterpart, John Carter, Warlord of Barsoom, conveys both his greetings and his gratitude. And further inform him that, should I ever find myself back on my natal *terra firma*, I will be certain to pay him a friendly call. And that he should practice his swordsmanship in anticipation of that day, for I would enjoy crossing swords with him under circumstances that are more equitable from the standpoint of atmospheric and gravitational conditions."

Later, Jason Gridley reported that a letter conveying that message was to be mailed to the Greystoke estate in care of General Delivery, Nairobi, Africa. Whether it was called for, I do not know. For no reply was ever communicated to Barsoom. Of Tarzan of the Apes, whom I first knew as Ramdar the panthan, I know nothing further.

As for the surviving eggs of Nulthoom, they arrived safely. What we did with them is a tale for another occasion.

About the Author

WILL MURRAY

WILL MURRAY was first exposed to Tarzan of the Apes when his father took him to see *Tarzan's Greatest Adventure* in 1959. He was too young to read and therefore too immature to understand what he was watching. But something must have struck a resonating chord in his young brain. During the following decade, he watched a ton of Tarzan movies, usually starring Johnny Weissmuller.

A decade later, Murray read *The Gods of Mars,* and became a fan of the works of Tarzan creator Edgar Rice Burroughs. After finishing the Mars series, he jumped to the Venus books, the Land that Time Forgot series, and ultimately back to Tarzan. These novels not only opened up for him the many worlds of Edgar Rice Burroughs, but also the greater universe of pulp fiction, where he continues to reside to this day, penning new adventures of classic pulp heroes such as Doc Savage, The Shadow, The Spider and others.

Fifty years later, Murray inaugurated a new revival of Tarzan in book form with his 2015 novel, *Tarzan: Return to Pal-ul-don,* which led to *King Kong vs. Tarzan, Tarzan, Conqueror of Mars,* and this sequel, *Tarzan: Back to Mars.* Like many authors of his and surrounding generations, he credits his writing career to the unparalleled imagination of Edgar Rice Burroughs.

At the 2021 Dum Dum held in Albuquerque, New Mexico, Will Murray was presented with the prestigious Golden Lion Award for his contributions to the furtherance of the memory and the mighty works of that supreme master of adventure, Edgar Rice Burroughs. He could not be more proud, or grateful to the fine people at Edgar Rice Burroughs, Inc., for their faith in him. Kaor!

About the Artist
JOE DeVITO

JOE DeVITO was born on March 16, 1957 in New York City. He graduated with honors from Parsons School of Design in 1981, studied at the Art Students League in New York City. Joe's art often displays a decided emphasis on Action Adventure, SF and Fantasy, and dinosaurs. Over a professional career spanning more than 30 years he has also periodically lectured and taught university illustration courses on painting and sculpting.

DeVito has painted and sculpted many of the most recognizable Pop Culture and Pulp icons. These include King Kong, Tarzan, Doc Savage, Superman, Batman, Wonder Woman, Spider-Man, *MAD* magazine's Alfred E. Nueman and various other characters. He has illustrated hundreds of book and magazine covers, painted several notable posters and numerous trading cards for the major comic book and gaming houses, and created concept and character design for the film and television industries. In 3D, DeVito sculpted the official 100th Anniversary statue of *Tarzan of the Apes* for Edgar Rice Burroughs, Inc., *The Cooper Kong* for the Merian C. Cooper Estate, Superman, Wonder Woman and Batman for Chronicle Books' Masterpiece Editions, several other notable Pop and Pulp characters, including Doc Savage.

Joe is also the founder of DeVito ArtWorks, LLC, an artist-driven transmedia studio dedicated to the creation and development of multi-faceted properties including *King Kong of Skull Island, War Eagles,* and the *Primordials.* He is the co-author (with Brad Strickland) of five books, which he illustrated as well. The first, based on Joe's original *Skull Island* prequel/sequel, was *KONG: King of Skull Island* (DH Press), published in 2004. The second book, *Merian C. Cooper's KING KONG,* was published by St. Martin's Griffin in 2005. In 2017 DeVito ArtWorks published the third book (the first under its own imprint), the very Limited Edition hardcover *King Kong of Skull Island,* the most comprehensive Kong history to date. *King Kong of Skull Island* covers the origins of the Kongs and the human civilization on Skull Island, the building of the great Wall, and the in-depth prequel/sequel story of King Kong himself. In 2019 the LE book was split into a two-part paperback version for the mass market: *King Kong of Skull Island Part One: Exodus and King Kong of Skull Island Part Two: The Wall.*

Having illustrated all of Will Murray's Wild Adventures of Doc Savage novels, Joe continues to enjoy his decades-long collaboration with Will on *Tarzan: Back To Mars,* their second Wild Adventures of Tarzan novel together.

"This one was challenging in that we wanted to use some excellent photos of Steve Holland for Tarzan and John Carter, but they were from unrelated photo shoots. I took advantage of weird lighting conditions on Mars to help pull it off.

"Additionally, I had always wanted to paint Tars Tarkas and was happy to finally get the chance. I grew up seeing him and his fellow four-armed Martians in innumerable illustrations. Thanks to Will's expert guidance with some key details, it was fun to finally contribute a version of my own that I hope Burroughs fans will like."

www.jdevito.com
www.kongskullisland.com
FB: DeVito ArtWorks / KongOfSkullIsland

About the Patron

RICHARD BURCHFIELD

I GREW up with three brothers on a hobby farm in central Minnesota, and have been very fortunate to go to school and work in the north, west, south, and east of this great country. Also, I have had the opportunity to hike and camp the magnificent national parks, Grand Canyon, Zion, Sequoia, Yosemite, Yellowstone, Glacier and more, and have great memories of the crown jewels of this country. Since I can remember, my mother, Rosita, influenced me with her love of reading science fiction. She introduced me to the wonderful worlds of Tarzan, John Carter, Conan, and more. I can recall escaping to Mars, Venus, Skull Island and the Dark Continent during Minnesota's cold winters in the 1960s and '70s.

To this day, when I see Tarzan, John Carter, Conan and others, I think of my mother and how she expanded my thinking and encouraged me to read and learn. In the late '60s, my father got us kids around the TV to watch the Apollo launches. It was a time when anything was possible. I had these great science fiction books and the real world was reaching for the stars. I have had a career in information technology since the early 1980s, and it's been an incredible transformation, witnessing how technology has impacted our lives.

Lastly, to be the sponsor of book covers for these great iconic characters, Tarzan and King Kong, and now Tarzan and John Carter of Mars, is a tremendous honor for me.

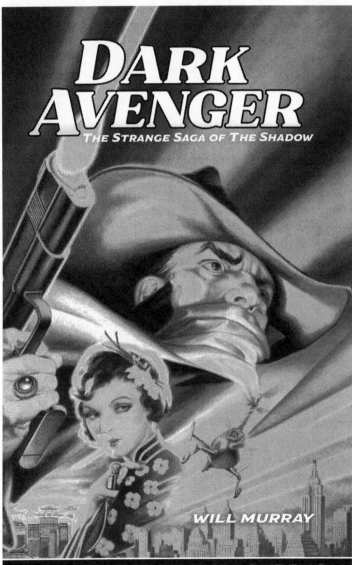

The Wild Adventures of Edgar Rice Burroughs'™

TARZAN®

Return to Pal~ul~don
by Will Murray

COMING SOON!